THE WITCH CHASE

THE WITCH CHASE

THE PACK MATES OF LUNAR CREST, BOOK FOUR

by

GINNA MORAN

ISBN 978-1-951314-38-5 (soft cover)
ISBN 978-1-951314-39-2 (hard cover)

This is a work of fiction. All of the characters, organizations, and events portrayed in this novel are either products of the author's imagination or are used fictitiously.

Cover design by Silver Starlight Designs
Cover images copyright Depositphotos

For Inquiries Contact:
Sunny Palms Press
9663 Santa Monica Blvd Suite 1158
Beverly Hills, CA 90210, USA
www.sunnypalmspress.com
www.GinnaMoran.com

DEDICATION

To Bailey Schonenberger,

Your support and love of my books means the world to me.

Here's to adding many more book boyfriends and girlfriends to

your life. XOXO!

1

CURSED ONE

"STOP! PLEASE! YOU CAN'T DO this!" The masculine voice sends a shiver down my back.

A scream rings through the air next, and I shudder at the high-pitched sound of the man's agony. He calls to his god for some sort of divine intervention. Goosebumps prickle over my skin the longer it draws on.

"Help!" the man shouts. A crash explodes in the hallway and

vibrant blue magic strobes in flashing light across the crack at the bottom of the door. He screeches again. "Someone help me! Please!"

I don't move from my spot. Nothing and no one in this fate-forsaken world can rescue him. I'm not this stranger's savior. In reality, I'm the complete opposite. I want this more than the witches who try to subdue him. I'm not planning to help, no matter how much he continues to scream.

"Stop it! Ouch! You're hurting me!" he screams again, the desperation in his voice stabbing me.

I flinch, squeezing my eyes shut. It'll only get worse, especially when I have to face him. If it wasn't for my deal with the Everdeen Coven, this man wouldn't be here. He wouldn't be the one chosen by the witches for their upcoming lycan spell. I just wish I could steel myself for what I know is to come. I always thought I'd be the one looking evil in the eyes. But I am evil. I'm no better than those who tried to steal my fate and future from me.

Now I'm taking his.

It won't be long.

"Silence him," Evelyn snaps, the sharpness of her words cutting me as deeply as the screams of the prisoner she forces into the sanctuary of the Everdeen Estate. Another streak of magic illuminates the crack below the door. "Now."

"Thank the fates." My comment comes out as a whisper, and guilt punches me in the heart.

I can't believe how much I appreciate her demand. This is all so twisted. I can't even imagine how much worse this can get, but I know I'll find out. Creating a curse from the beast roaring inside me can only be horrible. It'll rip away the man's humanity, destroy his body, and imprison his soul.

How am I going to go through with this and survive? I don't know. I have to. It's the only way I can get the help I need to save my stolen pack mates. Thoughts of Sagan and Bastien stab at my chest, threatening my heart. The feeling devastates me on a soul-deep level, making the man's screams more tolerable. Each day that passes by without them feels more torturous than the last. I can't bear to imagine my world without them for much longer or the horrors they experience every second of the day. Being forced to leave them behind in Lulupoterra feels as if a part of my soul was ripped from my body and is now held captive at the mercy of the Nightstars. I can't stand it. I get sick thinking about it.

So this is how it has to be.

Damaging my soul to save theirs. The price could be worse. No matter the cost, though, I'm willing to pay it. I'll do anything to bring my pack mates home.

"I'm going to—" A muffled wail hums through the sturdy door, the man refusing to give up, even when someone tries to force him to. My ears ring at the high-pitched anguish, shadowing the edges of my vision.

"Make him stop," I whisper, sending my own plea to the

fates. "Please, just make him stop."

Like someone answers my prayers, the man finally quiets down, his distress no louder than a whimper.

He begins to sob.

Shit.

I dig my nails into my palms, my whole body tense and on edge. Fuck. It takes everything in me not to find out what is happening on the other side of the door. It sounds worse than getting the man to stop screaming. He sounds as if he experiences a new level of pain, one that ruins his soul and will last forever.

A part of me wants to shut the bullshit out of my awareness, yet another part of me knows doing that shit is probably impossible now, despite how sexy Dax and Caz look staring at the door in front of me. I mean, it took me this long to avert my focus to them already.

Twisting his waist, Caz peers at me. "I'm sorry, Lyric. We should be helping to distract you instead of being distracted ourselves," he says, responding to my thoughts. Caz wears a towel slung low on his hips, his taut chest and chiseled biceps bulging and flexing with the movements of his body.

I shrug, trailing my gaze lower to his abs. If I concentrate hard enough, I might get more than his muscles to harden. "I can't blame you for that. This is fucked up."

"You agreed to what you thought was best, Lyric. Try not to blame yourself for having to pick between two horrible circumstances. I prefer this over the alternative." Rubbing his fingers through his hair, Dax shifts toward me as he stands naked beside Caz, giving me one helluva view of his hulking, muscular body.

I don't know if it's because I'm thinking about him naked or because of something else, but his cock grows to point in my direction. Unfortunately, I'm going to need more than just their eye-candy to break my thoughts from this madness.

"Which is why I made this suggestion. If you guys can't handle the task, then I will make our leader comply like a good girl." Antone's voice trickles into my mind as the shadow of his wolf looms behind me.

Caz clenches his fingers into fists and growls. "We've got it handled."

Another holler sounds through the door, dragging our focus away from each other. I press my lips together, trying to ignore the yells and also Antone's attempt to get my attention. I wish Flynn and Sterling would return already and let me know what's going on. Flynn promised they'd be away for no more than an hour, but I'm nearly certain that the time creeps closer to two hours passing by.

A furry body rubs against my leg as Antone stalks his way closer to the door in his wolf form. I thought being away from Lulupoterra might cause him to stay in his human form more often, but he embraces his wolf more than any of us, only transforming when I ask him to. And I can't exactly blame him. He feels the most powerful this way, and I'm sure the screams of the man don't help any with his nerves.

"I have no nerves toward what must be done for my brother." Returning to my side, Antone circles me again and licks my ass cheek with his long tongue, making me jump. "Now come on, Cherie, go take your bath with Dax and Caz. I will guard this room with my life. No one will intrude without getting a limb ripped off and devoured. I promise." Antone pads around me again and tries to poke his nose between my legs to get me to move.

I sidestep and run my fingertips over the length of his back, petting his black fur while keeping him in place before he awakens my she-wolf to play with him how he likes. And right now, we don't have time for wrestling.

"I think I should check to see what's going on." I say the words out loud for the others to hear, continuing my mission to bury my fingers into Antone's coat. "Whatever they're doing is freaking me out a bit."

Swiveling on the balls of his feet, Dax turns to me again. His honey-brown stare drops down my body, drinking in the view of me wearing only a short T-shirt and a lacy thong. "They're relocating the mortal. Leaving this room will only make them think their presence is welcome. Antone and Caz are both right. Your body needs our undivided attention."

How the hell can I argue with that? He's right. Their plan is far better than mine, and now that the screams fade by the second, I can pretend the seriously twisted shit the Everdeen Coven plans isn't going to go down.

"As does my heart and soul," I say, forcing my mouth to smile. "But I also need to give you mine as well. I haven't seen you smile in days."

Opening my arms, I wiggle my fingers at Dax and Caz, getting them to come to me. Caz dodges past Dax, and I hop into his arms. He spins, playing keep-away with me, and laughter bubbles from my mouth. I almost forgot how good it felt to laugh. To play around and tease my mates. To savor a teensy bit of competition between them.

I clutch Caz's cheeks and kiss him until he sets me on the counter. Dax starts the water and pours an excessive amount of some sort of potion Flynn says will calm our nerves. And seeing Dax dump the entire container must mean he is far more nervous than he lets on. He's turned into the expert of being open yet guarded with me, ensuring he only ever radiates the strength and love he knows can raise me up instead of overwhelming me with his own burdening thoughts. I just wish he would agree to let me carry some of the weight for him.

Caz stands between my legs and tugs my shirt over my head. I smile and kiss him the second I can, reaching down to untie his towel, letting it drop to the floor. Dax eases himself into the bubbling tub behind me, the soft groan of his enjoyment sending me rushing to strip out of my panties. Caz play-growls over the fact that I don't give him the honor and lifts me back into his arms, kissing me all the way to the tub.

"It's going to be a tight squeeze," Dax says, holding his arms out for me.

Caz laughs and hands me over. "Everything is for you."

I shift on Dax's lap to sit on his thigh. Inhaling a deep breath, I blow the bubbles away, showing off the fact that Caz is right. Even the water can't rise high enough to cover his enormous boner, currently looking like she-wolf bait to get me to play with him.

I reach out to touch and tease him as Caz joins us in the tub, not even caring that his legs rest on Dax's while he holds my feet on his thigh, massaging his fingers into my calf. A low growl reverberates through my bones, freezing my hand inches from Dax.

And fuck. It's like the Everdeens knew and waited until I was finally going to get a moment to just be with my mates. A flash of blue light shines from beneath the crack at the bottom of the door, and Antone's snarls suddenly cut off. My heart crashes to my rib cage, and I scramble from the tub, nearly slipping. Caz catches me, stopping me from eating shit on the tiles, and Dax throws a towel at me. I rush to the door, but Dax intercepts me in his wolf form, getting ready to charge out.

"What are you doing barging in on my wolves without my permission?" Flynn's voice hums through the door.

"It is time," Enrique says, his deep voice penetrating my chest, trying to steal my breath away.

I knew he'd be coming for me to fulfill my end of our bargain with the arrival of the screaming mortal man, but I had hoped I'd get at least a bit more time to prepare. While I've wanted to return to Lulupoterra for days to retrieve my mates, I need time to process exactly what's going to happen. I'll be responsible for cursing who knows how many people by agreeing to help the Everdeens create a lycan curse. But I don't see another choice. Our enemies grow out of control. Not only are Sagan and Bastien's lives in jeopardy, but so is the rest of our species. Nightstar won't stop until they have us as part of their army.

This terrible bargain—one that already hurts me on a soul-deep level—is worth the damage to my spirit. My heart aches so terribly at the absence of my mates that I swear I'm dying a slow, agonizing death inside while the rest of me clings to the rest of my pack, praying for survival.

The thought enhances the hurricane of emotions inside me, and I growl through my teeth, my she-wolf peeking through.

"Please control your pets and call upon your familiar, Flynn." Enrique's tone sounds more like a command than a suggestion. It prods at me harder like it stabs my wolf, setting off her nature to protect my pack. "You know the fragility of such a spell. We must hurry...unless you've changed your mind about reuniting Lyric with the rest of her pack. In that case, I—"

I twist the doorknob and swing it open, clutching the towel around me. I dart my gaze around the room, making sure Antone is okay, Sterling is back and safe, and Flynn...fuck I wish it didn't feel as if my heart wants nothing more than to leap at him, especially with how he glowers in annoyance because of my need to confront Enrique.

"I'll be ready in five minutes. Just let me get dressed," I say, flicking my gaze to the man who thinks I should belong to the Everdeens instead of Flynn all because he thought of my mother as his coven brother's pet.

Enrique claps his hands, summoning a billowing black robe embroidered with strange symbols. "Wear this and nothing else. You will need to transform on cue."

I catch myself before I open my mouth to tell him to fuck off, and instead, I saunter forward and take the heavy pile of fabric from his hands. Blue light flashes in his eyes, a cold contrast to his High Priestess, who summons warmth and power through red electric light that burns me to the core without even touching me.

"You will also need to leave your mates here," Enrique adds, backing toward the door like his words could set off my pack and send them on a witch hunt.

I reach my hand out and quietly scratch my fingers between Caz's ears. Enrique hesitates a moment longer like he thinks I'll argue. But I don't. I didn't plan to either. The faster we get this done, the better things will be.

"I will be joining her," Flynn says like he needs our pack to know I won't be alone.

Growls sound through the air, the anger of my mates

palpable as it threatens to leave me breathless.

I can't blame their response. Things have been rocky the last few days between everyone and Flynn except for Sterling. Sterling's go-with-the-flow attitude helps keep things from exploding, and it also helps knowing he agrees with me by trusting Flynn.

Enrique gives a sharp nod in response, thankfully not arguing. I wouldn't put it past him to test Flynn's resolve. We're in his coven's estate, hiding within the protection of their power after all. Enrique seems like the asshole type to throw something like that in Flynn's face.

"Five minutes," Enrique says, crossing his arms. "Any more time than that, and I can promise things will not go as planned."

Shit. Was that a threat? It sure felt like it.

I clench my hands into fists, ready to charge him. Like he can sense my annoyance, Enrique spins on his feet. He strides away and exits the small room. The door slams behind him, the crack of wood startling me in his wake.

The asshole.

"I swear. If we didn't need him, I'd bite his head off," I say, considering doing so anyway.

I don't get the chance to even step forward to act on my thoughts, because a warm hand hooks to my hip, spinning me around. Sterling greets me with a pouty kiss, gripping the back of my towel like he plans to rip it off.

"I'm sorry, blondie. We tried our fucking best to break the

shield so that you wouldn't have to go through with this." Pulling me into him, Sterling hugs me tighter. "Maybe I can convince them to use me instead."

"It has to be Lyric," Flynn says, his voice nearly a whisper. "Females are the key to creating the curse."

"Then use that damn doppelganger spell to turn me into her. If they don't know—"

I kiss Sterling's demands away, dropping my towel to distract him. I know if something like that was possible, Flynn would've already mentioned it. He'd probably do it himself to protect me from the Everdeen magic.

"I know you guys worry about me, but I want you to quit it. I've made this decision, and I stand by it. I will not allow any of you to risk yourselves on my behalf again. We've lost too much already. It is my job as your leader to take care of you and secure our future, and this will help. You have to trust Flynn to protect me. You know he's capable." I step back and shake out the ceremonial robe, studying the embroidered designs.

Sterling holds it for me, helping me put it on. "We do trust him, but it still doesn't make me worry less. I want us to do things like this together. It's hard to support you like you need when the witches constantly block us out. If you're with them, it does the same. It's going to drive me nuts worse than your sweet fragrance calling to my wolf like the drug you are."

"Then do something to distract yourselves. Strategize a plan for when we can return to Lulupoterra. Think about what happens after that. If that fails, fucking masturbate or something. You need to relax." I straighten my shoulders and adjust the ties on the robe, cinching it around my waist. I want so badly to just say forget it to everything, but it's impossible. We need this. "And please, try to stay out of trouble."

He play-growls. "You did not just suggest that we're the troublemakers, you naughty blonde. I can't even leave you for a bit without—"

I press my hand to his mouth, knowing if he continues speaking, I'll get distracted and the Everdeens will come back. I want to keep my mates away from them as best I can. I can't be sure my mates won't try something dangerous. I already know they want to rip the witches apart.

"Be good," I repeat, shifting my gaze to look at Dax, Caz, and Antone. Their hulking forms scream at me to try to make them. "I mean it. That's an order."

Everyone remains expressionless, but I sure as hell can feel their displeasure over my command. But what can I do? This is a lose-lose situation. I'd prefer they sulk and plot together to spank me later than have them get hurt.

Flynn holds out his hand for me, quietly pulling me into his arms. He doesn't say anything or look at the others. Lavender sparks flash in his irises, and he brings his lips to my ear, whispering a spell to transport us.

Blinding light steals my vision, and my heart feels as if it drops into my stomach at the strange sensation. I rest my head to Flynn's shoulder, trying my best to orient myself to the sudden relocation.

A muffled yell cuts through the air, and I jerk my attention to a naked man in chains with a strange rectangular piece of fabric over his mouth. His eyes widen, and he shakes the chains, trying to yank them from the wall. I'd be freaked the fuck out too if I were him, because I bet he's never seen someone transport with magic, though I'm sure getting stripped and chained up is just as terrifying.

"Evoka de sol eb." Two familiar women chant the strange words from behind an altar set up with unfamiliar herbs, what might be some sort of animal bones, a stone bowl, and other assorted things intended for whatever potion they plan to make.

Flynn squeezes my hand and guides me toward a circle drawn on the concrete floor in what I really fucking hope isn't blood. But my hope dwindles. I can smell the strange floral fragrance mixed with the tang of hot magic and the bitterness of iron. At least the circle isn't created from the blood of a victim but of one of the witches. My inner she-wolf encourages me to inhale deeper, imprinting the scent on my brain.

The familiar blue light of a portal spell blasts through the room, and I shield my eyes, glaring the best I can at the figures forming in front of me. Two more coven members appear, their small number making me think twice about my fear of what they can do. Evelyn and Enrique are obviously the most powerful of the six, taking charge and ordering everyone around.

Evelyn might be the High Priestess, but Enrique looks like he's on the verge of challenging her for the spot. Where her magic burns red and dangerous, his sparks cool blue, and blended together, their colors make an intense wave of purple energy that seems all-consuming.

"Evelyn carries stolen power." Flynn's thought enters my mind, answering my curious thoughts. His lavender eyes hold mine for a minute, darting over my face as he tries to decipher the battling emotions inside me. "She has chosen not to share it with the rest of her coven, which causes hostility with her brother. That's all I know."

I press my lips together, the information only summoning more questions in my mind. No wonder Enrique always looks as if someone constantly kicks him in the nuts. He probably thinks he's entitled to everything Evelyn has, and who knows? He could be. I don't know enough about witch covens to really have an opinion. I never had siblings either, so I don't know what it's like for them.

If Evelyn didn't suddenly fill the space in front of us, I would ask Flynn more about it. Energy bounces from her to me as if the jolts of magic test the strength of Flynn's power humming in the stone hanging between my breasts. I tense under her intense scrutiny as her gaze travels from my face to drink in the ceremonial robe around my body. Her lips twitch, a smirk pulling up the corner, and she nods her approval.

"Please take your familiar to her place, brother," she says to

Flynn, the term freaking me out, despite knowing Flynn agreed only to act as a coven member. He hasn't been formally brought in yet. This whole lycan curse is part of what I can only describe as a trial period. Whether he'll actually ever go through to blend and bind power? I fucking hope he doesn't. "Because we had planned this before your arrival, you will not be needed here. I hope you understand. I'll take exceptionally good care of Lyric. I promise."

I nearly lose my shit, positioning my body in a fighting stance, despite knowing one flick of Evelyn's hand can send me to the ground.

"I'm not leaving," Flynn snaps, tightening his fingers through mine. He straightens his back and narrows his gaze in warning. "She is not comfortable with you, and I will not add to the stress she already experiences from this bargain by not standing here and supporting her."

Evelyn's eyes flash with her warm power, and Flynn flexes his muscles, not backing down. They exchange a silent look, both threatening the other to give in. I clench my teeth, filling Flynn with my determination and a huge dose of my stubbornness. Evelyn doesn't stand a chance. This is our hill to fucking fight to the death on.

"Fine, if you insist, then you can control the Cursed One," Evelyn says, stepping back. She flicks a burst of magic at the man, jolting him. And what a bitch. He's already going to go through something horrific, yet she chooses to take out her frustration on him.

"Try not to feel too bad, Lyric. Brandon is far from pure and good. The Everdeens wanted someone with negative energy and a dark soul to absorb the curse. I made sure he wasn't innocent myself—abusive. Selfish. Violent. The world will not be saddened by this." Flynn strokes his fingers up and down the billowing fabric of my sleeve. "We're going to get through this, okay?"

I release a small breath. Thank fucking fuck. Sort of. While the knowledge about this mortal's history helps ease my nerves a teensy bit, it does nothing to help with the rising fear of what kind of true beast he'll turn into. If he's an immoral, sick fuck of a man, he'll be even worse as a lycan.

But what else am I supposed to do? This must be done.

I lick my lips and sigh. "I know. I just want to get this over with."

Flynn nods and tugs me past Evelyn's turned back and between the two unfamiliar male coven members who arrived— warlocks with strawberry blond hair and a stark contrast to the dark tresses of the rest of them. I try not to look at them as they obviously gawk at me like I'm some magical fucking unicorn. I'm tempted to react, but try to focus elsewhere instead. Unfortunately, the only safe things to look at are the ceiling or the floor. Everything else triggers something dark inside me.

Flynn turns me to face him and hugs me close, trying to squeeze away the trembles shaking across my body. He kisses my earlobe and whispers he is right here and not going anywhere. A blip of warmth caresses my soul with his words, and I tilt my face to meet his mouth with mine, hoping the brush of our lips eases the ache inside me.

Releasing me, Flynn turns toward the man. The space where he was standing grows cool with his distance, and I bounce on my feet, focusing on the sensation of his magic pulsing over my heart. He takes a few more steps and stops by the man, kneeling next to him. He pinches the man's chin to make him look up. "This will all be over soon, Brandon." The use of the man's name doesn't go unnoticed by the others, and they all look at Flynn with narrowed eyes.

"Heather, please mark the chosen, so we can proceed," Evelyn says, placing a stone bowl in the hands of the witch I met only once. Turning to the only other woman, she adds, "Trinity, join Samson and Godfrey in marking the Cursed One."

Heather dips her fingers into the stone bowl, covering her hand in burgundy liquid. A scream rips through the air from the naked man, startling me. I jerk my attention to see the other witches standing in front of him, the strange gag now gone from his mouth. Flynn chants something from behind him, freezing Brandon in place.

The sparkle of a blade catches my attention, and Trinity readies herself to carve something into Brandon's skin.

Ugh. I can't even remind myself how he isn't good to ignore his hollers.

"Undress, please. I need to draw the linking mark on your chest. It won't hurt," Heather says, touching my shoulder to grab my attention.

Brandon screams again, his ear-piercing anticipation toward his upcoming agony stabbing me in the heart.

I can't do this.

I can't stand by and participate in ruining a mortal's life, no matter how awful he is.

Tensing my muscles, I shove past Heather and to the other witches. "Stop! I'm not doing this. The deal is off," I say.

Enrique materializes in front of me, his face morphing with monstrous features. "You can't back out now."

"The fuck I can't," I snap.

Snatching my wrist, he yanks me back toward the blood circle. "If you don't do it, I will kill every single one of your mates."

My she-wolf awakens at his threat, and I transform, summoning the strength of my mates. No one has a chance to react. No one can stop me.

I launch at Enrique and sink my teeth into his neck.

2

POWER SHIFT

"LYRIC, NO!" FLYNN LOCKS HIS hands to the back of my neck and chants a spell, turning my body immobile.

Enrique scowls, clutching his bleeding neck. Power dances across his gaze, flickering with the same need I carry as we both desire to put each other in place. He thinks I'm some sort of animal to be trained when my wild heart wants to prove that impossible. He should fear me. Respect my power. And I feel the only way I can do so now is to treat him like my prey.

"Let me go!" I think, sending the thought hard and fast into Flynn's mind.

Flipping me onto my back, Flynn straddles my wolf body, pinning me despite his spell leaving my body incapacitated. "I will when you stop fighting. What you're trying to do will deem us enemies of the Everdeen Coven."

"They are." A growl escapes my mouth, and I try to break Flynn's spell again. "Look what they're doing. I don't know why you intervened. You didn't want me to go through with this either." Unless he was only saying as much to appease the rest of our pack.

"I still don't," he thinks, trying to fill my mind with the tranquility he emits from our soul bond. "It's the last thing I want. But killing Enrique won't put a stop to this. It'll only shatter the fragile alliance we created."

My heart races out of control as my wolf fights off Flynn's emotions. My mind wants to push him out while my soul begs him to stay. "Fuck the alliance—"

A snarl reverberates through the air, shutting up my racing thoughts. Flynn releases me from his magic hold, and I turn my head to stare at Evelyn standing with Dax by her side, his collar glowing red along with his eyes.

"We are running out of time, Lyric," Evelyn says, rubbing her fingers between Dax's ears. His hulking wolf body continues to growl and snarl, but he doesn't lunge. He remains obedient by her side. "Cooperate so everyone gets what they want. If you do not, you'll leave me no choice but to do something drastic. You had an agreement with my brother, bound by magic. If you fail to comply, we will have no choice but to test your warlock's power. And right now, I don't think he's capable of saving you and your mate."

This fucking witch bitch.

Closing my eyes, I transform back into a human and drop my gaze in defeat. My body screams to fight, to do whatever I can to get me and Dax out of here, but my humanity whispers that this is the only way to ensure my pack's safety.

Silently, I move away from Flynn and return to the circle. I don't look around or acknowledge anyone. Submitting to the witches kills a part of me, but it will be far worse otherwise. I channel my rage, drawing it inward to lock away for later. I have to pick my battles now, and risking Dax's life to avoid turning into a monster isn't one I'm willing to fight.

"Good girl," Enrique says, his snide comment purposefully testing my resolve.

I clench my teeth and shut down, losing myself to my thoughts. If I clear my mind and think about how I'll be reunited with Sagan and Bastien, I don't have to focus on Heather drawing something over my heart. I can ignore the screams of Brandon. I can ignore the witches and the strange spellcasting that sends tingles over my body.

"Eht flow dnib ot sih lous," Enrique and Evelyn chant in

unison, the eerie melody of their voices silencing every noise in the room, consuming my hearing completely.

They each step into the circle beside me, locking their fingers around my wrists. Tears burn my eyes as they force me to look at their Cursed One, chained and bleeding, a mark glowing on his chest as the other four coven members hold up their hands, staunching his curved marks with their power. Brandon's head lulls, his body giving out on him under the agony of the dark spell cursing his soul for eternity. Flynn's eyes sparkle with his magic, his gaze remaining locked on me.

"With this spell, your bite will ignite the curse by transferring a small amount of the magic in your blood onto him," Enrique says, spreading out my fingers. "Our power will leash him to us. With this lycan, we will be able to open the gateway to Lulupoterra. We can bring your mates home."

I don't react to his words and remain tall in my place, suppressing my nerves about what is to come.

The prick of Enrique's athame burns imaginary fire across my palm. I clench my teeth as Evelyn follows his lead, pricking my other palm with a sharp blade. They cool the sting with a black liquid and press our palms together.

"Eerf eht tsaeb et mon cocin teni Cursed One rad ges ti." Enrique chants the words, the deep tone of his voice swirling through the room. Blue magic sparkles around our hands, sending static over my body to lift my blond hair on magical currents.

"Eerf eht tsaeb et mon cocin teni Cursed One rad ges ti."

Chanting the spell next, Evelyn does the same, igniting power between us.

I shiver under the sensation, my wolf rippling over my skin, my inner beast clawing to break free. The magic dancing across each of my hands grows, crawling and twining up my arms to travel to the rest of me. I embrace the call of my she-wolf, giving in instead of fighting her for control. Fur sprouts from my body, buzzing with blue and red power, blending and morphing into a vibrant purple harsher than Flynn's soft lavender.

"Fates, she's beautiful," Enrique whispers under his breath.

I bow and stretch my claws, shaking out my tense muscles. Two hands touch my back and brush across my fur. It takes everything in me not to react, but all I want is to get this over with. The sooner we're done, the sooner I will reunite my mates with our pack.

"Sisters and brothers, we will finally take what is rightfully ours," Evelyn says, stepping away from me. "Look upon the beast of our brother and thank the fates who brought her to us. For she shall give us the power once taken."

"Blessed the fates," they all say in unison.

My muscles ripple, and my hackles rise on my back, watching as the Cursed One stirs, moaning as he becomes conscious. He blinks his eyes and scrunches his nose in pain. A growl rumbles from my chest, a strange, overwhelming need grabbing hold of me and refusing to let me go.

"Dnib eht tseab. Ekam mih enim. Volcu tre vit ods ti!"

Evelyn's voice rings through the air, setting me off.

It's as if I can no longer control my body as I charge forward at Brandon. He startles and screams, trying to jerk free of the magic coursing over him. Catapulting from the floor, I launch at him. The witches scatter, and Flynn squeezes his eyes shut, bracing for my impact. I send the Cursed One crashing onto him, pinning the two of them together. Brandon screams in terror, bucking his body and trying to free himself from the chains.

But he's no match for me. He can't fight against my she-wolf strength.

Opening my jaw, I bite down on his shoulder, sinking my teeth deeply into his chest. Blood coats my tongue, igniting something wild in me. If the pull of magic didn't rip me away, I might've bitten the man again. Just the idea knocks some sense into me, and I scramble away from the Everdeens and skid to where Dax remains collared. I crash into him, ignoring his deep growls. I snap my teeth to the back of his neck, dragging him with me, afraid for what's to come.

It breaks Evelyn's magic hold on him, and Dax snarls and shoves his head into my side, caging me against the wall with his massive frame. He stands in front of me protectively, but no one pays attention to us. The Everdeens focus on the man, writhing and wailing on the floor. They continue to chant something I can't understand, sending bursts of magic between him and me, stealing my breath.

My she-wolf releases me, and I cry out and curl in on myself, unable to do anything apart from just gulping in deep breaths that don't seem to fill my lungs. Dax lies down beside me, whimpering in his wolf form. He licks my aching hands, trying to comfort me as my body feels as if it'll rip in half.

A guttural roar echoes through the room, and I force my eyes to flick to the coven. Flynn creates a magical barrier around Brandon as his bones crack and shift. Dark, coarse fur explodes from his skin, growing across his deformed body. The lycan curse bends and breaks his body, stretching his frame over eight feet. Talons rip from his fingertips like long onyx daggers, and he impales them into the floor, trying to push himself upright.

"What have you done to me?" The eerie wetness of his voice gurgles his words as he tries to process the change in his form.

Evelyn raises her hands in the air, sending sparkling magic between her palms. "Ti ulmas vet og! Bow down to your masters."

The lycan roars and swings his long arms, trying to break the magical shield that protects the world from him. Power shocks him. Reeling back, he slams into the other side of the shield, electrocuting himself with Flynn's magic.

It doesn't stop the lycan, seeming to only give him more energy. He bashes his body back and forth, screaming and snarling, fighting with everything in him as the witches continue to chant their spell.

"Bow!" Evelyn shouts, stepping through Flynn's shield, unaffected by his magic. "Bow to me, my beast!"

Gathering an orb of red energy, Evelyn blasts it at the lycan, shocking him in the chest. I gasp as the air knocks from my lungs, and panic grips me. She does it again, and once more, the breath escapes me, shadowing the edges of my vision.

Something's wrong.

A scream escapes my mouth, echoing alongside the lycan's. Power sizzles through the air, zapping across every surface, lighting the entire room. Dax nudges his big head to my stomach, trying to get me to move, but I can't find the strength. Pain steals my breath.

"The spell is failing," Flynn shouts, his voice cutting over the hum of magic. "Release my familiar. Now!"

Enrique gathers blue magic to join his sister. "Just another—"

"Now!" Flynn drops the magical shield around the lycan with his words.

An eerie quiet engulfs the world around me, and I blink away the haze in my eyes. The lycan screams in silence, arching his back like a rainbow, shedding all of his new fur. His bones crack and shift, the sound like sand shaken in a metal can. He shudders and convulses in agony, his body rejecting the lycan transformation.

Heather rushes through the broken circle and snatches the dagger from her coven sister's hand. "You were unworthy, beast. Let your dark soul burn." Stabbing Brandon in the chest, Heather chants a spell, engulfing him in flames.

I gasp, my mind whirling, and I whip my attention to Flynn.

"You should've allowed us to finish," Evelyn snaps, getting into Flynn's face. She has the audacity to threaten him with a jab of her finger to his chest.

"And risk you killing my familiar?" Flynn gathers power in his hand, getting ready to fight. "Absolutely not. She is mine. I will not allow you to push her. You could already see the mortal's body rejected the curse."

"But we had everything right," Enrique says, touching Evelyn's shoulder. "It should've worked."

"You're wrong. You failed to include me. Have you forgotten that Lyric's soul binds with mine?" Flynn shoves past the coven and strides to my side. Ignoring Dax's warning, Flynn lifts me into his arms and drapes the discarded ceremonial robe over my body.

"Then you will fix this," Evelyn says, crossing her arms over her chest. "Now give Lyric to Enrique to care for while we get this right. I will put the spell into your hands."

"She will return to her pack." Flynn touches Dax's back as he slinks around us.

Enrique claps his hands, blinking from his spot only to materialize in front of us. "She needs rest. Allowing them to see her like this will unnecessarily complicate things. This is not up for discussion. Now help Evelyn or test exactly how powerful we really are."

Flynn doesn't fight, allowing Enrique to gather me into his arms. The world shifts. Dax's snarls and growls fade with the bright light engulfing us. I jerk my body, wanting nothing more than for Enrique to release me. I hate everything about his arms around me, like he will strangle the life out of me to steal my magic.

Dropping me on a cot, he glowers and steps back, crossing his arms over his chest. "You have just as much fight in you as your mother had. To think you being raised in the mortal world would tame your wolf was ignorant of me."

I scramble off the cot and away from Enrique, preparing to fight against him. "You say that as if you knew her."

He holds his hands up, showing me he's not out to get me, but that doesn't mean shit. He could have a spell ready and waiting for the moment I let my guard down. I can't risk it after the shit they pulled with the lycan. I need to show him that he can't fuck with me, and I'm only doing what he wants out of desperation.

"Oh, come on now," Enrique says. He keeps his hands up in surrender and inches closer, making me back up even more. "You know I would never intend to hurt you, sweetie."

"Then why do this?" Anger rushes through me. "Why make me help you with any of this."

"Like I told you before, you were intended to be ours until the fates gave you to the Tenebris Coven. It shouldn't surprise me that you, like your mother, bonded souls with powerful magic."

"What?" Confusion rushes through me at his words. "I don't understand. What are you talking about?"

He makes it sound as if my mother was in love with someone who wasn't my dad. It's hard for me to believe such a thing. And I don't even know why it is, all things considered. She-wolves were raised—or maybe even have evolved—to accept more than one mate.

"Your mother and Eliphas." Blue light sparkles in his eyes.

"Who is Eliphas?" I suddenly and desperately now want to find my dad. Anger rushes through me. Because I'm not so sure I ever will. My dad kept so much from me. I don't even know who he is anymore.

"You don't know," Enrique says, folding his arms over his chest.

"Of course I don't know. My mom died when I was little. My dad kept everything from me. I didn't even know who I was. At least, not until the witches of Fire Mountain came for me." I sigh, shifting nervously. Why am I even telling him this? Why admit the truth?

Enrique's eyes soften. "I can't believe Levi never told you about your biological father. They were so close. He was the one who helped Melody and Levi leave Lulupoterra."

I inhale a few deep breaths, wondering if my dad kept all these secrets because of Eliphas. It would make sense why they risked getting me away from the she-wolves and the games. But what I don't understand is how. How could this possibly happen?

"You sound like you have a lot of questions." Shit. Can he listen to my thoughts, too? "Why don't you take a seat, and I will answer anything you want to know. I mean, if I have the answers. It will help pass the time more quickly. I can feel your anxiety as if it is living outside of you. You can trust my sister with Flynn. They will get everything right, so we can get your mates. And when they do, we will take back the territory which rightfully belongs to us."

To us? Why does it sound like he thinks Lulupoterra is his? Fuck. How can this day go from bad to bat-shit crazy? I just want out of here. I want my mates.

He tightens his jaw. "You look skeptical, Lyric. I wish you would just trust us to get things back in order. With you and your pack by our sides, we can fix what has been damaged. We can rid our lives of covens who should never have been involved in our mission to shift more power to the wolves."

"Shift power?" My voice comes out strong, filled with anger at his words. "You're delusional. You don't want to shift power. You want control."

He whips his head back and forth. "You're mistaken. This isn't about controlling the wolves. It's about changing the fates to put them back on course. Together, we will make sure the wolves and our coven will thrive."

Why does that sound like a bad thing? Anxiety tightens my

chest, my instincts flaring with a wild need to escape. This was a huge mistake. I don't care if we need magical help from this coven. Their ties to my parents dilute my trust. They obviously weren't the ones to help them escape Lulupoterra. And as for their coven brother, a warlock they claim loved my mother, he's no longer around. But what happened to him? Where is he? What happened to my dad?

I glance from Enrique to the door, wondering what my chances are of it being unlocked. It's not like he uses doors very often. All I know is that I can't pretend any of this is okay. He thinks I'm some sort of answer to his power trip, but he's mistaken. My dad never did anything without a good reason, and if he didn't tell me about Eliphas or the Everdeen Coven, it meant he didn't want me finding them.

Clenching my fingers into fists, I glower. "I am not your ally, Enrique. We are not some sort of family or kin or whatever the fuck you think. Now, I will only ask you one more time. Take me to my mates. I don't need rest. I need them."

Enrique opens his mouth, but I lunge at him, refusing to give him a chance to argue. I'm over this bullshit.

"Take me to them!" I yell, swinging my fist.

My knuckles smash into the tile floor, sending pain radiating through my arm.

Enrique disappears with his cowardly magic.

3

REVENGE

I JOG AROUND THE WINDOWLESS room, trying to burn off my anxiety. I've tried banging the door down, summoning the magic inside me, and even shouting for my mates to get me out of here. Nothing works. The hum of magic radiating from the concrete walls gets on my nerves. If only I could figure out how to disengage it or whatever, I could kick the door open. The wood shouldn't be as hard as it is to bust down.

"Guys?" I ask, both thinking the words and saying them out loud.

Silence greets me. Whatever kind of magic Enrique spelled this room with cuts me off from my mate bonds that allow them to feel and talk to me. It's probably driving my pack mad—even crazier than it does me. They have no idea if I'm hurt or how the failed lycan curse affected me. If Bastien was here...fuck.

"Let me the hell out!" I yell, running up to the door and smacking my hands against it. "I know you can hear me, you coward! Face me!"

Groaning, I rest my forehead to the wood, closing my eyes and listening to the magic flowing over the walls. I imagine what it would be like to touch it. Feeling Flynn's magic exhilarates me, and I wonder if it has anything to do with my heritage.

I push the thought away. My heart aches at even the slight possibility that my dad isn't really my father.

"Shut up. He is. He raised you. Sharing DNA doesn't matter. He loved you. He protected you," I say, talking to myself. "He...kept you ignorant. But why?"

Shit. Now more than ever, I need to talk to my guys. They're as clueless as I am in regards to the warlock who enchanted my parents. Is it possible that was what this Eliphas guy did? Maybe there is more to it. What if the only reason my dad didn't tell me about him was because he didn't know? I hate to think of that kind of betrayal. My parents were madly in love, even years after my mother's death. And now that I experience the mate bond with seven men, I know how endless love really is.

With the thoughts of my mates, another wave of anger crashes through me. I grind my teeth and tense, ramming my shoulder into the door. My ears pop, the hum of the magic spilling from the wall and onto me, sending a shockwave through my body. I shiver at the sensation, the intense need to run consuming me.

I flatten my palm to the door and feel for more witch energy. "Guys? Can you hear me?"

"Thank the fates." Caz's thought swirls through my mind, wrapping around me in billowing warmth. "We've been trying to contact you for hours. Are you okay?"

"Are you injured, Cherie?" Antone asks next, not giving me a chance to respond to Caz.

"Of course she's not fucking okay, and yes, she's injured. I saw it. I felt it." Dax's deep voice sends goosebumps sprouting over my skin. "I wanted so badly to kill every one of the Everdeen assholes for putting our mate through this."

Instead of responding to his comment, I wiggle the doorknob, trying to see if it'll open. It doesn't. "Sterling?" I need to hear his voice, since he has yet to say anything. "Where's my horn dog?"

"Waiting for his bone," he responds, the lightness of his thoughts easing my panic. "So hurry your tight ass up and find us. I'm currently chained and naked, and the only thing that will make this even remotely okay is if you come and dominate me. Maybe bend over and let me slide my sword into your sheath. I fucking need you, my fierce badass mate."

I frown at his words. "Wait, why are you chained?"

"So that's what you're focusing on?" Sterling asks, sighing.

"I'd ask why you're naked but that's sort of a given. Now, will someone tell me where you guys are?" I tighten my fingers around the doorknob and brace my foot on the frame.

"Outside," Antone responds. "Chained like the pets they try to force us to be."

"Just hold tight. I'm coming."

Sterling groans. "Damn straight, you will be."

I shake my head and smile to myself. The cute bastard. He always manages to lift some of the weight of anxiety off my chest with his sexy, filthy mouth. Jerking my weight back, I yank as hard as I can, proving my suspicions about the weak wood right. The doorjamb buckles and splinters the wood. It flies open, sending me on my ass.

"Shit," I mutter, launching to my feet. I bounce in place and listen for signs of the Everdeen Coven.

Silence greets me. Their overconfidence in their magic makes this even sweeter. They have no idea who they're dealing with. Flynn thought my dad had arranged a powerful protection spell with a coven to keep me safe. He thought it made me resistant and able to break spells. But if it's not true, if this deflective and defensive ability derives from being born from magic and power, it could mean so much more. It could also make things worse. That would explain my soul bonding to seven others.

Pushing the thoughts away, I narrow my attention on my surroundings. I'm still wearing the ceremonial robe and nothing else, which leaves me vulnerable but more guarded as I stride down the short hallway to a set of stairs leading up. I expect the door exiting the basement to be locked, but it swings open without me even touching it.

I fist my hands, readying myself to kick some witch-bitch or warlock-fucker ass, but the living room is empty. I think the rest of the Everdeen Coven went with Flynn and Evelyn to perfect the lycan curse spell. As for Enrique? I have no idea. I'll bite his head off if he tries to confront me. I will not allow him to spend another second thinking that he's somehow entitled to a piece of Lulupoterra or worthy of an alliance with the wolves. Witches have enough. I will not stand by while they try to control me.

"You're not far, Lyric," Dax thinks to me, his voice pushing me to pick up my pace. "Just head out and follow the path. You'll find us at the back of the property."

"Do you see anyone? No one is inside. Enrique left." I jog through the front door and head around the side of the house. For being powerful witches, I expected a lot more from this estate. Maybe moats or high walls, or something to protect the property more than magic.

"He left?" Caz questions, his curiosity piquing with a wave of his emotions. "He was supposed to keep guard."

"You mean cock-block and cage our mate," Sterling mutters.

"It's..." My thoughts trail off as I spot my guys standing butt-ass naked in a line with metal collars around their necks. Heavy chains lock each of them to anchors in the ground.

I can't believe what I'm seeing.

"Are you fucking kidding me? Flynn!" I yell the words out loud, my fury colliding through me in a hot hurricane of anger threatening to steal my humanity. Because right now I want nothing more than to be a wild beast. I want to destroy the Everdeen Estate and show the witches who they're dealing with. "Flynn!"

I rush to Sterling, standing at the end of their line with his hands on his hips, his back straight, and his boner already growing as he spots me. The intense need to free my mates consumes me, and I lock my hands to his collar to try and break it off him. Electricity zaps the both of us, sending me reeling back.

"Fuck," Sterling and I say in unison.

I rub the tingles from my palms and spin on the balls of my feet to peer around.

Antone drags his chain, strolling closer to me. Reaching out, he locks his fingers to my shoulder and spins me toward him. His dark eyes rove from my face and down the rest of me, examining every inch of my body like he can't help assessing my physical state to see if I'm injured.

"You don't think we tried that, Cherie?" Antone says, grabbing my wrist. He strokes his fingers over my reddened palm. "They are locked by magic."

"Which I will break—because, fuck. Why do they have you chained like this in your human form? Is this some kind of sick and twisted game?" I hold my hands a couple inches away from the collar around his neck like I can get the thing to unlock with my mind.

"It's our choice to remain as men," Caz says, drawing my attention to him. "We will not bow as pets, no matter what they try to do."

Dax brushes his fingers through his hair. "So this is how we'll stay until we can show the Everdeen Coven they're sorely mistaken to even pretend we're their servants. They're only doing this because they know we'd kill them otherwise."

"Not only kill them. I'm going to tear them apart limb by limb, Cherie." Antone shoves his fingers into the metal collar on his neck. "I can't remember much from the days before you claimed my soul, but I remember Evelyn caging me and some others nearby. Being out here like this triggered a memory."

Fuck. I had forgotten that the Everdeen Coven had kidnapped other wolves from the territories. My mind has been focused on my pack and what we need to do to save Sagan and Bastien, I forgot there are others outside of us.

"Blondie, don't feel bad. You're our pack leader, and your

heart, body, and soul will put us above everyone else. And it's okay. They were against us. They still might be," Sterling says, swinging his chain back and forth. "Now, stop it with the pity of others and pity me. I'm feeling needy as fuck. Antsy. I feel like I'll die if I don't burn off some energy, and since I can't run...give me a bone?"

I laugh in exasperation. "Seriously, horn dog? I'm not getting caught screwing you like this. Just take a breath and give me a second. I'll break the chains first and then figure out the collars."

He play-growls. "This is torturous. I don't know what the hell happened with that lycan spell, but damn it. Your scent is driving me wild. It's more powerful than before. I have the sudden urge to mount your launch pad and shoot my swimmers off for the great race."

Shit. I swear it better not have messed with the block on the mating spell, helping us keep our shit together and working as a magical contraceptive to ensure no one knocks me up during this maddening heat that could last weeks unless something fails and I get knocked up.

"It's not that," Caz says, messing with his chain. "I think the others that Antone mentioned must be close, and the rise in potential competition is messing with you. She's the same to me."

"Either way, I need to be freed." Sterling locks his hands around his chain and yanks it hard, sending sparks of magic through the air.

Pain bursts in my hands as if the shock he gets from messing with the restraints was my own. "Sterling—"

Another zap of electricity zaps from Sterling's chain without him even touching it. He hollers and drops to his knees, his body shuddering. Panic cascades through me at the sight of energy bolts blasting across the chains, wild and uncontrolled, shocking him again. Static flows over my skin, and I concentrate on blocking discomfort. Magic jumps from Sterling's chain and to Antone's, shocking him next.

I gasp as the air escapes my lungs. It's like messing with the restraints interrupted the spell, turning it haywire with my guys getting trapped in the faulty magic. Caz and Dax both step away, trying to get space between them and the electricity, but it doesn't work. The magical current dances from one anchor to the next, dropping them to the ground. I wobble, trying to push away the pain. I fear if I can't stop the power, my mates won't survive much more of the sizzling electricity meant to punish them, stopping them from trying to break out of the restraints.

Shrugging from the ceremonial robe, I wrap the billowing fabric around my hands and rush to the metal anchors staked into the ground. I brace for the electric shock of magic and grab onto Sterling's anchor first. I screech at the pain zinging to my core but refuse to let go. I can't stand seeing and feeling my mates like this. The second I see the witches, I'm going to do as Antone threatened and tear them apart, starting with Evelyn. I will not stand for this mistreatment. They only hold one thing over us, and if it takes a damn lycan to open up the gateway to Lulupoterra, I will find our own, even if I have to track down Mr. Remington to do so. I'm done here.

With my anger, I yank Sterling's anchor free from the ground. The force sends me sprawling backward on my naked ass. I don't even get a chance to push up before a heavy body lands on me, pinning me down. I instinctively wrap my body around Sterling's and hug him, laughing as he play-humps me and buries his face into the crook of my neck.

"My beautiful blond bombshell hero," he murmurs, his lips shocking me as he plants them to mine. "Let me show my gratitude."

A shadow looms over the two of us, and a second later, Dax hoists the two of us to our feet. I clutch Sterling, not letting him go, and he groans in my ear.

"Come on. We have to move," Dax says, rubbing a hand to each of our backs. "We need to use this to our advantage. If the Everdeens—"

A flash of light blinds me at the same time a growl escapes my lips. Enrique materializes a few feet away from me, his eyes glowing with his blue magic. My she-wolf breaks free of the cage I lock her in, and I transform in Sterling's arms. It's not often I've felt the most powerful in my wolf form, but something about seeing the flicker of fear in Enrique's gaze sets me off, feeding my beast, turning me monstrous.

I launch toward the warlock and crash into him, snarling in his face. I can't see or think straight, allowing my innate nature to do whatever the fuck is necessary to get my pack out of here.

"You're making a huge mistake," Enrique snaps, his voice deepening as his features morph into the monstrous disguise witches and warlocks use to try to intimidate those they find a threat.

I growl my response, the guttural noise reverberating through my body.

Enrique reaches for my neck, trying to hook a magical leash to my collar.

Fury bursts through me, and I bite his hand, growling and shaking my head, trying to break his arm off. He opens his mouth to shout a spell. It sets me off completely. I can't even stop myself as I shove my snout in his mouth and sink my teeth into his tongue.

Revenge tastes far better than I expect.

I won't stop attacking until I satiate my beast, even if it means swallowing this fucker whole.

4

WILD NATURE

I NEVER KNEW I COULD crave blood and flesh and bone, but now that Enrique's magic zings across my tongue and awakens my senses, I imagine savoring his despair as I show him how powerful I really am.

"Don't you dare hurt her!" Flynn's voice cuts through the air, and magic crackles above me. "I'll consider it an act of treason against the Tenebris Coven. You will regret it."

"But she's going to kill him!" Evelyn screams, the terror in her voice like a sweet melody to my ears. "She must be stopped."

Crackling magic rains down over me like a protective dome. I don't know what I was expecting, but it wasn't for Flynn to shield me from Evelyn as I sink my teeth into her coven brother's shoulder. Enrique hollers, failing to block himself. For being a supposedly powerful warlock, his fighting skills suck.

"I will handle her. Stand back. You've made a huge fucking mistake, High Priestess. I should let my familiar punish your brother as she sees fit. What the fuck did I tell you? These are *my* wolves. They're my familiar's pack, and they are under my protection. You crossed a damn line." Flynn's shadow draws closer. The minty fragrance of his powerful magic tickles my senses, interrupting my kill mission. "We had a deal."

"Flynn, please. Just control your she-wolf. We will work this out." Evelyn's voice softens with her desperation. "You're right. We have made a huge mistake, but this wasn't done out of ill intent. Enrique knew her pack wouldn't allow her to rest. They're all still feeling the remnants seeping through the spell blocking her heat. It makes them...more aggressive. Demanding. You know damn well that she will not tell any of them no. She can't help it."

"That's no excuse, Evelyn." Flynn risks closing the space completely and digs his fingers into the scruff of my neck. His magical shield remains in place, keeping Evelyn out. "My wolves aren't animals or pets. They are my family and damn well powerful enough that you should be fucking thankful they have good senses. It's already taking everything in me to stop my beautiful familiar."

I growl and snap at Enrique's bloody face once more. He jerks and yells, scrambling to drag his beaten body away from me. Flynn squats beside me and strokes his fingers over my furry snout, inspecting me for any injuries Enrique could've caused.

"They almost killed our pack," I think to him, replaying the image of the magic shocking Sterling, Dax, Antone, and Caz over and over again. "I want them to pay for their crimes."

Flynn scowls at my words and stands, gathering a glowing orb of power between his hands. My breath catches at the sensation of our souls seemingly merging and twining, his power tapping into mine to give him strength.

Chucking it at Evelyn, Flynn knocks her off her feet and restrains her to the ground. "Vu ta ere ezeerf! You not only changed my wolves but you restrained them with magic. I demand restitution. You will give me Enrique's control over the lycan."

Evelyn's face contorts with her anger. "That's not—"

Flynn waves his hand, sending another burst of energy colliding into Evelyn's chest, stealing her words. "You will accept my demands or I will find another coven to align with. Perhaps one of the other three would suffice. I'm done playing your games. I thought you were powerful and understood our needs, but you fail to understand what it means to be blessed with a bond to an incredible being."

Evelyn grimaces, her red power flickering in her irises. She opens and closes her mouth like she plans to argue, but Enrique groans and pushes up on his hands and knees. Flicking her gaze to him, she shares a silent conversation before relaxing against Flynn's power.

"We accept," she finally says after another quiet moment. "You will fill Enrique's spot. Now release me, so we can prepare."

Flynn lets his magic fizzle out, and I close my eyes, transforming into my human form. The red haze of anger clears from my vision. Shrugging out of his shirt, Flynn closes the space to me and helps me dress. He touches my cheek, drawing his gaze down to my lips, but doesn't lean in to kiss me.

"Stay with our pack and let me know if you need anything. I will come for you when we're ready. Things are changing around here. I promise. I realized my mistakes in allowing the Everdeens to think I was lesser than them. I thought it would help us in the end, but it seems that the only way we'll get what we need is to do as they do and demand it—steal it if we have to." Flynn's voice swirls through my mind, stroking my innate wildness, getting my heart to slow.

I moisten my lips, his protectiveness and power turning me on. "Please hurry. We have to talk in private. It's about my dad."

He blinks a few times and nods. "Should I postpone?"

I shake my head. "No, let's get this lycan shit over with and get our pack back. My family secrets can wait."

Brushing his lips to my forehead, he pulls away. Taking my hand, he strolls with me to where our pack waits in heated silence, their rage nearly palpable. Flynn's muscles ripple under the weight of their glares, but he doesn't back down or cower away. He instead offers his hand and helps Sterling to his feet first.

"I'm sorry for my shortcomings. I will remove the collars as soon as I return. If you feel as if my mistakes are unforgivable, I'll understand." Flynn's jaw twitches with his words. "Again, I'm sorry. It shouldn't have taken seeing you like this to realize I should've never tried to pretend to be someone I wasn't for the sake of a worthless alliance. You guys are far more important to me."

Dax allows Flynn to help him up next. Giving him a sharp nod, he says, "I know you're not going anywhere, and I've accepted your place in Lyric's life but we all need to change and work together."

"I agree," Antone says, pulling Caz up.

"Blind trust is not something we can manage, Flynn. I know Lyric trusts you with her life and soul, but we've built trust within our pack through time and work. I want to do the same with you. The only way to do so is to have a say in the decisions you think are best. I need to know you intend to truly be a pack mate and not just a mate of Lyric." Caz touches Flynn's shoulder and looks him in the eyes. "Is this something you can manage?"

Flynn bobs his head. "I want to be a pack mate."

Caz whacks him on the arm. "Good, because we want you to be one too."

My heart melts at Caz's words, and I can't stop myself from hugging him from behind. "I love you guys, you know."

Flynn smiles at me. "I do, my beautiful familiar."

"So do fucking I." Sterling drapes his arm around Flynn's shoulders and gives him a shake. "Now come the hell on. I'm supervising the whole spell thing and watching your back."

"You sure?" Flynn asks, furrowing his brows. "You look like you could use some care from our mate."

"I might actually need some care from you." Sterling guides Flynn to turn around and leans in close. He whispers something in his ear, and Flynn laughs with a groan.

Caz turns around to face me and lifts me into his arms like it's all he can think about. Antone and Dax join the two of us, and no one says anything as the chains and collars vanish from sight completely. Nerves manage to blossom in my chest again, and I peer around the quiet landscape, half-expecting to see one of the other Everdeen Coven members, but they're not around. We're now alone and free while we wait to see what happens next.

"Lyric, I want to believe that Flynn has the Everdeens in control, but I think they're only backing down to counterattack later," Dax says, enveloping me in his arms, squishing me to Caz.

"Oh, I know they are," I murmur, wondering if we should

stick to telepathy rather than risk being heard. "I found out something...confusing. Do you remember when you told me that a warlock helped my parents? That he created the den for them?"

"Mmmhmm." Dax rests his chin on my shoulder. "What about that?"

I squeeze my eyes shut and hug Caz tighter. "I don't know how truthful Enrique was being, but he said the warlock—Eliphas—was in love with my mother."

Antone stands behind him and touches my cheek, pushing my hair behind my ear to get a clearer view of my face. "If she was anything like you, I can see why."

I scrunch my nose. "But that's not it. He said...fuck. Levi isn't my biological father. I'm only half-wolf."

"Are you sure?" Dax asks, stepping around to stand next to Antone.

I shrug. "How can I be? All I know is that it makes sense. I'm not like the other she-wolves, and it's not because of being raised in the Mortal World."

"But Levi never said anything. Neither did my father." Dax's golden eyes search my face. "I don't understand."

"If that's the case, Cherie, then your dad wouldn't have needed to barter with a coven for your protection," Antone adds.

Caz grunts his agreement. "I think you're right. If Levi had known someone would come for him who wasn't part of the packs, he would've planned better. He wouldn't have relied on the pack leaders finding you in time for the games."

A strange light flickers from the windows of the estate, drawing our attention to it. Caz tightens his arms around me. My heart picks up pace, my body humming at the sensation of magic flowing through the air.

"Something is definitely wrong, and I have a feeling it has to do with them," I say, motioning toward the flicker of blue and red light. "Eliphas was their coven mate."

"Shit," Antone mutters.

"We should use their current distraction with the lycan curse to our advantage." Dax shifts on his feet. "What do you think, Lyric?"

"That's a good idea. I want to find out more about Eliphas." I wiggle in Caz's arms until he sets me down. "Let's split up and see what we can find."

I expect one of them to argue, but Antone and Dax nod their heads. Caz takes my hand, claiming me as his partner, and no one argues.

"Meet back here in twenty, okay?" Dax says, kissing my cheek. "Howl if you need us. Next time I want it to be me who tears the fuckers down."

"Is this a grimoire?" Caz runs his finger over a leather book with a metal plate on the cover. Engravings of unfamiliar symbols decorate the front along with what I think might be the Everdeen Coven crest.

I lean over his shoulder and flip open the book. "I think so. Those look like spells."

"It's old as hell," Caz adds.

Nudging Caz, I get him to sit on the bed and open the spell book to rest on our legs. My hand takes on a mind of its own, and I start flipping through the pages, entranced by how the handwriting changes the more pages I turn.

"It's all written in Witchland Tongue." Caz rests his hand on mine, getting me to slow my mission of discovery. "We have to take it. Flynn will be able to translate it for us."

"Enrique will know it's us." Sighing, I turn the pages until they turn blank. "Maybe we can come back."

Caz combs his hand through his hair and peers around. Silence falls between us as he thinks about things for a moment. A dozen scenarios dance through his thoughts, and I shift my hand and rest it on his thigh.

"Come on. I don't want to get caught in here. Like I said, we can come back. I'm sure we'll figure something out," I say, lifting the book into my hands.

"Or maybe that's what we should do." A smirk crosses Caz's handsome face, lighting his features as a chuckle escapes his lips. "I mean, maybe we should get caught in here. It'd cause a commotion, and—"

"You're fucking brilliant." I grin and play-smack his arm. "Might as well have some fun. Show them how wild we can be."

"Get the fucker back for what he did." Caz sets the book

beside us on the bed and gets to his feet. Grabbing a small statue from the nightstand, he chucks it at the wall, shattering it.

I laugh and snatch his wrist, stopping him from picking up another. "That's not exactly what I meant. I mean...we could have some fun, and you know, things could accidentally get destroyed in the process. Can't blame us for that. Like Evelyn said, you're aggressive. Demanding. Horny."

He chuckles. "You sound like Sterling."

I stand up and run my fingers over his bare chest, the only thing he grabbed to wear was a pair of shorts, and that makes this even more fun. "And?"

Sucking his bottom lip between his teeth, he reaches up and caresses his fingers to my jaw, his beautiful dark eyes searching mine. "You're serious." It's not a question. He can feel exactly how serious I am by the rush of desire rising through me.

I smile in response and reach between us, gliding my hand over his growing erection. "I know things have been up and down between us, and you've been so patient with me, but I finally realized that you're never going to just take what you want because of how considerate and empathetic you are to my needs, which I love. But Caz, I want you. You're mine, and with how things are in our lives, I know there will never be a perfect moment."

He hums under his breath and slides his hand behind my head, pulling me to him to kiss. Electricity zings between us, igniting a wave of hot passion inside me. My desperate mouth crashing to his sets him off, and he lifts me up and sets me on the dresser. Swinging his arm across the top, he knocks all of the books, a vase of some sort of tied together herbs, and a glass bottle of purple elixir to the floor.

I laugh and hook my fingers to his waistband, pulling him back to me. Easing my legs open, I make room for him to stand between them. His bone-hard body presses against mine as his mouth captures my lips for another kiss. I moan and roll my hips, grinding against him while playing with his hair, mussing the strands.

"I love you, Lyric," Caz says, breaking from my mouth to kiss the sensitive skin of my neck. "I've known it since meeting you at Ripped Fitness."

Linking his fingers to the hem of my shirt, he tugs it over my head and cups my breast, playing with my hard nipple.

"Was it before or after I beat your ass in a fight for the evening schedule?" I tease, reaching between us to stroke my hand over his hard length.

He chuckles. "The second you pinned me, I just knew I wanted to claim you as mine."

"I bet you didn't expect it would be me to claim you," I tease, tipping my head back with a moan. The sensation of his flexing cock between my legs turning me on even more.

"I still plan to claim you," he murmurs, sucking my breast into his mouth, kissing every inch of me on his mission to map out my body with his tongue. "Because you're mine."

"Is that so?" I rub my hands over his shoulders and arch my back, my whole body tingling in anticipation as he works lower.

"You're mine," he repeats. "My leader. My soul mate. My best friend."

Warmth blooms from my heart to course through the rest of me. "I love you, my determined, patient, self-less mate. I'm yours. Always."

He hums and opens his mind completely, drowning me in a wave of emotions I knew were there but haven't felt as intensely as I do now. I savor it, loving how our bond steals my breath and smothers me in the best way. Everything inside me shifts until all I can focus on is Caz. It's like the world around us shuts off, leaving us in a blissful haven where our love and passion can run as wild as our wolves.

Arching my back, I stretch my body, bending my knees to expose my naked body completely. It's like my she-wolf knew what was in store for us, because I didn't bother changing out of Flynn's shirt. I've grown used to wearing the bare minimum, and it no longer even bothers me.

Caz traces his fingers over my pelvis, slowing his mouth to admire my body, ready and waiting for him to proceed however he wants. Working his finger softly over my clit, he draws a line until he can dip his finger inside me, testing and feeling my excitement for him. He closes his eyes, savoring me, and I pant and grip the wall behind me in anticipation.

"Your scent is incredible," he murmurs, inhaling a long

breath. "I'm sure you taste even better."

Sliding his other hand behind me, he pulls me to the ledge and kisses between my legs while sliding his finger in and out of me, touching me in a way that makes my legs weak. Hunger for me lights his eyes, and he watches my reaction, enjoying the pleasure scrunching my features.

He hums in his throat, sending vibrations through me, and I scratch at the wall behind me, trying to hold myself still. Caz sucks my clit, rolling his tongue in quick strokes over and over again, the rhythm and pressure taking me to my peak. I brace on the dresser, digging my fingers so hard into the wood that my nails turn into the claws of my wolf, damaging the top.

Panic rises inside me, but Caz grabs my hand and rubs his fingers over my palms, linking our hands together to calm the beast threatening to break free.

"You really are feeling wild for me," he murmurs, grinning like he's proud of himself for drawing out my deep-seated nature.

It helps me relax, and I smile and slide off the dresser, hopping right back into his arms. Spinning me, he tosses me toward the bed, and I unleash my wild side again, tearing at the duvet, sending feathers scattering through the room. Caz's gaze burns over me so hotly that I'm certain he'll set the fabric around me ablaze. Locking his fingers to the duvet, he drags me closer and flips me over. I wiggle my ass at him and laugh, crawling forward, getting him to join me. He tosses the duvet aside, and I grab a pillow, swinging it at the nightstand, sending everything off.

"Turn that way," Caz says, kneeling behind me, using his hand to nudge me to face the wall instead of the headboard.

I meet his heavy-lidded gaze in the long mirror on the closet door. Stroking his hand over the length of his shaft, he teases me for a minute, giving me a show. Anticipation courses through me, and I back up a bit like the damn wolf in heat that I am, craving to feel him inside me. We've bonded in heart and soul, and giving him my body is all I want. I don't care if this started out as a plot to steal a book. This moment means far more than I realized, and I feel as if declaring our love and claim to each other will help right all that is wrong in our world.

"I love seeing you," he adds, coming up behind me.

Damn it, do I enjoy the idea of watching us too.

Caz's eyes darken at my thought, and he leans over and kisses my spine. Aligning his body to mine, he teases me with his tip, moaning with such ecstasy I can feel it in my bones, his pleasure radiating through me as if it were my own.

I grip the sheet between my fingers and gasp as he slides into me completely, slowly at first, savoring the sensation of my body. Grabbing my hips, he holds me in place and rocks his body, picking up his pace. His pelvis bumps my ass, and I gasp with each penetrative thrust, the movement hitting me just right that I can't stop my mouth from shouting my enjoyment. It's like every nerve in my body lights up, prickling and igniting me in waves of wild and hot sensations, as fierce and uncontrollably powerful as we are.

Reaching forward, Caz grabs my hair, gathering it in his fist to keep it out of my face. I pant and keep my eyes on his, loving watching his bulging muscles flexing, how his pouty mouth remains slightly open with his puffs of breath. He's as sexy as the first day we met, and I lose myself to every good memory we've shared together, leading up to this moment. He's mine, and nothing can change that. Caz holds a piece of my heart and soul, and I know he'll protect me with his life as I will protect him.

Tingles build between my legs, my body reacting to Caz's as he gets close to cumming. Bowing forward, I rest my head to the sheet, his climax setting me off. Caz pulls out of me and cums across Enrique's bed, grunting as he purposely gets it on the sheets.

I laugh in surprise, covering my mouth.

"Payback," Caz says, grabbing the last pillow and setting it on top of the mess, pressing it into the mattress.

"Still doesn't feel like enough," I say, flopping over onto my back.

Caz lies beside me and snuggles me into the crook of his arm. "This is just the start. I—"

The door to Enrique's bedroom flings open and clatters against the wall. Caz growls, transforming into a wolf faster than my mind can register that Enrique glowers in the doorway. He doesn't have a chance to move as Caz launches from the bed at him. I scramble to my feet and grab a heavy metal statue from the floor.

I throw it hard at the mirror, shattering it, causing Enrique to lose his focus on Caz. Enrique hollers, but he can't manage to spit out a spell. Colliding into the warlock, Caz sends the two of them into the hallway. Electricity zaps through the air, and Caz screeches and snarls.

"Stop!" a feminine voice yells from the hallway.

A blast of blue light cascades through the air, and Caz flies back in the room. He rolls across the floor and hits the wall with a thump.

My heart slides into my stomach.

"Fuck, Caz!" I say, rushing to him.

He doesn't move.

5

GRIMOIRE

FURY KICKS ME INTO ACTION, and I charge toward Heather and Trinity. They stand together, creating a barrier between me and Enrique. Grinding my teeth, I charge them, hellbent on showing them that they don't scare me.

Trinity summons an orb of electricity in her palm, but Heather grabs her wrist, throwing off her aim. The power crashes into a bookcase, sending it tipping over and collapsing on the carpet. Commotion sounds from the hallway, and I sense Dax and Antone drawing near, their rage as hot as mine.

"She-wolf, I won't hurt you," Heather says, getting in front of her coven sister. "I want to check on your mate. Please."

Blue light explodes through the room, and Flynn materializes beside me. Growls reverberate through the hallway as Sterling joins the others outside the room. I automatically clutch Flynn's hand and yank him toward Caz, still lying on the floor.

"Help him," I say, my voice threatening to crack. "The witch attacked him for protecting me."

"What are you doing in here?" Flynn asks lowly, running his hand through the fur on Caz's side.

"Trying to find answers. I found a spell book," I think to him, worried my voice will give me away.

"And you want me to take it?" he responds, his eyes flickering.

"Duplicate it or something. They can't know." I press my lips together and pet Caz's furry head, watching as he comes to, the magic blast only knocking him out.

Flynn tightens his jaw and nods. "I'm going to need a bigger distraction, she-wolf."

I twist my lips to the side and nod. "Fuck, I'm on it."

Abandoning Caz and Flynn, I rush toward the hallway and the two witches keeping everyone back. They both tense, treating me like a beast despite being in my human form. Something about their caution and fear prods at my inner wolf. The thrill of being regarded as dangerous makes this so much sweeter.

"Where are the rest of my mates?" I call, shoving my hand into Trinity's chest, testing her strength. "I need them. My body aches so much for them." I sound whiny and desperate, totally needy. If I could see my mates, I guarantee I'd spot their ears perking up.

Heather sucks in a breath and holds her hands out, trying to keep me back. "High Priestess, I think the season spell is wearing off."

Evelyn claps her hands and materializes in the room beside me. I do the only thing I can think of. Grabbing the front of her shirt, I spin her and pin her against the wall. I growl in her face and lock my hand around her throat, keeping her focus on me. My reaction keeps the other witches' attention on me too as they prepare to intervene if they feel their High Priestess is in danger of my wrath.

"Tell them to let my mates through," I snap, quietly listening to Flynn and Caz from a few feet away. "I need them. I'm done with being kept apart. You trying to bind me to a lycan contract is bad enough. You can't keep messing with my pack and our needs. They're mine, not yours. Let them through."

Evelyn's eyes widen, her irises sparking red with her stolen magic. "You're right, sister. The spell must've faltered."

I bare my teeth and glower, leaning in to get in her face. "Don't talk about me like I'm not here."

"So they were breeding in my room?" Enrique snaps, his

voice rising in annoyance. "Get her out. Now!"

I nearly break my act, wanting to laugh so badly. Breeding? If pulling out and cumming all over his sheets is considered breeding, then sure. "We're sorry. We couldn't help ourselves." Whimpering, I squeeze my legs together, trying to ignore my embarrassment at having to blatantly admit to being horny and impulsive. It's one thing to act as such with my pack like after the witch bitch from Nightstar triggered my heat with a spell. But now? I really don't want to admit to the animalistic side of me that loves a good fuck. "It was the first one we passed."

"Lyric, settle down and let the High Priestess go," Flynn says from somewhere out of view.

Evelyn raises her hand. "It's okay. She's not going to hurt me. She's overwhelmed by her breeding needs."

"Please," I say, pretending to ignore Flynn. "The urge—it's all-consuming. Demanding. I can't resist. It's the only thing that can help with the ache."

My fake confirmation of Evelyn's thoughts from earlier strokes her damn ego like lighter fluid to a flame. Her jaw twitches, her raised eyebrow saying everything without her having to say the words. She loves that she thinks she was right about me. The cocky witch. It takes everything in me not to slap her and yell that I'm only acting, but I need to keep her focus for a bit longer. I can't see Flynn, but I can sense him. He pretends to keep Caz away in my peripheral vision.

"I need my mates. All of them," I add. "Let them through."

Flynn grunts and magic flickers. A small scuffle tries to grab my attention as Caz dodges past Flynn in my direction.

"Good work, she-wolf," Flynn whispers into my mind.

"Please!" I screech and shake Evelyn, shoving her to the wall one more time.

She doesn't have time to react as I step away and clench my fingers into fists. Her attention jerks away from me and lands behind me.

"I'm here, Lyric. I'm ready to take care of you again," Caz says, his deep voice booming through the room. His arms slide around my body, and he presses into my back. "No one will stop us. I'll destroy anyone who tries."

"Caz." Flynn's sharp voice whips over us, and I twist and glance at him.

Pulling me into him, Caz slides his hand down my back, our bodies flush together. The spark of passion we shared lights between us. I fake the loudest moan in existence, the noise being the only thing stopping me from reacting by jumping into his arms.

Utter silence greets me, and my skin prickles. I realize my reaction might've sounded a little too good, because I swear to the universe, I can hear all my mates' hearts picking up pace. Their scents trickle around me, inviting me to join them in the hallway. We all might be on some magical birth control, but damn it. I'm starting to believe that maybe the spell really is faltering. The desire pouring into the room is intense in the best way.

My body reacts in excitement. Fuck.

Sterling and Dax both groan from the hallway, now in their human forms.

"Damn," Antone mutters, and I catch sight of him looking for a way past the witches. I already know he plans to wrestle me into submission the second I allow him to, especially now that I've allowed Caz to claim my body.

It's enough to get Evelyn to move from her place. "Flynn, your wolves are on the brink of losing control. What do you want to do?" she asks, inching as slowly as she can away from the wall like any sudden movements might send me and Caz fucking on top of her. "If we let them go into a mating frenzy and just let them breed, it will help control them."

"No. Lyric doesn't want that," Flynn says, finally getting his shit together. With one look at his eyes, I can tell he was just as enamored by me, losing himself in our pack's desire. He tugs Caz back and hands him the ripped duvet. "Cover up and go join the others. I want you to meet us in Lyric's room, okay? Don't go anywhere. Some space will settle you all down. Take a cold shower."

I think it's me who is in need of a cold shower.

Caz releases a fake growl but doesn't argue with Flynn, accepting the blanket without wrapping it around his naked body. It's then I realize why. It's like the grimoire radiates power, tickling my senses. Flynn did it and without being noticed. He managed to replicate the book, because I see another copy of it lying on the floor.

Caz touches my cheek. "Is that okay, Lyric? I don't have to go."

I slowly nod. "I'm sure it's for the best."

With one last kiss to my cheek, Caz strides from the room, joining the others. I watch all four of them stroll past the door, looking in on us like they need confirmation that we're going to be okay without them.

"Hey, Caz," I think to him, sending him a small memory of our fun. "We will cuddle later. Promise. I want more time to enjoy you as my mate."

"Damn. What the hell did I miss? I want in on it," Sterling teases, back stepping to wag his brows at me.

I smirk and shoo him with a wave of my hand. "Possibly."

"You can't resist double the peen forever." Sterling's hum echoes from the hall, sending warmth between my legs at the idea. He's right. I'm starting to imagine all the ways I can take care of my guys' desires at once. It's like my wolf craves it, especially knowing how good they can make me feel. "I know you dream about it."

Suppressing my urge to follow after them, I think, "Keep our pack out of trouble and you can have whatever you want."

He play-growls. "Damn it. I love it when she gives me hope. You guys better do as I say, and she might let you participate. That ass...fuck. It's mine again. Dibs."

Flynn squeezes my hand, drawing my attention away from Sterling and his ass-obsession. I sigh and sink into his open arms, wanting so badly to cuddle and just breathe in the scent of safety I find in his arms. If Enrique didn't stride into his room and curse, I'd whisper for Flynn to pick me up. Instead, I twist and glower, preparing myself to put the asshole in his place if I have to.

Evelyn snaps her fingers together like she's calling an animal. "Lyric, why don't you come with me to our altar room, so I can give you a bit more of the potion to suppress your desires?"

I grimace, hating the sound of that. "I'm fine now. I was just worked up over *everything*. My warlock will watch out for me."

"You don't trust us," she says, placing her hands on her hips.

"Of course I don't fucking trust you. Nothing good can come from the coven who thinks they are entitled to benefit from me because of my dad. If that were the case, wouldn't you think your coven brother would've ensured we met sooner? You wouldn't have collared me in the first place. You—" I groan, digging my nails into my fingers. This wasn't how I had planned to tell Flynn.

"Wait, what are you talking about, Lyric?" Flynn asks, touching my chin, getting me to look at him.

"You told her, Enrique?" Evelyn asks, her eyes narrowing at her coven brother. "We talked about this. It wasn't the right time."

Is she kidding me?

He throws his arms out. "I was trying to gain her trust."

Pointing, Evelyn says, "Behind my back? Like with the lycan bargain? Like with Eliphas and Melody?"

She blasts power at his feet, making him stumble back. He falls on his bed and scowls as his fingers touch the sticky sheets. I burst out in uncontrollable laughter, wishing my mates could see his reaction. Juvenile? Maybe. Worth it? Absolutely.

"I'm beginning to question your loyalty, Enrique. You've done nothing to prove you respect me as your High Priestess since our brother faced the wrath of the fates. Now until you can show me you have our coven's best interests above your own, you will be cut off from the power of our coven." Evelyn's hair blows around her head, her usually perfect black bob tousled by her magic. "Maybe this will appease you and your pack, Flynn. My coven and I would really love to form a union. Please know Enrique acted alone."

"You—"

"Etum ruoy hita vi!" Waving her hand, Evelyn flings magic at Enrique, shutting him up.

His eyes widen, and he tries to get up to charge, but Evelyn and Flynn both grab onto me. Power lights up the room and swallows us. My head spins at the sudden relocation from Enrique's room, and I clutch Flynn, bracing against his sturdy frame.

A deep intake of breath sounds from the corner of the room.

Goosebumps prickle over my skin, making me shiver. I swivel my torso to follow the subtle rattling of chains and spot a naked man kneeling in the same spot I watched the mortal man die earlier. But this man doesn't look scared. He only reacts with a huge smile that lights his rugged features, his unkempt beard needing a trim.

"My beautiful goddess, you've returned to me," the man says, bowing forward.

Shit.

Evelyn twitches her nose and offers him a smirk, the gesture softening her features. "Of course I have, my pet. You are so very special to me."

"Is it time?" he asks, keeping his forehead on the floor.

"Almost. I wanted to introduce you to Lyric. She will be the one bestowing you with a gift of power worthy for those who serve us well." Evelyn saunters closer and bends down, touching her palm to the man's back. "Will you say hello, my dear pet."

The guy finally lifts his head to stare at me. "Hello."

Damn. This is awkward as hell.

Forcing my mouth to smile, I say, "Last chance to change your mind. The last guy died at my feet." I don't know why I say the words, but seeing how eager this man is weirds me the hell out.

The man straightens his shoulders, giving me an unwanted view of his pitiful flaccid cock. At least he won't have much to miss in his lycan form if the curse takes. "Because he was not worthy of the gift of power. I am. I'm ready."

Before I can open my mouth, Flynn spins me back to him and cuts me off with a kiss. I fucking hate and love being interrupted with affection, but this time, I know it's for the best. My humanity needs to stop feeling guilty. This guy clearly wants to risk his life for whatever Evelyn promised, and I should be grateful. Because with him, we'll be able to re-enter Lulupoterra. I'll be able to bring my pack mates home.

Flynn eases away from my lips. "We will return within the hour. Lyric needs to cleanse and prepare for the spell."

Evelyn nods and rubs her hands together, summoning a glass vial of some sort of green potion. "Don't forget this. I worry about you stepping in between the she-wolf and her mates, despite her being your familiar."

A small growl escapes my throat, rumbling through my chest. My need to shout at her that he wouldn't get between us, but he'd join us, consumes me. I want to prove to her she knows nothing of how our pack works.

Flynn chuckles, his wave of amusement simmering my annoyance. "I'll be fine." He takes the potion from her and shakes it. "Thanks for this."

Scooping me into his arms, he carries me like a blushing bride to the door. Whispering his transportation spell into my ear, he relocates us outside my bedroom with a blink of my eyes. Silence greets us, though I can sense my mates behind the door. Flynn's magical shield protecting us hums with energy, calming the anxiety always threatening to tighten my chest.

"Hey, do they know?" Flynn asks, tipping his head toward the door. "I mean, about Eliphas."

I nod with a sigh, my eyes blurring with tears. Blinking them away, I gather my nerve to speak. It's harder and harder to say the words out loud, but Flynn needs to hear it just like the rest of our pack. "I didn't want to believe it at first, but it makes sense. I just—how is it possible? How could my dad never tell me? My parents grew up with the same pack mentality as everyone. My mom knew she'd conceive children for her chosen mates. Each mate claims his kin and accepts his pack mates' children as pack members and nephews. I just—why is everything this complicated and fucked up?"

Flynn rushes to open the door of the room, spinning me to kick the door closed. Like the rest of my mates know I need them, I'm suddenly enveloped in the middle of the best group hug of my life as lips kiss the trembles away from different parts of my body.

"What the fuck is wrong with me?" I ask, trying not to sniffle. "I don't cry. Crying accomplishes nothing." At least, that's what my dad used to say. *Bottle up those damn tears and put your emotions to good work, Lyric. Sweat it out. Let it push your ass up to fight instead of letting it bring you down.*

Damn it, Dad. He should've known how impossible a task that'd be without him telling me what to do and how to get my shit together.

"Sure it does, blondie. It kills boners, so we can do shit like this without getting in a sword fight. And Dax is a bit too close. He might swing and send Caz into the wall, which will make me jealous. I know how you get when one of us gets hurt. Bandages and blow jobs. A little tender love and extra care. We all know your sweet pink portal will transport us to paradise."

I tip my head back and laugh, bonking it against his shoulder. "All you've done is make me want to watch your cock fight for a chance to claim my treasure trove."

He releases a sexy, growly rumble from his throat and steps back, his cock growing seemingly on command. "All right. You heard her. Who wants to test the strength and determination of the great Excalicock."

Dax chuckles and breaks away from our hug. "Whatever it takes to see our mate smile."

Sterling straightens his shoulders. "All right, bestie. Work your magic. Get your Merlin whirlin'. I need an extra inch to battle that ass annihilator."

Fuck me.

I wiggle from Flynn's arms and get between Dax and Sterling, holding my palms up to each of them. "I only have an hour before we do the lycan curse. I'd prefer to spend it loving rather than fighting."

"There is also the matter of the grimoire, Lyric," Caz says, speaking up.

I shift on my feet to meet his gaze, realizing he holds the

book with his hand separating the pages. "You found something."

"It's not all written in Witchland Tongue, Cherie. Only the spells." Antone meets me with his dark gaze, his face remaining expressionless.

I blink a few times. "Why didn't you guys tell me immediately? What did you find? Let me see."

Sterling groans and Dax cuts him off, returning to my side. Clutching my face, he steals my attention, not allowing me to focus on anyone else. His golden eyes search mine, and the others fall silent as we lose ourselves in each other's gazes until my heartbeat slows, and I can get my wild emotions under control.

"Lyric, I want you to know that no matter what is in the book, it doesn't change anything between our pack and the fates choosing you to be ours. Your dad—Levi loved you so much." Dax strokes his fingers along my cheek. "I know he did. You were the most important person to him."

My mouth dries at his words. "So...it really is true."

He tightens his jaw. "It is. This book doesn't belong to Enrique. It was Eliphas's."

I sigh and close my eyes.

"That's not the only thing, Cherie," Antone murmurs, stepping up behind me.

Once again, my pack engulfs me in their strong arms.

"Just spit it out," I say, my muscles tense. "Tell me everything."

Sterling sighs against my shoulder, stepping up to deliver what might be earth-shattering, life-altering news, and the type of revelation that should remain buried and locked away.

"We're nearly certain it was the Everdeens who killed your mom and Eliphas," Sterling says, sliding his arm around my back.

"We think they were also responsible for the doppelgangers that weakened the protection spell in Lunar Crest," Caz adds. "They made them look like they were from the Fire Mountain Clan."

"They're also responsible for the shift in power that allowed the Nightstar Coven to move in and take over Lulupoterra." Dax's words rumble against my earlobe.

I stiffen. "Fuck. What do we do? I can't give them power over a lycan. They'll use him against us. They probably only want to open the gateway to try to take out Nightstar Coven to try to control the packs as their own."

Resting my face against Dax's chest, I breathe in his scent, trying to let it consume me.

"We won't let that happen, she-wolf," Flynn says, speaking up for what seems like the first time since we entered the room. And maybe it is. "I have a plan."

I turn my gaze to him. "Does it mean not going through with the lycan curse?"

He shakes his head. "That's the easiest way to open the gateway, but that's not my plan. Preparing the spell with Evelyn gave me an idea and the grimoire has exactly what I need."

"Going to need a better explanation than that, bestie. Your mind is too jumbled to decipher," Sterling says.

Flynn grabs the spell book from Caz and flips through pages until he spots what he needs. "I can make a cure to the lycan curse. We can take control back."

My eyes widen. "A cure? But at what cost?"

Flynn's eyes flicker with his lavender magic. "A powerful sacrifice."

Damn it.

He shakes his head at my reaction. "Don't lose hope so soon, she-wolf. I know exactly who we'll use."

6

THE CURSE

"IT'S ALL OF US OR nothing." I cross my arms, standing just inside the altar room where the mortal man grovels naked by Evelyn's feet.

My stomach twists and my chest tightens. I don't want to be here, let alone participate in some of the darkest magic in the universe, but it's something I have to do if I want to take our lives back and free our species from the cruel power of these witch bitches.

Evelyn opens her mouth to argue, and Heather touches her shoulder, offering me a kind smirk. "It wouldn't hurt any, High Priestess. Her pack can support her. You know a mate bond runs deeper than body and mind. They're connected by their souls. I can see it."

Heather's eyes sparkle with her blue magic as she drinks in the sight of me standing protectively in front of my mates. Something about the witch seems different from the others. She's kinder, though misguided by her loyalty toward a coven who wants nothing more than to bring harm.

"If you believe it is in our best interest, then I will accept your assessment of the pack, dear sister. Your brother would be so proud that you care about your niece despite his shortcomings." Evelyn flicks her gaze to me. "Your mates may join us, but if any of them try to interfere—"

"My wolves won't be a problem," Flynn says, cutting between Antone and Dax, his arms full with a bag of ingredients. "Now that your treacherous brother is not trying to intervene, they've settled down."

"He will learn his place," Evelyn says, still standing up for Enrique. "I assure it. You know how these things go when a coven loses a leader and another must step up."

Icy dread trickles down my back, and I shiver at her comment. Flynn tenses, his biceps bulging as he sets the bag down next to the altar in front of the circle of fresh blood. Without having to hear his thoughts, I know he thinks of his coven and the tragedy they faced, being set up.

"I can only imagine," Flynn responds, keeping his voice even.

Now that Evelyn brings up the power struggle within her coven again, I realize that it could very well have been one of the five covens that separated Lulupoterra from Magaelorum that set the Tenebris Coven up.

"If it was, we will find out and tear them apart," Sterling thinks, keeping his comment between us.

Flynn bobs his head without a word. He continues setting things up, dropping ingredients into a stone bowl until he lights it aglow with his lavender magic. The mortal man peeks up from his place on the floor, still bowing to the false idol he found in Evelyn.

"My wolves, please take your places outside the protective circle and transform to give your leader your strength. She will need your bond to help guide her through the magic." Flynn looks up. "What Lyric is about to accomplish is draining, but know that no matter how she looks, she is safe in my care."

"She better be," Antone mutters.

"He already knows his nuts are on the line if he fucks up," Dax responds, giving Flynn a pointed look, his gaze speaking volumes.

Caz huffs a breath, though he keeps his emotions from me. "Good thoughts, assholes."

"Yeah, fuckers. My badass blond bombshell is going to be better than fine. She's going to be fucking magical and get us one step closer to bringing our pack mates home." Sterling leans against the wall and graces me with a reassuring smile. "And then double the peen. Sagan will have desperately missed us both."

I try not to react, narrowing my eyes at him instead of laughing like I want. Because he's fucking ridiculous.

"Lyric, please take your place by my side. It's time to begin," Flynn says, extending his arm to me to take my hand. He guides me with him into the bloody circle.

Evelyn helps the mortal man up, and her two coven brothers—Samson and Godfrey—join her side. Heather and Trinity come and silently stand before me, waiting for Flynn's direction.

"It is an honor to lead a spell circle, combining the magic of the Tenebris Coven with that of the power of the Everdeen Coven," Flynn begins, handing the stone bowl to Heather. He circles behind me and eases the ceremonial robe from my shoulders, letting it billow at my feet. "Please bless my beautiful wolf familiar and her pack mates, giving them the strength to bestow the gift of power to a man chosen by the fates."

"Blessed the fates," everyone says in unison.

Silence draws through the room as the witches follow Flynn's instructions, using a potion and blood to bind my strength to the man to help him survive a curse. Without the screaming and fighting like before, it doesn't feel as if I'm damning the man to a life of misery. Whatever Flynn had done to help

Evelyn worked. My heart remains in control, and I don't even flinch as I'm pricked with an athame.

"Eerf eht tsaeb et mon cocin teni Cursed One rad ges ti," Flynn says, his voice echoing through the room. "You will embrace the power of the beast."

The others join hands around us, chanting the same thing as Flynn. "Eerf eht tsaeb et mon cocin teni Cursed One rad ges ti."

My transformation grabs hold of me so quickly that I don't realize I'm a wolf until the world sharpens and the man gasps in astonishment. Like before, the need to sink my teeth into his flesh consumes me, sending a strange energy buzzing over my body. I launch forward, growling, my she-wolf wild and out of control under the influence of magic. My mind can barely grasp what I'm doing, but Flynn snatches my wolf body, and restrains me in his arms.

His fingers sink deeply into my coat, scratching me with his affection. "Be gentle, she-wolf. It will only take one bite."

Setting me on my paws, Flynn keeps his hand locked to the scruff of my neck, guiding me forward. The witches continue to chant, making my stomach flip. A growl escapes my mouth, and I can't control the feral beast claiming my humanity. I don't know what's wrong with me. It's like my wolf and human rationale go to war. My wolf wants to devour this man instead of turning him into a lycan. Maybe because of the threats lycans pose or because I'm helping the same witches who want me caged. Either way, it doesn't matter. No magic is strong enough to tame my beast.

Lunging forward, I break away from Flynn's hold and knock the man onto his back. He covers his face protectively, yelling out for the first time. His fear scents the air as sweat beads on his forehead. No one can react fast enough to my wild nature. Sinking my teeth into the man's shoulder, I bite down hard, filling my mouth with blood.

The man convulses in pain, his back arching.

I growl and bite the man again. I can't help it.

My wolf wants him dead.

"Lyric, stop!" Flynn yells, grabbing onto the fur on my back. "That's enough!"

Biting down on the man's neck, I try to rip out his throat.

"Lyric!"

Power shocks me to my core, and pain collides into my soul, shadowing my vision.

The last thing I see is the man turning into a lycan.

Magic consumes me.

Screams ring in my ears, stealing my senses away. I can feel the pain of the lycan as if it is my own. I blink, trying to rid the darkness from my vision, but it doesn't work. I'm lost in the magic consuming my soul, trying to cage the beast inside me.

"Blondie, hey. Can you hear me?" Sterling's voice swirls through my mind, twining around me like a tether to pull me from the abyss. "It's all over. Your mind is just trying to process. Magic doesn't try to control you."

Then why can't I open my eyes? I feel far worse than I had during the first attempt. Not only do I feel as if my body split apart and fell back together, but I also feel as if a part of my soul has been ripped away, leaving me feeling as if something's missing.

"Come on, blondie. Try and open your eyes for me. I know you've been through a lot, but I miss your beautiful blue gaze devouring me like the piece of meat I want to be for you." A warm hand touches my lower back, sending tingles over my body.

"Keep talking to her," Flynn says, his voice soft like the caress of his lips on mine. "She needs grounding. The spell took a huge toll on her this time around."

"You hear that, blondie? He wants me to keep talking to you, and the only thing I can think to say that might entice you to open your eyes is all the things I plan to do to you the second I can. I'm pretty sure my bestie might not recover from hearing such things. He needs to be ruined a bit more by you." Sterling's hand glides up my back and combs my hair off my shoulders. "I'd be happy to help if you want. He can really jump into sharing is caring with me."

Flynn chuckles. "I'm trying. You know how intimidating the others are. Dax barely tolerates me."

"Because you gotta work your magic," Sterling says, the

lightness of his voice begging me to open my eyes to see his beautiful smile. "Teach him that you can only turn a great time into something fucking fantastic."

My body reacts to his words, and I groan, fighting against the heaviness of my eyelids.

Sterling's hand wanders down my spine and to my ass. He squeezes my ass cheek. "Mmm, you like the thought of that, don't you blondie? Open your eyes and maybe we can give you a little tease. Work the warlock up for one helluva bang."

"You're way too damn excited over the idea," I murmur, pouting my bottom lip. "I just cursed a man to witch servitude and all you can think about it using Flynn's magic to get off."

"Ouch, blondie," Sterling says, leaning over me. "You know I intend to get you off first. I've missed you. Do you know how long you've been out?"

I turn my gaze to Flynn. "You tell me. I know this horn dog will only say eternity."

Flynn smirks and touches my cheek. "Only a couple hours. It's dark, so we will meet with Evelyn in the morning to talk about what our next step is in opening a gateway. The rest of your mates are strategizing different approaches and making territory maps."

"You're not helping, Sterling?" I ask, trying to push away my nerves.

"They have it covered, blondie. Now don't make me beg for you to kiss me and stop thinking about things we don't need to worry about at the moment, okay?" Sterling massages his fingers into my back. "Let's just—"

A zap of power flickers in the air, and Sterling yelps, hopping to his feet. Flynn laughs, rubbing his hands together, clearly behind Sterling's reaction. Sterling growls and stalks toward Flynn, preparing to tackle him.

Flynn raises his hands in surrender. "I give up. I'm no match for you. I was only trying to kill your boner so our gorgeous mate can process."

Sterling narrows his eyes. "I was going to suggest we relax and cuddle."

Laughing, Flynn says, "Yeah, right after you ask to bone."

Charging forward, Sterling attempts to tackle Flynn, but he's quick on his feet, spinning out of the way. Sterling flings his arm and smacks Flynn right on the ass, making him jump. I crack up, and prop up on my elbows, watching their playful wrestling match on the floor.

Another pop of power flickers through the air, and Sterling startles at the shock. Flynn doesn't have the chance to move before Sterling flips him onto his stomach.

"Smack his bare ass, horn dog!" I call, scooting to the edge of the bed. "It's only fair."

"You're helping him?" Flynn asks, waving his fingers to try to shock Sterling again.

"Damn straight, she is. You know she has a thing for those less fortunate." Sterling hooks his fingers to the waistband of

Flynn's jeans and drags them down. "Now you heard her, hold still so I can do what she wants."

Flynn laughs and shakes his ass at Sterling. "You can try, asshole."

Sterling swings his hand, but Flynn chants a spell, freezing his arm in place. I practically cackle, my voice cutting through the air. Sliding off the bed, I saunter toward Flynn and Sterling, totally checking the two of them out.

"Careful, she-wolf. I hear your thoughts. If you even try to spank me, I'll—"

I smack Sterling's ass, breaking him out of the spell. Flynn doesn't have the chance to react as Sterling's palm swats him right on his bare ass cheek. I scramble away, rushing across the room, running from retaliation. Sterling tackles Flynn, and the two of them wrestle, trying to spank each other, making me laugh even harder as it turns into a damn competition.

"I'm starting to get jealous that you guys are leaving me out," I tease, perching on the edge of the bed. "Can you at least take your shirts off? Give me a show?"

Sterling takes my dare and grabs Flynn's shirt, ripping it down the front to show off his body.

"You're in fucking trouble now, Sterling," Flynn says, his voice shaking with his laughter.

Waving his hand, Flynn chants a spell under his breath. Sterling's clothes explode into a million pieces, raining down on us like confetti. I laugh and cheer, catching the tiny pieces. I jump to my feet and dump them onto Sterling's head. He straddles Flynn in surprise, completely naked on top of him.

And suddenly, we're all thinking about it.

Who knew their playfulness would be so sexy? Or how great they get along...how much I enjoy seeing them tear each other's clothes off.

"You naughty blondie," Sterling murmurs, tipping his head back.

"I'm the naughty one? I can clearly see how much you're enjoying wrestling my warlock. I can feel it too. It's hot." I trace my fingers across his shoulders. "I had no idea how much I'd love seeing two of the men I love together. Messing around."

"Teaming up to rip our mate's clothes off," Flynn adds, resting his hands behind his head, not even caring that Sterling hasn't moved off him yet. "Actually, I can handle that."

A burst of energy hums across my skin as my long shirt tears at the seams and falls to the floor. I place my hands on my hips and glare at Flynn. Sterling wags his eyebrows and reaches around to grab me by my ass. I don't resist as he flips me over his shoulder and right onto Flynn's head. Flynn hums and hooks his hand to my hips, stopping me from scrambling away. I link my fingers through his hair, keeping him inches away from my naked body.

"All right, horn dog. I demand you finish your task. It's unfair that we have to be the only one's naked. I'll hold him down." I laugh and slide back, sitting on Flynn's chest. "You might have magic, warlock, but I have Sterling, and he's just as creative."

"Fuck, I love when she talks about me like this." Sterling kisses my shoulder from behind. "Just cover his mouth, blondie. Keep those magic hands of his restrained. He's getting naked."

Flynn chuckles, far more relaxed than I've ever seen him, and I bow forward and silence him with a kiss. He lets me pin his arms over his head, shifting and moving, pretending like he's resisting Sterling's mission.

But I can feel how much he likes our team effort. How he feels as if we're all bonded and truly a pack, despite him not being a wolf. I can also feel something strange and exciting blossoming.

"That's love, blondie. Bromance. I don't know if you're aware, but you soak me in your lust and appreciation for the warlock." He kisses my other shoulder. "And the fact that you love that I can feel and accept your feelings for Flynn as if they're my own..."

Flynn arches up and squishes me between Sterling. "Aw, bestie. I love you too, man."

I grin and trail my hands down their hard pecs. "You should just kiss already. Seal your sweet words with a real bonding moment."

Biting my lip, I wait to see their reactions. Curiosity washes over me coming from them, and they shift slightly to look around me at each other. Anticipation quickens my breathing as I get caught in the middle of...something unexplainable. My body tingles, desire building warmth between my thighs. Sterling flares his nostrils, inhaling a shuddering breath. Arousal hardens Flynn's cock, and it presses against me. I'm in the middle of one sexy sandwich that awakens a carnal need inside me.

"Lyric," Flynn says softly, his voice a whispered breath against my neck. "You love the idea."

Blush heats my cheeks, and I lift and drop my shoulders. "Is it too much? I had no idea the thought would turn me on."

"Me either," Flynn and Sterling say at the same time, their muscles flexing at their admission.

I raise my eyebrows. "It does? You guys aren't just saying that because you're always down to give me what I want?"

"That's me, blondie, not him. He loves resisting way too much." Sterling flicks Flynn on the shoulder. "Isn't that right?"

Flynn chuckles. "Mostly. Not about this, though. I don't know. It's indescribable. I can't tell if I feel this way because of Lyric or myself."

"I'm a fucking catch. Loyal. Sexy. Of course it's not only because of Lyric. I mean, look at me." Sterling curls his arm, flexing his bicep.

My smile widens, and I lean in and kiss him. "You're also an amazing kisser. So giving. Self-less." I ease away and turn toward Flynn. "And I have to say, you're pure magic. That mouth of yours..." I shiver. "Your protectiveness and kindness fills me up in the best way. The thought of you two...I love you."

"You forgot the magic cock, blondie. Instant orgasm

maker." Adjusting me in his arms, Sterling sets me sideways between them.

I moan at the sensation of his hand sliding over my thigh. "Careful, Sterling. Flynn might not be ready for this kind of adventure."

Sterling motions to Flynn's hard body. "Tell that to the warlock's wand."

I lace my hand around Flynn's thick shaft and stroke my fingers from the base to the tip and back down. Humming his pleasure, Flynn cups my breast and rubs his sparking fingers over my nipple, the electric sensation tightening my sensitive skin.

"I want everything you want, my beautiful familiar," Flynn murmurs, leaning in to kiss my neck.

I reach for Sterling and stroke his cock too, loving feeling their early excitement dripping over my fingers, adding slickness to my exploration. Slipping a finger between my legs, Sterling moans, feeling the pleasure he elicits as our minds open completely. I spread my legs wider and turn my attention to Flynn, watching his pleasure scrunch his face.

The two of them lean in closer to kiss me, and I give in to their desire, kissing each of them slowly, sensually. Easing back, I watch their gazes break from mine to land on each other.

The intensity of their stare burns across my skin, and I squirm in excitement, craving to see more, to experience the new kind of bond they share build from their love of me that blossoms into a new love and appreciation for each other.

Flynn shifts closer, drawing his fingers between my legs to join Sterling's. He rubs my clit, sending another spark of electric magic through me, and I moan so embarrassingly loud as Sterling and Flynn brush their lips together in the hottest kiss I've ever seen. My lips tingle, and I swear I imagine the taste of Flynn's minty breath as his tongue glides between Sterling's lips.

"Whoa," I whisper under my breath, my whole body buzzing, the pleasure they give me bringing me to my peak.

I can't help letting their cocks go, and arch my back with my oncoming orgasm. My body tenses, every nerve-ending exploding in pure ecstasy.

Reaching out, I grab onto each of their shoulders and pull them in. They kiss me at the same time, their tongues gliding across mine and each other's, our passion lighting our bodies ablaze.

"Lyric, I want you," Flynn says, showering me with so much need that I nod my head.

"I want both of you...if that's okay," I whisper, the words coming out soft and shy, a part of me nervous about revealing my suddenly intense desire.

"My beautiful blond bombshell," Sterling says, sliding his arm under my legs, lifting me off the floor with him. "That is better than okay for me."

"Me too," Flynn adds, following us to the bed.

"I want to give you whatever you want like you do with me." I grab their hard-ons and drag my tongue from Sterling's tip to Flynn's.

Sterling's eyes widen, his expression cheering his thoughts before the cute bastard can even say the words. "Double the peen? Don't joke with me, blondie. This fantasy is all I've been dreaming about lately."

I hum under my breath. "Is that so?"

"Fuck yeah." Sterling flops on the bed in front of me and pulls me close, slapping my ass as he kisses me. He eases away and swats me again. "Come on, bestie. I will give your magic scepter the chance to slide in through the backway to paradise. That sexy ass of hers is like the keyhole to heaven. Seriously."

I laugh and reach for Flynn, pulling him to lay behind me. "You are such a good friend," I tease, playing with Sterling's erection, teasing my clit with his tip.

"The best," Flynn murmurs, leaning over me to kiss Sterling again.

Fuck me. It's hot as hell. I'm so ready to lose myself in the pleasure we'll share through our mate and familiar bonds.

Flynn whispers a spell, sending lavender sparkles through the air. I moan at the tingling sensation of the lube he summons, the thrill of taking care of both my guys in the way they desire turning my passion into need. I feel as if I'll already orgasm at just the anticipation. Flynn's hand slides over my hip as he reaches around, sending an intense vibration across my clit as if magic pulses from the tip of his finger.

Sterling moans, sliding into me from the front, feeling the

same vibrations I do. He kisses me, his thoughts so hot as he thinks about how warm and wet I feel and how he can't believe how amazing this moment is.

"Are you ready for me?" Flynn murmurs, using his other hand to work me over, getting me ready for more.

Arching my back, I press my ass against his boner. Sterling reaches over my hip and digs his fingers into my ass cheek, spreading me wider as Flynn eases his tip in, the lube and magic sending me over the edge before he ever gets started.

My muscles tense with mind-blowing bliss, and I kiss Sterling with desperation, gliding my tongue over his, my body clenching and bursting with pleasure that won't end. It steals my breath and makes me tingle in places I never knew were so sensual and sensitive.

I lose myself to the pleasure swirling between the three of us, feeling more loved and adored, appreciated and desired than I've ever felt.

"This is fucking mind-blowing," Sterling murmurs.

"Magical," Flynn adds.

I stretch and kiss each of them again. "Perfect."

Our moans of love and passion fill the air as we savor the ecstasy we each experience, our souls twining together in a way I'll savor for the rest of time. Sterling and Flynn work in sync, giving and sharing affection with me and each other until we orgasm at the same time, our bodies caught up in the whirlwind of bliss.

"Our sexy, beautiful mate," Sterling murmurs, cuddling me close. "I can never get enough of you. You've showed me how truly magical you really are. Your love and protectiveness, how you unexpectedly brought us together to share bonds unlike any other pack...we're going to change our world. I know it."

"She's already changed mine," Flynn says, rubbing his hand along my side. "All of you have. I finally feel like I have a purpose."

"You two—our whole pack—that's my purpose," I say, taking each of their hands. "It wasn't clear until now. I will not let anything or anyone ruin this for us." Sitting up, I scoot to the edge of the bed. "You help strengthen me and each other, and I can't stand the thought of our pack being apart any longer. We need to find Evelyn and go."

Flynn and Sterling stop me from rushing toward the bathroom, and Sterling asks, "Are you sure you're good to go? We can't all follow. You have to pick only one of us besides Flynn."

A knock sounds on the door, drawing our attention. "She's not picking." Antone's voice trickles through the protective magic, thinned by his presence. "I'm going to get our brothers."

I frown. "We haven't even disc—"

Antone cracks the door open. "There's nothing to discuss. Now get dressed, Cherie. There are some things we need to do to prepare. I'm getting Bastien and Sagan back, even if it's the last thing I ever do."

7

PACK MENTALITY

"THIS IS CRAZY." I HUG my arms around myself, bouncing on the balls of my feet. "Why can't he just portal us in groups? Don't you think it's safer to stay together?"

Dax sighs and rubs the back of his neck. "Of course it's safer to stay together. The last thing I want is to separate from you, but it's important to get in and out without being noticed."

"Evelyn said that to go in unnoticed, the break in the

gateway can only happen once. Each time the lycan must cross weakens the Nightstar's spell. They will notice and attack. It's easier for Flynn to protect only two of us instead of our pack." Caz rests his hands on my shoulders, peering into my eyes. His pouty mouth puffs out slightly with a breath, and I almost kiss him, feeling his need to try to make me feel better about the situation course through me. Leaning in, he rests his forehead to mine. "I know this isn't ideal, but you're in good hands with Antone. He knows the pack territories as good as any of us."

I give him what he yearns for, brushing my lips to his just as sweetly. "I still don't like it."

"And I fucking hate it," Dax says, clenching his teeth. My words trigger his steely expression to break, and he tips his head to look at the ceiling. "Believe me. This is complete bullshit, but it is what it is."

I press my lips together and peek over at Antone, Sterling, and Flynn talking quietly with each other. They look over hand-drawn maps of the territories Dax had put together with Caz and Antone. Like they sense the weight of my stare, the three of them look in my direction. Flynn's sharp features soften first, and he offers me a smile. Sterling winks, and Antone raises an eyebrow, not giving me much else. He keeps his emotions completely locked away, which annoys me a bit. I don't like not being able to read him. I want to know the true reason why he's the one going to Lulupoterra. I know it doesn't completely involve getting Bastien. I just know it.

"Almost ready, she-wolf. Try to relax," Flynn whispers into my mind. "Your pack mates have a solid strategy that'll get us in and out as safely as possible."

My stomach flips at his comment, my heartbeat skipping erratically with my nerves. I want none of this madness. Why couldn't the fates give us a break? I'm afraid of failing my pack because I've learned to rely on them, and now I have to prove I'm still capable of doing things on my own. It's weird knowing that, and my dad would have a few choice words, but they're a part of my power and strength. We're a pack.

I shake out my hands and bounce on my feet. "You know, Dax. I'm a bit surprised that you don't insist on going with us if you hate it so much. Did something happen that you're not telling me about? You guys do shit like that, so don't lie. I'm not in the mood to spank it out of you."

Caz releases a cross between a laugh and a groan. Turning me, he nudges me toward Dax. "I told you she'd question it."

Dax engulfs me in a hug and snuggles his face into the crook of my neck. He remains open, letting me feel his warring emotions, my comment getting to him. I feel a bit bad over it, but they need to know that I still haven't changed my mind about being kept in the loop.

Sliding his hands to my ass, Dax lifts me up, curling my body around his. His lips caress mine, silently pleading for me to give in to his affection. I do, deepening our kiss, sliding my tongue over his, tasting the sweetness of his mouth. My body ignites with a deep-seated need to be with him, but I force my she-wolf to chill out.

I growl under my breath at myself and wiggle until Dax sets me back on my feet. "You drive me crazy. You can't kiss me like this and expect me to leave you."

Dax pulls me back to him by my hand, pulling it up to rest over his beating heart. "Lyric, I want to go and be by your side. I do. But this wasn't worth the fight with Antone. He has his reasons, and I respect them as his pack mate."

"Reasons? What reasons?" My brows pucker, and I swing my gaze from Dax to Antone and back to Dax. "Tell me."

Dax straightens his shoulders, guarding himself from my oncoming badgering. "Ask Antone. It is not my place."

Heaving a dramatic breath, I spin away from Dax and march toward Antone. He stands rigid in front of Flynn, allowing him to hook some sort of pendant around his neck. I can tell Antone is bothered by having something else put on his neck, but he suppresses his complaints. It almost makes me reconsider confronting him. Almost. Instead, I do as he does and steel myself toward the world.

Sterling catches my gaze first. "Blondie, I think you—"

A guttural noise escapes my throat, cutting him off from trying to interrupt my mission for answers.

Raising his hands in surrender, Sterling steps away, not wanting to face my wrath by association. He sidesteps and locks his hand to the back of Flynn's shirt, dragging him away with him.

Antone jerks his head up, meeting my glower with narrowed eyes. The muscles on his arms twitch as he flexes his biceps, and he gets into a fighting stance, looking ready to confront me if he feels the need for it.

I close the space and gather the front of his shirt between my fingers, pulling him into me so no space gets in our way. I stand tall on my tiptoes to stare into his dark eyes, wishing there was a step nearby to give me a bit of extra height. Antone is bastardly enough to use something like a height difference to test my dominance, and right now, I need him to know his place is as my mate and not as the man who enjoys testing me.

The longer I capture his stare, the more my heart aches, memorizing the nearly identical features he shares with his twin. Licking my lips, I lower my voice and say, "I know Bastien is your brother, but why do I feel as if something else is influencing your decision to face the Nightstar Coven?" I brace my free hand on his shoulder, stopping my legs from wobbling.

"Are you admitting that you wouldn't have picked me, Cherie? Haven't I proved myself capable of protecting you? Am I not of use with my medical training and knowledge of Lulupoterra? You claimed me as your mate, now you must accept that I can stand by your side as an alpha-mate." Antone laces his fingers around my wrists, tightening his hold until I loosen the fabric of his shirt. "Now be my good girl and let the warlock give you the protection amulet that'll prevent the damn witches from trying to collar and leash us. I need you to trust me to care for you and guide you through this fucking mess."

I clench my jaw, annoyance running through me as he embodies the douche he was when we first met, making my questions sound unnecessary and invalid. I smack my palm to his firm pec. "It is not the time to treat me like your little brat, Antone," I snap, shoving him back hard enough to pin him against the wall. "I trust you and don't need you to try to make me feel like shit to make yourself feel better."

His body reacts to my gesture, and I can't stop the magnetic pull of his presence as it ropes me in until I stand flush against him. "Since we don't have time for me to do with you as I please, if you demand to know, I've volunteered so the others wouldn't have to. I'm the newest member of this pack, and we still haven't completely bonded. If something happened to me...it wouldn't devastate you as much as it would if something were to happen to the others."

Shock steals my breath away. His words trigger an icy rush of hurt to crash over my heart, tightening my chest. I can't believe that's what he thinks. I can't believe he considers himself disposable all because we haven't had a chance to explore our bond. It's utterly and insanely infuriating.

Anger rushes over me, and I surprise the hell out of Antone by latching my fingers to his athletic pants, yanking them down to expose his cock to me. Everyone's gazes burn into my back as our confrontation grabs their attention. Silence fills the room, the others standing in the same surprise as Antone does. I steel myself to the part of me that is hesitant to proceed with my plan to show Antone that I can ruin his thinking with my bold act. If screwing him will prove that he is just as important to me and our pack, even after everything, I will climb him like a damn tree and hump the hell out of him in front of everyone. Fuck, I'd probably give in to his wild nature and allow him to screw me in our wolf forms.

"Damn," Dax and Caz say at the same time, my thoughts loud enough to project to all of them.

Antone grabs my waist and spins me toward the wall, caging me to it. Hooking his hand to the back of my thigh, he stretches my leg up to press his throbbing boner against the flimsy fabric of my panties now showing from the long shirt I chose to wear like a dress.

My body reacts, and tingles bloom wetness between my legs, dampening my panties for Antone to feel. He presses his cock harder against me, and I can't help the moan escaping my mouth.

"Cherie, you have no idea how much I want to have my way with you," he mutters, a growl escaping his throat to vibrate across my ear. "But no. You can't have what you want. This is my way of ensuring if things go wrong, you'll be okay."

"But I won't be," I argue, panting against his mouth. "You're my mate and my bond to your soul is far more powerful than the one our bodies will create."

"Cherie, stop." His words come out as a plea. "Please."

I swallow and grab his beard with my fingers, not letting him step away. Yanking his head forward, I crash my lips to his, kissing him hard and desperately. I want him to feel this kiss with swollen lips even after I'm through. My deep-seated nature consumes me as his mate and leader. All I can do is try to force him into submission, because it seems to be the only way I can ever get through to him and his hard-ass, dominant thinking.

He growls another warning, but I ignore him and suck his bottom lip into my mouth and nip it, stretching it as I pull away. I still grip his beard, keeping him close so that we share the same heated breath.

"I'll remember this denial to bond how I want," I say, my threat making his nostrils flare.

"Just as I'll remember this threat." Dropping my leg, Antone kisses me once more and steps away, leaving my mind and body spinning in a vortex of confusing, hot, and especially infuriating emotions.

The damn bastard.

I don't get a chance to retaliate as blinding light erupts in the room, peppering my vision with stars. Evelyn materializes in front of Flynn with the man I gave the lycan curse to. He offers Flynn a bow, and Flynn flicks his gaze to mine, clearly uncomfortable with being treated as royalty or a god or some shit.

"Can you make him quit that?" I ask, striding across the room. I adjust my shirt and mess with my hair, using my focus on Evelyn to snuff the desire still clinging to me from Antone. "We're no different than him. It's the god-complex you hold over others that makes us want to tear you apart with our fangs."

The man's eyes widen and he drops to his knees, kneeling in front of me. "My savior. How blessed I am to be in the presence of the being that graciously gave part of her essence to entrust me with power unlike anything the mortals know."

Ah, fuck.

I reach down and grip his shirt, dragging him up. "Knock that shit off, and tell me your name, so I know what to call you."

"I am your pet," he murmurs, his voice soft with awe. "You may call me whatever you please."

Ugh. I swing my attention to Evelyn. "What did you do to him?"

Her mouth twitches into a smile. "Nothing to concern yourself over. We have far more important things to worry about, don't you think?"

Damn her.

"Fine, I'll just call you Pete," I mutter to the man.

Flynn moves to get behind me, silently hooking the pendant around my throat to join the piece of his soul I hold in my other necklace buzzing over my heart. Now that everyone is gathered, I can't help thinking about what is to come. The uncertainty kills me. Leaving my mates behind is complete agony. I'm afraid, yet I'm far worse off knowing that it's already taken too long to get Sagan and Bastien. What they're going through? Fuck.

The thought is enough to battle my fears and replace them with determination.

"Five minutes, she-wolf," Flynn whispers into my ear.

I swallow and nod, turning away from Evelyn and Pete as they join Antone and Flynn, staring at the wall. Sterling beats Caz and Dax, scooping me up to shower me with a dozen kisses. Spinning me, he sandwiches me to the wall and surprise humps me, bouncing me against his pelvis.

Bubbling laughter escapes my mouth, and I hug him. "Save this for later, okay? I want Sagan to know that I'm ready for your brotherly competition."

He chuckles and kisses me. "His water hose will explode in your backyard garden so hard. He's going to thank me for eternity for getting you on board."

I crinkle my nose with my smile. "You should try it sometime."

He raises an eyebrow. "I'm down for anything with you, blondie."

Setting me down before I lose myself to my wild imagination, Sterling nudges me toward Caz. He hugs me next, burying his face into my shoulder. I tilt my head, inviting him to kiss his way up my neck, until our lips finally meet for the softest, most sensual kiss I think I've ever had. It only lasts long enough to make me crave more.

"Good," Caz whispers against my lips. "I'll give you everything you want when you get back.

I nod and nuzzle my nose to him. "And I'll give you everything you want if you can ensure the others behave."

"You're worried about us misbehaving?" Dax steals me away from Caz and combs his fingers through my blond hair, tugging me to him for a kiss. "I'm nearly certain it's impossible for *you* to behave."

I giggle and shrug. "You can thank my dad for that. He encouraged it."

Dax's eyes flit back and forth over mine as he searches my gaze. "We're going to find him, Lyric. We're going to read you-know-what again and find answers, okay?"

I bob my head. "Okay."

"Now kiss me once more before I figure out how to kidnap you from this room so that you can't ever leave me again." Dax molds his lips to mine, kissing me with a desperate intensity I can feel penetrate my soul.

It takes Flynn and Antone coming up behind me to get us to break apart. I open my arms one last time, inviting Sterling and Caz to join us, and the five of us hug as a pack, absorbing each other's strength, power, and support.

"We must hurry," Evelyn says, her sharp voice snagging my attention.

My eyes widen as a portal erupts in the wall, setting the room aglow. Flynn and Antone each take one of my hands, and Flynn holds onto the lycan with Evelyn by Pete's other side. My heart pounds in my ears as we step forward, leaving the sanctuary of the Everdeen Estate.

My skin prickles as my eyes adjust, and I stare in shock at the land before me.

Lunar Crest has been destroyed.

My pack's home is nothing but a hellish wasteland.

8

WASTELAND

"THEY DESTROYED EVERYTHING," I WHISPER, my heart breaking like the dozen fallen trees bent, broken, and pulled from their roots around us.

Tears uncontrollably cloud my vision as I take in the sight of the collapsed buildings I started imagining would be my future home to raise children with my mates. Where the magnificent main building once stood now lies burned and blackened rubble. The heavy scent of my territory's destruction taints the air, stinging my nostrils. I don't know what I was expecting, but it was far from this. The destruction is beyond anything I could ever imagine.

Fury ignites inside me. How could the Nightstars care so little about a place that was so beautiful? Why would they take control only to destroy it? I don't get it. I thought this was about power and control. I thought they wanted to turn the wolves of Lulupoterra into pets to take the last thing we had left.

"We can rebuild, Cherie," Antone says softly, his velvety voice swirling through my mind. "It's just a building. You hated the pink room, anyway."

I twist and poke his chest. "That's not the point. These witches—"

Flynn covers my mouth from behind. "There is nothing we can do now. Use this anger to ignite your strength. We need to remain focused."

I inhale and exhale a couple long breaths, knowing he's right. I need to guard myself not only physically but mentally. If Lunar Crest looks like this, I can't imagine what the rest of Lulupoterra looks like. Whatever witch or warlock stepped in to fill Invidia's High Priestess position seems even more brutal. My mates have been here for days, which feels more like years.

"Fuck," I think to Flynn and Antone. "We need to get to them now."

"Transform, my pet," Evelyn says, speaking to Pete. "It is

worse than I thought. I need you to follow my strict orders. You must go forth and find the Nightstar Coven. Do not engage unless you have to. Kill all other lycans you come across, but leave the wolves."

Pete stretches forward on his hands. His bones crack and shift as hair sprouts from his skin. Long talons burst from his fingers, sinking into the compacted dirt. With a deep growl, his face elongates into a snout and sharp fangs extend down past his jaw.

Shit, he's freaky.

Evelyn beams a smile, looking at the beast as if he's the handsomest thing she's ever seen. Pressing her fingers to his temples, she shocks him with a burst of red magic and says, "Refs o tog won, my pet. You can track their magic. Go."

Without waiting, Pete takes off in his lycan form, jumping and weaving around anything that gets in his way.

"I will keep track of our beast," Evelyn says to Flynn, straightening her shoulders. "It is up to you to ensure our bargain is fulfilled. Once Lyric brings me a she-wolf, we will collect your stolen wolves...unless you want to risk going after them alone."

My heart sinks into my stomach at her words. How could I have forgotten about this part of the deal I made with Enrique? Why would I even think that just because Evelyn put Enrique in some sort of coven time-out that she would change her mind? This confirms that the whole fight between them was an act. It had to be. She blamed her brother to keep us here. Damn it.

Clapping her hands, Evelyn disappears without another word, not giving me a chance to argue or threaten her. Flynn's eyes widen, and he grabs onto me and Antone, chanting a transportation spell to take us to the river with the gateway to the other territories.

Flynn creates a magical shield around us and links his fingers together on the back of his head. "She knows better than to use magic like that. Now the Nightstars will come looking for who disturbed the area. And with you, Lyric...fuck. We need to hurry."

Antone closes his eyes and inhales a deep breath. "I can track a she-wolf. I suspect if the place looks like this, the She-Wolf Games are over and new packs have been created."

Flynn nods his head. "Controlling entire packs by magic would be far too difficult, especially if a female was pregnant. I suspect the females have been taken back to their home territories and the Nightstar Coven waits the gestation out."

My stomach knots with nerves at the thought of Antone and Flynn capturing a she-wolf for Evelyn. It makes us no better than the coven we fight against. "Wait, no. We will find Sagan and Bastien and bring them home ourselves. We're here already. We don't need any more help from the Everdeens."

Flynn purses his lips. "Lyric, we—"

Snapping his mouth shut, Flynn whips his attention to the area around our protective shield. Snarls cut through the air as two wolves fight somewhere within the forest of blackened trees. My heart ricochets against my ribcage, flinging back and forth as if it tries to decide whether to explode through my chest or to escape my back to fly in the other direction.

Antone kicks off his pants and stretches his naked body, transforming into his hulky wolf form. His sleek black coat shines in the lavender light of the shield, and I can't help sinking my fingers into the softness of his fur, clutching onto him. The hackles on his back rise as we listen to the fight crash through the trees in our direction. A wolf yips in pain and something thuds into a tree nearby, raining soot around us.

A tan, gray, and black wolf darts through the trees, his familiar markings sending me stepping back into Flynn's chest. I suck in a breath at the sight of Alonzo racing to put space between him and a wolf I can't see.

Alonzo is so focused on his escape that he doesn't realize he's about to charge right into Flynn's magic. Panic whips through me, and I throw myself forward, breaking the shield. Alonzo growls and barks, skidding and trying to stop, but his paws fall out from under him, and he crashes into me.

"Lyric!" Flynn shouts a spell, sending magic colliding into Alonzo. The tri-colored wolf tumbles off of me and into a tree.

Antone launches at Caz's brother, pinning him down. Everything happens so fast that I see the hulking shadow too late.

Sharp teeth sink into my calf, biting hard enough that I drop to the floor. I twist my body, swinging my arm, and I punch the enormous body of Fergus as he snaps, trying to grab me with his teeth.

"Yer gonna need to hit harder than that, lass," he thinks to me, his annoying voice whipping through my mind with his mental invasion.

"Fi vet tati—" Flynn yells out, his spell cutting off.

My attention breaks from Fergus's for a split-second to see another former competitor collide into Flynn. It's the moment Fergus needs to overpower me, and he flips me onto my stomach and pounces on my back. His soft coat turns into the heat of a naked body, and he flattens himself against me, his cock hardening and he flexes it between my legs, his twisted thoughts shooting panic through me.

He tightens his hand in my hair, yanking my head back. "Yer mine, lass. I'm going to fucking enjoy hearing you scream."

Squeezing my eyes shut, I throw away my humanity, transforming into my wolf form. Fergus loses his grip on my hair, and I twist my neck and sink my teeth into his arm. He hollers and tries to jerk away, but I refuse to let go. Dragging me up with him, he swings his arm as hard as he can to throw me off. I release him mid-swing, knocking him off balance, and he fumbles and tries to catch his footing. Rage shades my vision in a red haze, and I launch at the fucker, crashing into him just as fur starts to sprout over his body.

I bite his side only to release him to bite his hip. The pain falters and slows his transformation, and I snarl, summoning every damn horrible thing he tried to do to me and feed it to my wild beast. Something all-consuming comes over me, the taste of Fergus's flesh and blood sweet on my tongue.

He arches and locks his fingers around my head, trying to block me, but a blast of magic from Flynn catches him off guard. The second his hands loosen, I jerk my head down and bite as hard as I can between his legs, swinging my head back and forth in a game of tug-of-war against the sensitive skin of his body. Fergus screeches, his voice high enough to deafen my hearing for a second, my wolf's hunger on a mission of total cock destruction. He will never use his fucking dick again. He won't even have one. No balls either. I'm putting a stop to his bloodline, and ensuring he or any possible assholes he could produce die here with the bloody, limp, pathetic penis I drop to the ground with his scrotum.

Fergus thrashes in his half-wolf, half-man form. "You fucking bitch! I—"

Growling, I launch at him and bite him in the throat, cutting off his airway. He bucks and fights, trying to break free, but I refuse to let him go. Even after he falls silent and limp, I still don't release him. I can't. I'm afraid the second I do, he'll roar back to life and try to hurt me again and again.

"Cherie, he's dead," Antone whispers, licking the side of my face, nosing me with his snout. "You have to let him go. We need to move."

"Please, Lyric. We need your help. Harlow—she—I—

please, will you come with me?" Alonzo's voice hums through the air. His soft pleas for Harlow are the only thing allowing my she-wolf to give my humanity back.

Flynn helps me to my feet, sliding my torn shirt over my head, covering me the best he can. Antone circles me in his wolf form, weaving between my legs and licking my calves as if to check to see if I'm injured while remaining in his wolf form. After this attack, I doubt he'll transform back. Not when he feels most powerful in his beast form.

"What happened, Alonzo? Where is she?" I ask, shifting on my feet to meet his brown eyes, similar to Caz's.

He purses his lips together, his face morphing with utter sadness, I have to blink to keep my own eyes free of tears. "Come on. We have to hurry. I'll take you to her."

Alonzo leads the way to a part of Lunar Crest I haven't had much time to explore outside of the She-Wolf Games. Flynn holds my hand protectively while Antone skulks through the trees, keeping an eye on our surroundings.

"We're just up the mountain in the caves," Alonzo says, peering at us over his shoulder.

I rub my lips together, a dozen thoughts flitting through my mind. "I don't understand what's going on. The last time I saw you, Invidia had you collared and under her spell."

"A collar is only as good as the witch who controls it. Killing her would've freed her control over him and unless one of her coven mates leashed him, he'd have his free will," Flynn says, keeping his voice low.

"Most of us ran," Alonzo says, releasing a low whistle at the bottom on the steepest part on an incline. "My pack and I saved Harlow and brought her here...but she was in heat."

Ah hell.

"We were all freaked out and worried the witches would sic the alpha-mates on her, using her season to track her," Alonzo continues, sighing as a rope ladder cascades from a hidden cave. "It was her idea. It was supposed to give us time to figure out how to kill the witches and take control back, but...now you're here."

"Pssst, Alonzo. Get them up here before someone smells Lyric. Her scent is wafting even to me." A familiar man swings the rope ladder back and forth.

I crinkle my nose. It's one thing for my guys to comment about the scent my body produces to let them know I'm ready for babies, but hearing someone else? Ugh. I swear they better stay in check. I know how hard it can be for my mates, and if someone even looks at me with desire...Antone will beat the shit out of them. I know him.

Flynn rubs his hands together and chants a spell, shooting a web of magic into the air. It sticks to the air like invisible strings hang it from the sky. Flicking his fingers, he sends me shooting off my feet and into the air with Antone. Antone spirals at me from where he was lurking in the trees. I manage to snatch him, and I cling onto Antone's huge body as if he'll break my fall back to the ground.

Wind whips around us. Flynn uses magic to send us into the mouth of the cave. I stumble into the arms of who I'm nearly certain is one of Alonzo's mates. The man rights me and jumps back, holding his palms out in surrender as Antone releases a warning growl. I scrub my fingers through the soft fur between his ears, calming his nature to protect me from the entire universe.

"Lyric? What are you doing here? Thank the fates! I've been so worried about you. Have you seen Emerson? Any of the others?" Harlow pads her way toward me from a pile of blankets at the back of the cave in her wolf form.

She bows forward and transforms into her beautiful human self, greeting me with a huge smile. I rush to her side, and we hug each other. I haven't known Harlow long, and we don't always see life the same way, but she stood up for me. She and Emerson helped me out. We wanted the same for our futures, truly leading the packs and not turning into weak baby-makers manipulated and unable to protect ourselves.

I pull away and cup her cheeks, blinking my eyes to stop my emotions from taking over. "Alonzo told us what happened. Are you okay?"

Harlow closes her eyes, her bottom lip trembling. A tear slips on her cheek, trailing to her jaw. Pulling her close, I hug her again as she begins to sob, crying into my hair. Another body comes up behind her as the same man who caught me hugs her from behind. My heart melts just a little bit.

Harlow laughs a shaky breath. "I'm sorry. My body is out of whack, and I'm scared. I always imagined I'd be with the other she-wolves, experiencing this incredible stage in my life. We shouldn't be hiding in this cave with no support from our packs."

"Girly, it's going to be okay. We will never abandon you, even if this wasn't how we imagined life. You will never be last in our lives, okay?" The man eases away and wipes his thumbs over her cheeks.

She bobs her head and sniffles. "I know, Nathanial. It's just hard. I know you never planned on joining a she-wolf pack."

"Just because we hadn't planned on it, doesn't mean you're not important to us. I'm excited," another guy says, helping Alonzo and Flynn into the cave.

"Jeremy is right, sugar-pie. Plus, I have enough love to share it with you. I feel like the luckiest man to know you're okay with sharing that handsome man over there with me." The guy waves his hand at Alonzo.

"I think we're all lucky, Cage," Alonzo says, grinning.

He strolls over and plants a kiss on the man's lips before kissing Harlow and rubbing her slightly bulging belly. From what my mates told me, the gestation for us is short and we can have two pregnancies a season, so Harlow will grow fast.

"Lyric brought the warlock," Alonzo adds, turning to me.

"Now we can fight and take Lulupoterra back. Our pack can go home. We can raise strong, loving, amazing children."

The dynamic of their pack only surprises me a little. I knew Alonzo had mates already and they didn't believe in the She-Wolf Games because they didn't want to risk being separated from each other. As for Harlow? She wanted a pack to dote on her and teach her how to be strong, one willing to change with her as she realizes there was more than pretending to be a good she-wolf.

Flynn glances to me, and I bare my bottom teeth. In this moment, I hate that I have to bring more bad news. Because we can't fight right now. If we could face the Nightstars alone, we would. We need Evelyn, and the only way she will help us is if we hand her a she-wolf. There is no fucking way I'm going to hand her Harlow. Not now. Not ever.

I clear my throat, shifting on my feet. "Um, we're going to try our best, but—"

"One warlock is not enough to face this coven." Antone strolls from the mouth of the cave in his sexy, rugged human form. He automatically comes up behind me and hooks his fingers to my hips, peering at Harlow. "They have the traitor alpha-mates on their side. Lycans. Magic powerful enough that it took a bargain to even get us here."

Harlow tilts her head, glancing between me and Antone. "You guys have bonded."

That's what she's going to focus on?

I frown. "Don't worry. We're going to figure it out. We've come for the rest of my pack, but—" Snapping my mouth shut, I shake my head and turn to Flynn, hovering outside of the circle everyone creates as we stand together. "Flynn, there has to be another way. What if all the she-wolves have mated? I can't do that. We can't do this."

Antone releases a growl. "It's the only way to get Bastien. He's suffering here, Cherie. They're surely worse than the Everdeen Coven."

"He's right, she-wolf," Flynn says, rubbing his palms together. "But I understand your hesitation. I know you want to do right by your species. This is why we've come here."

"We came for Sagan and Bastien," I argue, peering around the dimly lit cave.

Flynn closes the space and turns me toward him, resting his hand to my cheek. His lavender eyes soften as he searches my face. "No, I meant here. With Harlow. Don't you see? If she stays here and the Nightstars find her, they will punish all of them for hiding. They'll collar them and turn them into their slaves. We've seen how they've treated the wolves already. If we take Harlow with us, we will at least have a chance to ensure her safety. We can—"

"I'll do it." Harlow's voice rings through the cave. Striding away from her pack mates, she reaches for my hand. "I don't care where we go, Lyric. I can't stay here. It's too dangerous. And if it's somewhere with you...I have faith that everything will be okay. It was the fates who brought you here and to us. I know it. This is the first time anyone had been out of this cave in days, and to have you just stumble across Alonzo? You have to take me.”

“But—”

“Please, Lyric. I’ll go with her. She’s carrying my child,” Alonzo says, his brows pinching together. “I’ll worry about her. We just need a way out.”

Alonzo’s three mates look at him and Harlow, sadness shining in their eyes. My heart breaks that they have to make this decision in the first place. I couldn’t imagine being in their place. The more I think about how unfair it is, the angrier I become. My breathing quickens, and I tighten my jaw, forcing my head to nod in agreement.

“This will only be temporary,” I say, biting the inside of my bottom lip to stop it from quivering. “We will come back, stronger and ready to fight. I swear.”

Nathanial straightens his shoulders, meeting my gaze. “And we will stand with the Lunar Crest pack.”

Antone releases a small growl and flares his nostrils. A moment later, a blinding light erupts in the cave, stealing my vision. Flynn yells and gathers magic. Harlow’s pack shifts into wolves with guttural growls. They launch at the lycan intruding their den.

I jump in their way.

9

TRICKY WITCH

A MAGICAL SHIELD ERUPTS BETWEEN me and Alonzo's pack, stopping them in their tracks. Two huge, hairy arms wrap around me and drag me back. Pete's muzzle rests on my shoulders and he snarls at the wolves.

"Damn it, Pete. They think you're going to hurt me. Put me down," I snap, shoving my elbow into his hard chest until he sets me down.

Flynn takes me into his arms protectively, keeping a palm full of magic in case he must intervene again. The wolves slink back and forth along the barrier, growling, seemingly unable to relax with those they think come to threaten us.

"What a beautiful she-wolf," Evelyn says, stepping forward to stroll past me and Flynn. She ignores the growling wolves and strolls through Flynn's shield, scattering the magic across the floor, unaffected by it because he built it to keep the wolves out, not her in. Stopping in front of Harlow and Alonzo, she gives Harlow a once-over. "And a soon-to-be mother. How exquisite."

Harlow whacks Evelyn's hand away, not allowing her to touch her stomach. Flynn rushes with me to get beside her, cutting her off from doing or saying anything more. I don't know if it's because he's afraid Harlow might change her mind or what, but I kind of hate that I don't intervene.

"I know you're excited, Evelyn, but wolves are very protective of their mates. Harlow will not resist as she and Alonzo want away from here, but I cannot in good faith agree unless you swear to me that you will not separate them from their young." Flynn tightens his jaw, daring Evelyn to ponder over the idea instead of just agreeing.

"Of course I would never. Wolves are stronger together," Evelyn responds, her eyes flickering with her red power.

"You will keep the she-wolf with her mate as well," Flynn adds. "They are family. Alonzo is Caz's brother, and Harlow is Lyric's friend. If my pack becomes unhappy—"

"As long as they obey as they should, we will not have a problem." Evelyn smirks and turns to Harlow. "You will have a room with a nursery. Is that acceptable?"

Harlow slowly nods. "What do you expect from me in return?"

"Loyalty, my dear. Protection. Using you to aid my coven with magic. Wolves are very...powerful." Evelyn glances at me in her periphery. "Lyric can explain more in detail later. We must go. My lycan located the lost Lunar Crest pack mates, and we must hurry."

I bring my hand to my heart as if it might crash from my chest otherwise. "You found them? Are they with the Nightstar Coven?"

Evelyn shrugs her shoulders. "Not that I could tell. The Nightstars remain in the last territory far from everything. They seem to be busy figuring out how to proceed without Invidia."

"Then who are they with?" I ask, frowning.

Antone growls and closes the space to me. Leaning in, he meets my eyes with his dark gaze and silently thinks, "The fucking alpha-mates. We never even needed Evelyn to help fight. I can take down every last one of them."

I purse my lips at Flynn. Antone's right. We can take down the alpha-mates without help. The idea that Harlow and Alonzo agreed to serve Evelyn spills dread through me. It was all a trick. She waited until Harlow agreed to even tell us.

The fucking witch-bitch. She's going to regret ever messing

with me. She'll see.

Clenching my fingers into fists, I straighten my back and face Evelyn. "Just take Harlow and Alonzo to the gateway and wait for us."

Evelyn dips her chin. "My pet—"

I scowl. "Pete will come with us. He is far more helpful."

Motioning to Flynn and Antone, I get them to stroll with me to where Pete quietly waits for his command. Evelyn might've tricked me once, but there is no fucking way I'm falling for her bullshit anymore. If she takes Pete, she'd leave us here.

"If we don't return in thirty minutes, come for us. You are obligated to hold up your bargain to help us if we need it," Flynn says to Evelyn, wiggling his fingers, sending magic sparkling to the cave floor.

Antone lifts me into his arms and grabs the rope ladder. "Come on, Cherie. Let's save our pack mates.

"You forgot to mention fuck the alpha-mates up," I say, letting him flip me to his back.

He flexes his muscles and turns to Flynn. "You hear our mate? We're taking these fuckers down."

Darkness steals the day, leaving the glow of the river as our only light to illuminate the vast canyon around us. Stars litter the sky, sparkling like billions of tiny diamonds. Flynn whispers a spell under his breath, drying off the four of us.

The lycan trudges forward, his nails clawing into the soft

ground of the riverbed. He sticks his snout to the ground and inhales a deep breath. "We head east. They're not far from here."

Where here is? I have no idea. I've never been into this territory before.

"Moonlight Canyon," Antone says, keeping the thought between us.

My eyes widen. "This is Harlow's territory?" Wow. It angers me even more that these traitors not only sent Harlow into hiding but also had the nerve to take control of her territory. They were probably the ones to help destroy mine as well, flexing their power as if they're the bastards in control.

Antone growls his confirmation before stretching his arms over his head. He bows forward on his hands, transforming into his beautiful black wolf. Padding forward, he sniffs the air. Flynn laces his fingers through mine, quietly standing close. I can tell he wants me to remain human with him so I do. The lycan leads the way, galloping ahead of us. He tracks whatever scent he smells, leading us along the riverbed.

"I don't want you to fight if you don't have to," Flynn murmurs, keeping his voice low. "Seeing you beneath that asshole earlier—it killed me. I don't know what I'd have done if he had hurt you."

"Flynn, I've trained my whole life to fight. You know me damn well enough to know better than to ask the impossible from me. Bastien and Sagan are my mates. They're your pack mates. Asking me to stand by while you and Antone handle it is like telling me you don't think I can take care of us as your leader."

Flynn sighs and brings my hand up to his mouth to kiss my knuckles. "Of course I think you can. Can you blame me for trying, though? You're always the first one to run into dang—"

A collection of howls echoes through the night as if the alpha-mates are calling to the full moon as it rises over the canyon. Flynn tenses and wraps his arm around my shoulders, but I shrug out of it and put a foot of space between us. I need my full range of movements to fight, no matter how badly he wants to protect me.

One by one, the howls fade until the deep, familiar guttural growl of Sagan reverberates through my bones. The canyon intensifies the noise, stealing my breath away. The only times I've heard him sound so scary were during a fight.

Tensing my muscles, I brace to hear the oncoming snarls. Metal crashing into metal sounds through the air like chains rattling together. I pick up my pace, recognizing the sound of the spelled muzzle, once used by witches to control the wolves. If Sagan wears one, he'll be in so much pain. I know this from my own experience. The thought of that kind of agony forced upon my mates hurts me to my soul. It takes everything in me not to scream out Sagan's name to tell him I'm coming. I just want him to know I haven't forgotten him. We never abandoned him or Bastien.

Antone picks up speed, darting forward like a black shadow

in the night. Catching up to the lycan, he runs beside the beast instead of running ahead. A whistle rings through the air, reminding me of a dozen times before. It's the same call the leaders did for the start of the She-Wolf Games and whenever they called the competitors together. But now? Fuck.

Snarls and growls rip through the air, the sound of two wolves fighting pushing me to run faster. Sagan yelps in pain, but his fighting noises only intensify. I can't decipher who the other wolf is, but I know without even having to see Sagan, that he's the one at a disadvantage. The alpha-mates would never fight fair, especially against a wolf strong enough to fight every last one of them into submission.

"Flynn, you have to transport us. I don't want Antone facing them alone, and he won't wait for us," I call, my voice fading on the wind.

Locking his hands to my waist from behind, Flynn chants a spell, sending bright light flashing in my vision. I tense as the growls intensify in volume, my mind struggling to orient itself to being relocated. Silence suddenly falls on the world around us, and I blink, trying to adjust my vision to the change in light.

"Fuck," Flynn mutters under his breath.

My gaze falls on Sagan, lying on his side, bloody and panting. Stopping me in my tracks, Flynn pulls me back into his chest. It's now that I realize he accidentally relocated us right into the middle of a ring of alpha-mates.

"Flynn, get Sagan out of here," I mutter under my breath.

He shoots a blast of magic into the sky, sending a dome of magic around us, keeping the alpha-mates back. "But—"

I yank away from him and get into my fighting stance. "That's a damn order!"

Rushing to Sagan, Flynn hooks his fingers under his huge body and chants a spell, relocating him without me. His disappearance shatters the protection spell, leaving me standing in the middle of a dozen growling wolves. My skin prickles with goosebumps, fear trying to incapacitate me. If they capture me...fuck that. I'll bite off every single one of their cocks and shove them down their throats.

"Where is Bastien?" I ask, shifting my weight from foot to foot. "If you give him to me, we will leave without a fight."

"Do you really think your warlock will make it back in time to save you?" Killian asks, his thoughts penetrating into my head.

I whip my attention to his wolf form and glower, realizing why they're here. He technically won a spot on the Moonlight Canyon pack. This is his territory, though Harlow should be the one in control.

"You have three seconds," I snap, fury rippling over my muscles. Reaching down, I pick up a broken chain and wind it around my hand. "One."

Killian transforms into a man while the others remain wolves. "Two," he says for me, testing my gall with his cocky-bastard attitude.

"Three!" Antone shouts the word from somewhere outside

the circle.

A roar echoes through the air, and Pete bursts through the trees in his lycan form. Killian scowls and rushes me, abandoning the wolf beside him as Pete tears into its stomach with his fangs and throws the wolf away.

Twisting on my feet, I perform a spinning slap kick, smashing my foot into the side of Killian's head. He stumbles forward, trying to engulf me in a bear hug, but I jerk my knee up, splitting his chin open. My rage intensifies my strength, and my moves come as naturally as they did when I was training every day.

I move forward to stomp my foot into Killian's throat, but two hot, strong arms swing around me, lifting me off my feet. Yelling out, I throw all my weight forward, loosening his grip on me. The second my feet touch the ground, I jerk my elbows up, giving me space to shift my body until I manage to hook my leg behind his. Twisting, I knock the both of us down, landing on the ground first. This asshole might be strong, and he might know how to fight as a wolf, but he sorely lacks skills as a man.

I flip over and land on top of him, sucker-punching him in the nose twice, my jabs so fast, he can't even protect his face. Shoving my palms into his chest, I push myself up and stomp his pelvis, squishing his flaccid cock under my heel. Yowling, Killian tries to snatch me by my ankle to throw me off of him. I put more weight on my feet and launch off him, spinning around for something I can use to knock his ass out.

Antone launches over me and lands on Killian, tearing into

his throat. Thrashing, Killian tries to transform into a wolf, but Antone's too powerful. I turn away, my stomach twisting as Killian goes limp.

I search my surroundings, wanting nothing more than to find Bastien. He has to be around here somewhere. I feel it deep inside me, his soul calling to mine even if we can't see each other.

Licking my lips, I moisten my mouth and shout, "Bastien!"

A whisper of my name trickles through my mind, and I gasp in a small breath. He sounds so weak, yet I can't feel his pain. Another wolf tries to launch at me in my moment of distraction, but Antone collides into him, fighting the fucker off. The other wolves focus on Pete, and I pray to the universe that he's strong enough to withstand the viciousness.

"Bastien," I call again, focusing on opening my mind. "Tell me where you are."

Bright light illuminates the world with Flynn's arrival, and my heart jumps to my throat only to freefall into my stomach. A few dozen yards away, Bastien lies facedown and naked in the dirt, his body beaten and bruised with dozens of teeth marks marring his skin.

Rushing past Flynn, I dart toward Bastien, my whole body aching at the sight of him. How could the alpha-mates be so cruel? What the fuck is wrong with them to be so cold-hearted that they would put my caring, sweet mate through this torture for entertainment?

A cursed muzzle hooks over his head, and chains lock his

arms behind his back. I wince at what looks like a dislocated shoulder, but it's too dark to tell for certain. Without hesitating, I lock my hands to the spelled collar of the muzzle, burning my hands. The pain doesn't stop me as I flick open the buckles and ease off the muzzle as carefully as I can as to not burn more of his skin.

I drop to my knees and work my hands over the chains next, unwinding them to free his arms. "Fuck, Bastien. I'm so sorry. I'm so, so sorry."

He groans, his eyes fluttering open. "Ma Belle," he whispers, my name only a breath from his mouth, his throat bloody and burned so much from the spelled silver, it seems to affect his ability to speak.

"Flynn!" I scream. "Flynn, hurry!"

Flynn catches up with us, lighting a glowing orb in his hand. "Shit, Bastien. Hold on. I'm getting you out of here."

Lifting Bastien in his arms, Flynn uses his magic and disappears. I straighten my back and spin around to look at the wolves fighting the lycan and Antone. Rage tints my vision red. I stretch with my transformation, my she-wolf bursting free. Charging forward, I race in my wolf form, my inner beast wanting nothing more than to destroy the rest of the alpha-mates.

Pete yowls in agony as two wolves bite into him, one trying to gut him and the other sinking his teeth into the back of his long leg. I set my focus on the gray and white wolf, readying myself to attack. Launching forward, I latch my teeth around his tail and rip him away from the lycan. The wolf twists and snarls, snapping his teeth at me. Lowering my head, I shove my body beneath his and flip him off his feet. We roll together as he tries to pin me, but I manage to sink my teeth into his throat. I squeeze down, keeping my wolf body stiff. I refuse to let go, even with his pleas of surrender.

"You're fucking dead," I think to him. "Fucking dead."

The wolf goes limp under me, knocked out from the lack of air. Light flashes through the world again, and I jerk my attention up, expecting to see one of the Nightstar witches, but it's only Evelyn joining Flynn. The two of them raise their hands into the air, gathering magical energy between their palms, sending static through the air.

"Emat eht tseab. Ezeerf ot vi olon vita!" they chant in unison.

Magic rains down on the alpha-mates, the lavender and red colors dangerously beautiful as they blend. All at once, the alpha-mates topple over, slumping on their sides. The lycan groans, shifting back into a man, his body bloody and beaten, but he still manages to stay on his feet. I gulp in a few deep breaths of air, searching the area until I spot Antone shaking off the dirt from his black coat.

"Do you want to sentence them to death?" Evelyn asks, rubbing her hands together. "You must make your decision quickly. The Nightstar coven will be here at any moment."

A huge part of me wants me to shout yes, but with one look

into Flynn's eyes, I know it would be the wrong decision. I'm not the only one who'd have to live with these deaths on my soul.

I shake my head. "I want to relocate them to another territory and trap them there. They can take care of themselves."

Antone transforms into a man. "Take them to the old Hunter's Trail territory."

Hunter's Trail? I recognize the name. It was my great aunt's territory, but it has since been cut into and divided for new leaders. What's left of it is only a small reminder of Paige and her former pack.

"The leaders kept it as a reminder...before we discovered Paige wasn't killed," Antone adds.

Evelyn nods. "We can seal it off."

Hooking his arms around me, Flynn lifts me up. "Come on, she-wolf. I'll take you and Antone to your pack mates. The Everdeen Coven can handle the rest."

My heart swells in relief. We did it. I can't believe it.

My soul finally feels whole.

10

REUNITED

"THEY'RE GOING TO BE OKAY, Cherie," Antone whispers, hugging me from behind. We stare at Sagan and Bastien, lying unmoving on the bed. "Flynn only sedated them with magic while they finish healing. Why don't you come and eat with us? Or we can spar. You have a ton of energy you need to work off."

I quietly shake my head. My heart throbs at even the thought of leaving them alone. A part of me fears that this is only temporary and the Nightstar Coven might come for them, stealing my pack mates from me. "I'm going to stay here until they wake up. I don't want them to be alone. But you should go grab something to eat and then rest. You need to take care of yourself too, Antone. I need you in the best shape."

Turning me around, Antone pushes my hair back as he combs his fingers into it. His eyes narrow, and he looks ready to toss me onto his shoulder to carry me out of here kicking and screaming. "You're such a brat, not letting me take care of you. Don't think you'll continuously get away with this."

I stand on my tiptoes and brush my lips to his without getting out of control. "That's my job, you bastard. Now go on and be my good omega. Don't make me fight you into submission. I need you to just listen to me for once. You'll be rewarded later. I promise."

He smirks and kisses me once more. "You're my perfect leader, Cherie."

Antone swats my ass as he exits the room, leaving me alone with Sagan and Bastien sharing my bed. I close my eyes and listen to the sound of Dax, Sterling, and Caz greeting Antone and Flynn not far down the hallway. I know they all wanted to come in here and support me, but I just need a moment to breathe. I need some quiet as I savor having Sagan and Bastien home with me. Giving them my attention when they wake up will hopefully ease the trauma just a little, at least for a moment. No matter how strong I know they are or how tough their brothers assure me they can be, I know they have their breaking points. I only wish I could use the magic I supposedly have inside to fix this.

Sauntering across the room, I carefully creep onto the bed between their two hulking bodies. They're both dirty and covered in scrapes and bruises, but the worst of their injuries have been healed with magic. As for their souls? I can only pray to the universe that all this torment hasn't broken their spirits. I won't be able to tell until they wake up and open their minds to me.

Fuck. I'm scared. Tears burn my eyes at the thought. I need to get my shit together and be the leader they need me to be. The mate they deserve. The woman they claimed and bonded with, entrusting their entire existence in my shaky hands.

I push my thoughts away and grab the bowl of warm water with a washcloth Antone left behind. Setting it between my legs on the bed, I soak the soft fabric, needing to keep busy. I take turns cleaning each of their faces, doing my best to be especially gentle around the deep bluish-black bruises across their bodies. The sight of their throats where the skin still glows a tender red twists my insides with pain. My poor mates. I just want to hold them and love them for the rest of time.

I inhale slow breaths to suppress the heartache threatening to leave me sobbing and a mess. Steeling myself to ensure they don't feel an ounce of my whirlwind emotions, I gather my nerve to speak. "I want you two to know that I am here, and I swear to the fates that I'll never let anyone separate you from me again," I say, keeping my voice low. I brush my fingers through their hair and kiss Bastien on the forehead and Sagan on the cheek. "Whatever happened to you...I will help you through it. Our pack will help you as well. You don't have to deal with it alone."

Tears blur my eyes with my words, and I stroke my fingers across their chests, my hands mirroring each other as I trace their muscles. The sounds of their strong heartbeats fill the air, and I cherish the beautiful melody. Nothing has ever sounded so perfect, thrumming in sync with mine.

Bastien's eyes flutter open first, and I shift and take his hand, pulling it up to my chest so that he can feel my thrumming heart. He doesn't move or look at me, quietly staring at the ceiling in a weird, almost trance-like state.

"I'm here, Bastien. We brought you home to our pack. You're going to be okay," I say, staring at him in anticipation. "The torture and torment are over. You're safe."

Jerking upright, Bastien clenches his jaw, baring his teeth. He snatches his hand from mine only to lace it around my throat. Flipping me onto my back, he squeezes the sides of my neck without cutting off my airway and glowers down at me. My eyes widen in shock, my body refusing to react. If it were anyone else, I'd fight back. But I'm afraid to hurt him in his state of confusion.

"Bastien, hey. It's me. It's your mate," I think to him, trying to keep calm, taking slow breaths despite the shadows crowding the edges of my vision.

I lock my fingers around his wrist, trying to tug his hand off without having to force him away. His hand restricts the blood flow through my body, and I can't figure out why he doesn't restrict my airway. It's like he's forcing me to submit and not trying to kill me.

"Bastien, let go of me. I don't want to call for help. I'm your leader. Stand down," I say, thinking the words to him, afraid if I use my voice, he'll cover my mouth.

A flicker of blue magic dances across his irises. "You're not my leader."

Ah, hell.

Gathering my nerve, I release my hold on his wrist. Breaking my leg free, I jerk my knee up into his gut at the same time I shove my hands into his chest. He hollers as I flip him over my head and onto the floor. I scramble to the edge of the bed and launch myself off the side, landing on top of him. He growls and tries to grab me by the neck again, so I reach behind me and grab his cock. He freezes without me having to even threaten his manhood with a little squeeze, and his body hardens in my hand.

"Bastien, stop attacking me. I am your mate. You don't need to make me submit to you," I say, hardening my voice. "This isn't Lulupoterra. I'm not a threa—"

The world spins as Sagan grabs me by the hair and yanks me off Bastien. I don't even have a chance to react as he drops me onto his knees, yanks my panties down, and slaps my ass with his palm.

I lie stunned, trying to process what just happened.

And my damn vagina. What a kinky bitch. I shouldn't be getting turned on.

"That's how you put her in her place, Bastien," Sagan says, his deep voice rumbling through the air. "Give it a try."

I jerk up, my good senses returning to me, but Sagan flattens his palm between my shoulder blades, pinning me in place. He shifts me just a bit, and I suck in a breath at the sensation of his shaft flexing under my breasts.

Bastien releases a low rumble from his throat. "My way works just as well."

"You say that as if she wasn't going to try to rip your cock off," Sagan retorts. "Which she needs to be punished for. Now go on before I do it. I'm starting to think you don't want our mate."

What the fuck?

A large hand spanks my ass, knocking the thought right out of me. I'm confused as hell by what is happening, but my damn body decides now is not the time to fight. They know I'm their mate, yet they're not treating me as they had before. This is something one of the fucker alpha-mates would do.

Bastien hums under his breath, rubbing a soft circle over my stinging ass. "Will you obey me as your alpha now, Ma Belle, or do I need to do it again?"

"Again." Did I just say that? Fuck yeah, I did.

I don't even care that they want me to submit, probably

bend me over, and screw me from behind. All I want is to give them what they want now and figure out what is wrong later to bring my sweetest pack mates back to me.

The sound of Bastien's slap, followed by an equally powerful one from Sagan, rings in my ears, weakening my body. I shiver, the sensation prodding at my wild nature. Heat courses over me, traveling the length of my body and rushing right between my legs. I clench my vagina and squeeze my thighs together. I crave more. I need more.

"She loved that," Sagan says, gliding his fingers down my ass until he slips one between my legs. "Isn't that right, gorgeous?"

I moan in response, hanging limp with my hair cascading toward the floor. Sagan works his finger in and out of me, feeling what he does to my body. My mind turns to mush, my voice refusing to work as pleasure zings through me.

Sagan suddenly stops and smacks my ass again. "Tell me."

I bite my lip and remain silent.

Fingers lock through my hair and Bastien stretches my head up, forcing me to look at him. "Answer your alphas."

This time, I glare. "No, I didn't love that. It wasn't enough. If you think you can be my alpha, then prove it."

One second I'm bent over Sagan's legs, and in the next, I'm on my stomach in the middle of the bed. Fingers hook to the hem of my panties, ripping them off me completely. The bed bounces, and I turn to roll over only to have Sagan grab the back of my shirt to pull me to my knees. He stands in front of me, towering over me, his hard cock pressing against the fabric of his athletic pants. My wild nature ignites inside me, and I jerk my hands forward and yank his pants down, wanting nothing more than to make him cum.

A moan rumbles from his throat as I lick my tongue across the base of his shaft and to his tip, tasting his building desire drip into my mouth. Bastien comes up behind me and drags my shirt over my head to cup my boobs. He pinches my nipples hard enough to make me gasp, and Sagan slides his massive cock into my mouth.

"Look how far she takes you," Bastien says, combing my hair from my shoulder for a better view. "I think she needs a reward for being a good mate."

"Just for a minute." Sagan rocks his hips to my face, moaning as I tighten my lips and roll my tongue.

Sliding his hands from my breasts, Bastien works his way down my torso until he rubs his fingers over my clit, making me gasp in pleasure. My body lights with dozens of zinging sensations, their fierce passion stroking my she-wolf the way she likes. With his other hand, Bastien shifts his hard cock, teasing me between my legs, gliding his shaft over my slick excitement without going in. I bounce slightly on my knees, my body screaming with desire so much that I squeeze my legs together in an attempt to relieve the crazy intense ache inside me.

Sagan slides his cock out of my mouth and strokes it in front of me. "Flip her over."

Bastien turns me around and kisses me, pulling me to the bed on top of him. Sagan grabs my hips and pulls me back. I land on my knees between Bastien's legs, bracing my hands next to his legs. Gathering my hair, Bastien holds it out of the way and flexes his cock.

I lick my lips. "More."

Sagan smacks my ass. "Only when you give Bastien what he wants."

Lacing my hand around Bastien's boner, I guide it into my mouth and bob my head. He moans and guides me at the speed he wants, and Sagan presses against me, bowing forward to kiss my spine. I moan and hum with Bastien in my mouth, savoring the sensation of Sagan gliding his tongue across my ass until he reaches between my legs. He swirls his tongue over every inch of me on his quest to make me moan and then sucks my clit into his mouth, the pressure sending electricity through me.

"You taste so good," he murmurs, spreading me wider with his hands to work his tongue back up. "I bet you feel even better."

Aligning his body to mine, he braces on my hips and thrusts inside me. I gasp and moan, my voice vibrating against Bastien's cock as I suck him all the way to my throat. Pleasure explodes through me, my inner beast content. I enjoy taking care of Sagan and Bastien, no matter what their needs may be. They might act differently, but their true nature peeks through the strange magic turning them into dominant alpha-mates. They don't just use me to get off. Bastien whispers his love for me into my mind, and Sagan slows and reaches around to play with my clit, rubbing fast circles until I orgasm before him.

Sagan thrusts hard and fast, hitting his hips to my ass until he grunts and cums. Bastien drags me to him and rolls over, sinking inside me, wanting more of me. My moans come in quick bursts, my voice ringing through the air. Sagan flops beside me, his heavy-lidded gaze filled with lust and desire. His hand glides down my side until he can pull my leg, opening my body to let me feel more of the pleasure Bastien has to give. His cock hits me just right, his pelvis rubbing my clit in quick successions as he fucks me unlike he ever has before. My body tenses with another orgasm, and I cling onto Bastien.

Their minds suddenly open to me, and a wave of their confusing, intense emotions crashes over my soul, stealing my breath. Their love feels darker, dangerous, like the residue of the Nightstar Coven clings to their souls.

Despair ties around my heart, squeezing it in my chest. "You're bound to them," I whisper, my lust fading with the realization that this is more than a spell. It's far worse.

"Flynn!" I scream, my mouth acting before my mind catches up.

Bright light erupts through the room, blinding me. The weight of Bastien's body flies off me, and he hollers as he hits the wall. Dax swings the door open, sending it clattering to the wall.

He rushes into the room with Caz, Sterling, and Antone behind them. They all tense, unsure of what's going on.

"Did he hurt you?" Flynn asks, heaving a breath.

"She's mine!" Bastien yells, transforming into a wolf.

"She doesn't concern you," Sagan adds, snatching my wrist to pull me to him.

Antone launches past Flynn in his wolf form, snarling at his brother. Flynn lights magic in his palms, preparing to blast Sagan with it. A dozen emotions explode through me, kicking my mind to catch up with what's happening.

"Stop! Everyone stop! I'm fine. No one hurt me," I shout, covering my face with my hands.

"Then what's wrong, Lyric. You're terrified." Dax strides forward, giving Sagan a warning look before he growls.

"Yeah, blondie. You were so hot and bothered and—" Sterling huffs a breath. "And then bam. Boner dead."

I shake my head, sending my hair flying back and forth. "It's not about me. It's about them. The Nightstar Cov—" Anger steals my grief, tensing my body. "They bound their souls to them. I can feel it. They tried to sever them from me."

Flynn's eyes flash lavender. "Are you sure?"

"Yes, I'm fucking sure!" I don't mean to snap, but this is so messed up. "We need to fix this. Now."

Flynn turns his back on me and tips his head to stare at the ceiling. "It'll take some time."

"We don't have time," I say, sliding to the edge of the bed.

"Just tell me what we have to do."

Flynn's shoulders droop and he turns around, his tattoos rippling with his movements. "If they're bound to the witches, there is only one thing we can do."

My heart crashes into my stomach.

Hopelessness consumes me.

I don't even have to ask him to know the answer, and it's something I'm afraid we might not be able to do.

"Flynn...please. There has to be something. Anything. If they're bound, can't the witches take them back?" My voice shakes.

"I won't let that happen," he says, turning to the others. "We won't. We're free from the Everdeens, but I can still use their power to help us. I have a plan."

Dax flexes his muscles. "Which is?"

Turning back to me, he says, "First we need to find out what happened to Levi. I'm afraid only he has the answers we need."

"And then?" Caz asks, speaking up.

"We go on a witch chase," Flynn says.

I straighten my back. "And when we hunt them down, I'll kill every last one of them."

11

Witch Hunt

I STAND NEXT TO FLYNN, watching as he creates a make-shift altar on the top of my dresser. He could use the Everdeen Coven's altar room, but the last thing we need is for them to know we're going to search for my dad. We need answers, and he might be the only one who can give them in regards to everything going on. And if he's with the Fire Mountain Clan? Maybe we can use them to our advantage.

I doubt Evelyn would stand by and do nothing as we take care of the Nightstar Coven on our own and take back Lulupoterra. She will try to step in and stake her claim. I know it. Enrique proved it. She thinks she's a wolf in sheep's clothing, but she'll realize that I'm the alpha, and I will take her down. She will regret the shit she pulled manipulating me into getting Harlow involved. Harlow was desperate. I will teach Evelyn never to fuck with someone when they're down.

"Can you open the grimoire to the page I marked?" Flynn asks, kneading his fingers into a large stone bowl with something dough-like. "I need what's in the envelope on the right. It's like Eliphas set everything up for us to go on a witch hunt. There is blood from many covens within the pages. Fire Mountain is on the top, written as F-Y-R-E. It's a bit odd, but I'm sure it's them."

"Maybe he suspected the five covens who shielded Lulupoterra were bat-shit crazy and power hungry. Maybe he planned to kill them himself." I turn the pages, gazing at the different spells, passages, and pictures until I find the black ribbon holding a place in the back. I draw my finger over a small weathered envelope attached to a page covered in spiral script. I carefully lift the flap and slide out a yellowing piece of fabric with a brown stain. "Are you sure this is going to work? Shouldn't we have the original for this?"

Flynn bumps my shoulder. "This is the original."

"You brilliant warlock," I say, stretching up to kiss him.

Gracing me with a smile, he nuzzles his nose to mine and takes the blood-stained fabric from my hand. I watch in anticipation, staring as he scrapes at the brown spot with an athame. The dried blood sprinkles across his strange dough, and he continues to knead it in with his fingers. The substance sparks and sizzles, ignited by his power, and I inhale a sharp breath, feeling him tap into the magic I carry around my neck in the soul stone. The dough melts into a liquid, turning into what looks like fresh blood. Whoa.

"That is so crazy," I say, peering over the bowl. "I could watch you make potions all day. I've never even thought much about what goes into your magic, but you're incredible."

Flynn chuckles and wipes his hands off on a white handkerchief. "Thanks, but this is nothing, she-wolf."

"What else can you make besides truth serums, blood whatever that is, and...magical fucking lube?" I ask, grinning as his cheeks tint with his sudden flush. "I'm starting to think you're under-utilized in our pack, and we might need to fix that...if that's something you'd be interested in. I mean, I loved being with you and Sterling. I can imagine what fun we can have all together."

"Lyric, you're going to get yourself into trouble." Flynn's eyes flicker with bolts of lavender electricity. "Don't let Sterling hear. He's already come up with a list of possible...pack bonding experiences."

I shiver at the deep breathiness of his voice, his desire

trickling to me through our familiar bond, despite him trying to remain in control. "You don't have to be worried about me. I know you worry about the whole everyone wants to fuck me idea, but I look forward to any sort of magical adventure you can come up with. I love you guys. I want to take care of our pack like you take care of me."

"You owe me that you-know-what spell, bestie." Sterling cracks the bedroom door open and pokes his head in. "I told you she was ready for pack life."

Flynn groans and flicks his fingers, shooting sparks at Sterling. Ducking, Sterling dodges out of the way of the shock and transforms into his breathtaking silver wolf. Flynn doesn't even have a chance to brace himself as Sterling mounts him from behind and humps him like the playful horn dog he is.

I crack up and lock my fingers into Sterling's coat, dragging him back. Breaking from my hold, Sterling skids around and launches at me, knocking me onto my back. He shifts into his cocky-bastard self, his naked body flush against mine. He snatches my leg up and dry humps me through my clothes, making me laugh harder.

A soft tap on the doorframe draws my attention away from Sterling. I spot Harlow hugging herself in the hallway. Her watery eyes gleam in the light, and a pout puckers her lips. I don't see Alonzo behind her and guess he's with Caz, catching him up, while Dax and Antone work on Sagan and Bastien's new alpha-mate complexes to ensure they can come with us.

What they're doing exactly? I don't know. I'm scared to even ask.

"You guys are so cute together," Harlow says, forcing her mouth to smile. "I'm so happy you have such an amazing pack. I've always worried about you and how you would deal with...everything. I guess, what everything was supposed to be."

Sterling rolls off me, and Flynn tosses him some shorts from the dresser drawer. We seem to be naked more often than not, so Flynn ensured my guys have a ton of clothes. Pushing up, I get to my feet and cross the room, pulling Harlow inside. I close the door and guide her toward the bed, inviting her to sit with me.

"You will reunite with your pack, Harlow. I swear to it. Things are going to change. You will not be obligated to serve this fucking coven." I keep my voice low. Flynn has the room magically shielded from the Everdeens, but I can't help being cautious. "The position you're in is unfair. They tricked me."

Harlow sucks in her bottom lip between her teeth. "I would have agreed to come regardless. I'm only nervous. I've never been away from Lulupoterra."

"Like I said, I swear it won't be forever. We will take our home back. I just need you to hold on." I hug my arm around her. "Now why don't you get comfortable? My warlock is about to perform some serious magic."

Harlow raises her eyebrows and stares at Flynn, tightening her fingers around mine. I realize she's probably scared as fuck because of the wolves' experience with witches, and I hug my arm around her shoulder, reassuring her everything will be okay.

We watch in silence as Flynn finishes up his tracking spell, using the blood from the Fire Mountain witches. I bounce on my feet, nerves getting the best of me. I can't believe this is happening. Flynn is going to locate where my dad is. It's a longshot, but I pray to the fates that we can manage to get him back. I'm sure they are as mad as the Everdeens about the war the Nightstars have waged and will want what we do.

Flynn lays a shirt down next to his bowl and smooths out the fabric with his palms. Dipping his hands into the bloody liquid, he scoops up a palmful and drips it onto the fabric.

"Vota le trekita vol tatu," Flynn chants, igniting the blood in a purple glow.

It dances across the shirt without absorbing into the material, swirling into a design I recognize. Holy shit. I can't believe I've seen it before. I looked at the symbol all my life growing up. It was painted on the wall of my dad's gym, was also painted on a huge canvas that hung in our living room. My dad even had the symbol engraved on the bottom of his watch. I always thought it was the gym's logo. But it's not. It's something else entirely.

I get to my feet for a closer look, listening to the string of words Flynn chants like a song, holding his hands above the glowing symbol. Like my hand can't control itself, I reach out and touch the top of the symbol. Flynn's eyes widen, his words faltering. No one has a chance to react as the glowing liquid crawls up my hand and sizzles across my arm.

I screech and jerk away, trying to fling it off. Burning pain stings my skin as the liquid swirls into the same symbol before sinking into the smooth skin of my inner arm, branding me. Electricity buzzes through my hair, the static swirling my blond strands around my head. Panicking, I rush toward the bathroom, ignoring everyone calling my name. I shove my arm under the faucet, trying to wash away the symbol, the puckered texture strange and warm, though the burning pain fades.

"Fuck, Lyric. Let me see," Flynn says, coming up behind me. "Why did you do that?"

I lift and drop my shoulders. "I don't know. It was like I couldn't help myself. The symbol...it called to me. I recognize it."

Stretching my arm out, I inspect the brand mark, tracing my finger around the points of a diamond shape split in two with a line that stretches from one side of my arm to the other. A swirl design crawls from the top point of the diamond, curving like two crescent moons facing each other with one larger than the other. The design is simple, but the complex feelings battling around my soul scream there is much more to this symbol than I could've ever imagined.

Flynn gently touches his finger across the brand, shiny and looking to be already healed despite being fresh. "Where do you recognize it from?"

"Her dad's gym," Sterling says, speaking up. "I recognize it too. Levi said it was for protection."

"It's a witch mark," Flynn says, rubbing his hand to the back of his neck. "Some of us have tattoos like myself." He points to the geometric heart on his chest next to where my familiar tattoo appeared on his skin. "And others get brands. Some birthmarks. It depends on what the coven agrees on. But it should be impossible for Lyric to have this specific one. It's the symbol of the Fire Mountain witches. I was putting it on the shirt to help us track their location. It was meant to trick the magic of their cloaking shields."

I frown. "I don't understand. If it's supposed to be impossible, how is it on me?"

"Your father—your biological father must have renounced his coven and given up their power to join another coven. It's nearly unheard of. Covens kill traitors. They—" Flynn snaps his mouth shut and spins on his heels, rushing back to the makeshift altar. "Evelyn's magic. It doesn't belong to her. I think she stole it from Eliphas." Flipping through the grimoire, he reaches the last written page and searches over it, drawing his finger over the script. "Fuck. I'm right. If Eliphas remained part of the Everdeen Coven, it would still have the mark. They stole this from him."

I frown, rubbing my hands up and down my arms. "What do we do? If they find out we know..." I flick my gaze to Harlow, sitting frozen on the bed. It's now that I realize she's been spelled by Flynn.

"She can't know," Flynn says, scooping up everything from the altar, dropping it into a bag. He tucks away the grimoire and hands me the bag to hold. "Call your mates, Lyric. I need everyone ready to go in five. I'll handle Evelyn, okay?"

I nod, turning to Sterling. "Go with Flynn."

He nods without question, taking Flynn's hand. The two of them disappear in a blink of light, breaking Harlow from the spell. She tenses, peering around the room, her eyes widening at Flynn and Sterling's absence.

"Thank goodness, you're awake. I think you passed out. Flynn and Sterling went to get Evelyn to make sure you're okay." I hate lying to her, but I don't know what else to say. "I'm going to get your mate, okay?"

Harlow only nods.

With one quick look around my bedroom, I rush to the door.

Dax stands on the other side with his hands on the knob. Our eyes meet, his golden gaze trying to figure out what's wrong.

I hold my hand out to him and tug him with me. "We need to find the others. It's time to go."

12

Lupine Woods

I STAND ON THE FAMILIAR main street of my hometown, shock and confusion overwhelming me. This can't be right. How the hell can the Fire Mountain Clan be in Lupine Woods? Were they watching us all along? None of this makes sense. Why would they drag my dad away? Why hadn't he just picked us up and moved if he thought there would be trouble?

"What the actual fuck?" Dax strolls a few feet ahead of me,

staring down at the small town nestled in an expansive forest. Unless someone travels through the woods, there is only one road that cuts through the town as the highway is miles off.

"You know this place?" Flynn asks, striding to stand next to Dax.

An arm drapes over my shoulders as Bastien takes Flynn's place by my side. "This is Lyric's hometown. Isn't that right, Ma Belle? Tell the warlock."

I glower, trying not to get annoyed by his attempt to talk over me, treating Flynn's question as if I need permission to answer him.

Antone locks his hands to Bastien's shoulders and pulls him away from me. "Show our leader respect. Isn't that what you told me?"

Bastien swings his fist, trying to punch his twin. Antone ducks and rams into him, knocking him off his feet. Sterling and Sagan run to them at the same time. Punching Antone between the shoulder blades, Sagan winds him, giving Bastien a chance to clock Antone in the jaw. Sterling locks his arms around Sagan from behind, dragging him back. It takes Caz and Dax intervening to get Antone and Bastien to separate.

Fuck. Me.

Marching to Bastien, I get in his face and jab my finger into his chest. "I never in a million years thought I'd ever have to say this to you, but stop being a damn asshole."

"Are you going to let her talk to you like that, Bas?" Sagan says, goading Bastien on as he tries to break out of Sterling's hold. "Maybe you should just bend over and let her spank your ass next. You'd enjoy being her—"

"Sagan!" I shout, jerking my attention to him. "Even though I know what the fuck is up with you, I will not stand here and excuse this. You're going to be the one experiencing my slap—to your fucking balls—if you don't keep your mouth shut. The next thing you say better be 'yes, gorgeous,' or I will put you in your place. You're not a fucking alpha-mate. You're my fierce protector and sweet lover. I will not let you forget it."

Bastien tips his head back and laughs. "Fuck, do I want to pin her down until she shuts up."

Oh my fucking-fuck.

I dig my nails into the palms of my hands, trying to keep my cool. It was one thing to dominate me in bed, but this? I don't know how much longer I can wait. I'm about to go running through the nearest mortal town in my wolf form, howling until a damn lycan shows up before demanding he take me to Lulupoterra.

I open my mouth to warn Bastien that his balls are in trouble, but a huge lion roars, charging in our direction from the trees. All of my guys transform into wolves, and Flynn shouts a spell, creating a protective barrier around us.

The massive lion slows but doesn't stop, stalking closer like he's about to test the power of the shield.

"What the fuck is a lion doing in the forest?" I whisper,

glancing at Flynn.

Flynn straightens his back. "The witches here must use a pride from Magaelorum for protection. It's not unheard of. Sometimes bears, tigers, and even the dragons barter contracts."

"What the fuck?" I whisper mostly to myself. Why am I surprised? I'm a damn wolf.

A flash of blue light sparkles next to the lion, and a woman blinks into existence. Red magic similar to Evelyn's grows in the palms of her hands. The lion roars beside her, the sound ringing in my ears.

I blink a few times, staring at the familiar woman. Her blue eyes meet mine and she cocks her head, glancing from me, to my pack, then to Flynn, before returning her gaze to mine. Her long strawberry blond hair blows in an invisible breeze, created from her magic, and she steps a foot forward.

"Lyric, you've come home. I wasn't sure if I'd ever see you again, knowing Levi had planned to take you home to find your chosen pack." The woman shifts her gaze to my mates again like she can't help herself. "Where is Levi, anyway? I never thought he'd leave your side."

I open and close my mouth, my words lost to me. I can't remember this woman's name, but I've seen her around my dad's gym. She would bring in her sister—no, her niece—for self-defense classes.

"It wasn't willingly," I finally manage to say, my muscles tensing. "One of the Fire Mountain Clan witches kidnapped him, and I know they're here. Are you one of them? Don't lie to me."

The woman frowns, tilting her head in confusion. "Why would I lie to you? I was entrusted to protect you and Levi until you two returned back to Lulupoterra. It was my coven brother's final wish. Did Levi not—"

"Where is he?" Fury rushes through me, and I stride forward, breaking through the magical shield. "Where's my dad? I know someone from your coven took him. The Fire Mountain witches sent doppelgangers after me. It was my pack who found me and not my dad taking me to my pack. I had no idea I was even a she-wolf."

The lion roars, flashing his long fangs, but the woman raises her hand, keeping him away.

"So don't give me this bullshit. If you won't take me to my dad, I will find him myself." Stretching my arms over my head, I prepare to transform into my wolf self.

Flynn comes up behind me and hugs his arms around my waist. "High Priestess, please forgive my familiar."

"You're not going to talk to her about me like I'm some kind of pet," I snap, shrugging from Flynn's embrace.

"I would never consider you a pet, Lyric," the woman says, keeping her eyes trained on me. "It's McKayla, by the way. There are no titles here. No covens, packs, prides, or anything of the such. We're all one clan—witches, shifters, fae, vampires, merpeople, and the like—have come together to build this sanctuary away from Magaelorum, kind of like the wolves have Lulupoterra."

I cannot even wrap my mind around her revelation. "But my dad." It feels like if I can wish for it enough, her answer will change. Like if I will it, he'd be trapped in some dungeon with an evil witch clan in need of saving.

McKayla's features soften and she reaches out and touches my shoulder. "I'm sorry. He's not here, Lyric. Had I known...I'm just so thankful you found your pack. I—"

"McKayla Lioht?" Flynn's voice snaps through the air, startling me. "You're McKayla Lioht, aren't you?"

Blinking her eyes a few times, she shifts her gaze to Flynn. Silence falls over everyone, my mates remaining tense and ready, absolutely quiet, as Flynn and I handle this.

"I go by McKayla Fyre now. I have long since disowned the Lioht Coven," McKayla responds, folding her arms over her chest. "They could never follow my vision, craving power over anything else."

A wave of crazy-intense emotions collides into me, stealing my breath away. I heave and bend forward, Flynn's fury and shock making it hard to think. It sets off our pack, and my mates growl and move behind us, inching their way closer.

"Flynn," I murmur, trying to suppress his debilitating emotions. "What's wrong?"

Without looking at me, Flynn gathers glittering power in his hands. "McKayla Lioht is supposed to be dead!" he shouts.

His face morphs, his teeth elongating into fangs as his body bulks up. His intimidation magic sends him towering over the petite witch, who gathers magic of her own.

"What do you mean I'm supposed to be dead?" McKayla asks, taking a step back.

Everything clicks into place. Flynn's anger. His sudden shift in emotions. The need for revenge. I knew Flynn's coven was wrongly convicted of some serious crimes, including the murder of a High Priestess. He wanted to use me to help him clear his coven's name.

And now, as I look at McKayla, I realize the truth.

Fuck.

"My coven was convicted of crimes against the Liohts. My High Priestess, my parents, my coven mates—almost all of them burned by dragon fire. They were convicted of murdering you!" Flynn's rage and grief battle through me, igniting a feral need inside me.

McKayla raises her arms into the air, shouting a spell, but I crash into her. I pin her down, covering her mouth with my hand. Her lion guardian roars, but the rest of my pack surrounds him, keeping him away.

Flynn materializes over me, his eyes storming with his lavender magic. "You're going to fucking fix this. I'm taking you to the High Council and clearing my name. Now."

Jerking my body, I swing my arm into the back of Flynn's knees, knocking his legs out from under him. I never thought

I'd ever have to stop him from getting the justice he and his coven deserve, but dragging McKayla to Magaelorum might not be the answer. My dad would smack Flynn upside the head and tell him if she's running, there's a reason, and none of us should jump into anything without knowing how deep the hole goes.

"Don't move," I snap at McKayla, pointing my finger. "If you try anything, you will regret it. I need to talk to my warlock for a moment."

Anger burns from Flynn to me, and he scowls like I've just betrayed him in the worst way possible. Catapulting from the ground, I tackle him and grab his hands at the same time I kiss him, sliding my tongue into his mouth. If he can't speak or use his hands, he can't do something crazy with his magic.

"Lyric, don't make me fight you," Flynn thinks to me, his teeth grazing my tongue like he might bite. "I have to do this. You should stand beside me. My coven was slaughtered because the High Council thinks we killed her. If I prove they were wrong, I can save my sisters and brother in the Magaelorum prison. I can go home."

"Home..." My thought fades as the thought shoots me in the heart.

He stills beneath me, realizing what he just admitted. I knew he wanted to return to Magaelorum when he saved my life, but I thought that changed when he joined my pack and realized I was his familiar.

"If you go home, I can't go with you." I whisper the words

against his lips, needing to say them out loud. "I know it's selfish of me to say this, but you promised you'd never abandon me. Forcing McKayla to go to Magaelorum like you plan would do just that."

"Lyric," he murmurs, groaning under his breath. "You don't understand."

His heartache displays clearly on his face as he thinks about what I've said. I want to feel badly about bringing it up, but Flynn is my mate. I will fight with everything in me to keep him.

"I do, Flynn. I've lost people too. Look what we're going through to get them. I want to help you. I will help you get your coven back and clear your name. But the way you're planning to do it? I thought I was the careless one. McKayla left Magaelorum for a reason...right?" I stretch my neck, peering up at her, waiting for her response.

She slowly nods her head. "I got involved in something which made my coven unhappy. It would've ruined their good standing, so I left. If I had stayed..." Shuddering, she pushes away her thoughts. "I just—I'm sorry. I had no idea they'd claim I was murdered. I thought I was wanted for treason."

"The Liohts stole my coven's magic," Flynn says, growling with his words.

McKayla closes her eyes, pursing her lips. "I'm so, so sorry. I know nothing I can say will make up for your loss, but please. There is another way. If you turn me in to the High Council, you will sentence me to death."

I pull Flynn upright with me, sitting between his legs with mine around his. Clutching his face with my hands, I caress my thumbs over his scruff, locking him in my gaze. His eyes sheen with his emotions, the sparkle of lavender intensifying.

Leaning forward, I kiss him again. "Enough people have died because of the Liohts. Because of all the witches trying to rise in Magaelorum. Let's hear her out, okay? It doesn't hurt to have someone on our side when everyone seems against us."

Sighing, Flynn engulfs me in a hug, burying his face into my hair. A soft whimper sounds from next to us, and Sterling noses his big wolf head between us, joining our hug. The others break their circle and follow his lead, enclosing us with the strength of our pack. Flynn shakes in silence, not speaking. I focus on sending him all my love and strength, blending it with our pack's to bathe Flynn in what we have to give.

Because we've all experienced loss and tragedy. We've all faced injustices and have been wronged. Despite the horrors of our lives, we must still carry forward. But together, we can share the heartache and loss, the heavy, sometimes unbearable weight of the evil in the world. We carry our baggage together and grow even stronger together. The universe can't take our pack bonds from us, no matter how hard anyone tries.

Pulling himself together, Flynn eases away from me and scratches Sterling between his ears. The cute bastard licks Flynn across the face first and then licks me, slobbering across my cheek. Flynn hooks his arm under Sterling's front legs and flips him onto his back. I scrub my fingers into his chest fur and work my way down his belly until—

"Damn it, Sterling. Put away your red lipstick. There is no way I'm touching it as a human." I smack him on his chest, and he barks and wiggles.

"So, transform into a wolf," he teases, thrashing in Flynn's arms to flip over. "I guarantee you'll appreciate my rod of the Rovers then."

Flynn cracks up. His laughter fills the air, lightening the heaviness in my heart. "You're a crazy bastard, Sterling. I'm nearly certain you're going to have to show her more than two inches of the red menace."

I whack him next. "Don't encourage him."

A small cute noise hums through the air, drawing my attention back to McKayla. She could've vanished and ran from us during our moment, but she didn't. It's how I know she's not lying about my dad or anything else.

"Levi did such a wonderful job raising you, Lyric. I don't think he expected you to bond with so many, but you do have your parents' hearts." McKayla wrings her hands together, stepping closer. "And a warlock as well? You really are Melody's daughter. Eliphas would've been so in love..." Her words fade into a whisper, clenching my heart.

"My dad never told me about Eliphas. So it's true? The Everdeens said I was his daughter. They tried to claim me but Flynn bonded with me." I have so many questions.

Her face contorts with anger. "Of course they did. Those traitors ruined so many lives. Eliphas abandoned his own blood bonds with that coven to escape. And you know what they did?"

She doesn't have to say the words for me to know.

"They murdered Eliphas and stole the magic gifted to him from the Fyre line to collar Melody to try to force her into creating a curse. They killed every man she loved except for Levi and it forced her to give her own life to protect you two. She and Levi knew you would need a strong pack and the witches guaranteed it." McKayla blinks, her eyes watering with tears.

Fuck. Her words set off a bomb inside me, exploding my entire past apart. My dad never liked to talk about my mom's death, and now I know why.

"They had to have used extremely dark magic, sacrificial magic, to locate you and get through the shields unnoticed," she adds, hugging her arms around herself. "The town is constantly shifting locations to prevent it being found. Those who leave and return are informed by magic of where to meet one of the elders to return. We've been protecting those seeking sanctuary for over a century now."

"So you just assumed my dad left? You didn't even bother to look for him? Or me for that matter?" Hurt and disappointment floods through me. I try not to be angry, but what kind of place is this if they don't look out for those who live here? She claims it's a sanctuary for fate's sake.

Dax drapes his arm around my shoulders, pulling me into

him, engulfing me in a hug. "Lyric, I'm sorry. We had no idea this was the Fire Mountain Clan. Levi—and my father—swore they were our enemies."

"Because word can't get out about what we do here," McKayla says, butting in. "If word got out, many would try to destroy us. They don't believe in the unity we've found. They'd prosecute those who refuse to live under the Magaelorum Law and those who want to create new ones."

I tip my head back and look into Dax's golden eyes, needing his guidance as my mate. He knew my dad on a different level than anyone. Our fathers were best friends. "What do we do now? My dad was supposed to have answers. He was supposed to help us take control of Lulupoterra."

Dax studies my eyes, his thoughts racing a mile a minute. His first instinct is to return to the Everdeen Coven and slaughter them, seeking vengeance on my behalf. His inner wolf hungers for destruction but his humanity tames his wildness, giving him a voice of reason. We both know waging a war on the Everdeen Coven could result in loss for us if we're unprepared. Doing so still won't give us the answers or help we need.

"I think we should return and pretend we know nothing of this situation," he finally says, peering past me to confirm with the others. "We can use this knowledge against them and find out what happened to your dad."

"We will return and tell them that we weren't actually looking to establish a home in the Mortal World and went after the

Fire Mountain Clan. We'll ask for their help in locating them in exchange to help them seize a portion of Lulupoterra. They won't be able to resist." Flynn turns to McKayla. "You could help us. You could use a communication spell to alert the High Council of the Everdeens' supposed act of treason."

"It will also show you're alive." I break away from Dax and turn to the witch. "You could help get justice for the Tenebris Coven."

McKayla's eyes sparkle with magic and she slowly nods. "Okay. I'll do it. Melody once said she was carrying the woman who would change the packs forever. If the fates brought you here, I can't deny them."

I throw my arms around her. "Thank you. Thank you. Thank you. You won't regret it."

She smiles and looks to the lion. "Inform the elders. It's time we move."

13

Fragile Alliances

"WHY DON'T YOU STAY WITH me and let the others handle it?" Sagan grabs my hand, stopping me in place. "You might distract them."

My instincts tell me to yank away, but my heart screams to knock that shit off. "I'm not going to distract them, Sagan. Now come on. I don't want to waste much time. We need—"

Reaching up, he covers my mouth with his hand. "You

heard that witch. Your mom ensured you'd have a strong pack to handle things, and I really, really want you to distract me."

I lick his palm, but he doesn't pull his hand away. "Not to handle things for me," I mumble against his fingers. "To handle things with me."

"Come on, gorgeous." Sagan nudges me back, herding me toward a tree with sprawling branches. None of our pack mates say anything, but Dax gives me a look, letting me know all I have to do is say the word, and he'll step in.

I subtly shake my head at him.

"I've been through a lot. I just want you to spend some time with me. Alone. I've missed you. Your taste. Your scent. It's hard for me to stay in control." He reaches between my legs with his other hand. "What do I have to do? Ask to slip my womb broom into your cum closet?"

I laugh in exasperation, smacking my hands into his chest. "Seriously?"

"It works for my brother," he replies. Leaning in, he brushes his lips to my ear. "Or should I just spank you again?"

Warmth blossoms between my thighs, my body remember-ing how good it felt when Sagan and Bastien had their way with me.

He inhales a deep breath, teasing me through my clothes. "Only good?"

A howl rips through the air, stopping me from responding. I jerk away from him, the lust fading with another call from

Sterling. Sagan growls and snags the back of my shirt, pulling me back. Blue light flashes within the trees, followed by another and another.

"Little she-wolf, come here. Let me take a look at you," a man with long white hair says, strolling with another man and a petite girl with pink hair and fucking wings behind him. "Evelyn told me you were stunning. Is this the wolf lucky to have mated with you?"

Shit. He thinks I'm Harlow.

Snarling, Sagan yanks me back protectively. He engulfs me in his arms, spinning away. My mates growl in warning, skulking through the trees. The warlock narrows his eyes, peering around. I don't have a chance to react or make my pack stand down.

Sterling launches from the trees and attacks the warlock, sinking his teeth into his arm. Roaring, the man next to the warlock bursts through his clothes, transforming into a lycan. Sterling releases the warlock's arm and scrambles back, only to dart around to try to get to the lycan from behind.

"No!" I shout, snapping a heavy branch from the tree.

The warlock gathers brilliant blue magic in his palms. "Et to volati s—"

Swinging the branch at him from behind, I clock the warlock in the side of the head, knocking the spell right out of him. Dax darts through the trees in his mahogany form, crashing into the lycan, sneaking up on him from behind as Sterling tears at his leg from the front. Something pink erupts in the winged girl's hands, and I swing the branch at her next, sending her fluttering through the air. Bastien and Antone jump from opposite sides, snapping and snarling, attempting to pull her down. Caz barrels in front of me, forcing me into Sagan.

"Pilc reh rewop. Pord eht fae!" Flynn blasts the girl with an orb of lavender energy, sending her colliding with a tree. Flicking his hand, he uses magic to shove Antone and Bastien away as the pink glob of jelly splatters across the ground, smoking and eating away at the dried grass.

What. The. Fuck.

"How dare you attack an invited guest," the white-haired warlock snarls, growing in stature while stretching his mouth open to reveal his elongated fangs. His long hair floats in the energy of his power, and he raises his hands, getting ready to chuck it at Flynn.

My heart bursts with heat, my soul zinging as Flynn calls upon my magic, enhancing his. He meets the warlock with a threat of his own, his body rippling with his flexing muscles The tattoos on his arms swirl and dance across his skin, glowing with power.

"Enough!" Red and blue light flashes through the air as Evelyn and Enrique materialize before us. Evelyn's gaze darts to mine, her surprise of finding us out here clear in her expression. All my mates growl, circling the Everdeens and the new group, waiting for my command.

I'm tempted to say to hell with it and let them attack, but

we came back for a reason. If only seeing Enrique with Evelyn didn't burn sizzling rage inside me. I knew the witch was lying. I fucking knew it.

Evelyn glances away and refuses to acknowledge me, instead, turning to Flynn. "I didn't expect you back so soon."

"Because we lied to you," I snap, trying to keep in control. I've never wanted so badly to call someone out. "We weren't setting up a safe haven for my pack. We were on a witch hunt. Now that I have my pack together, I want to find the fucking coven that kidnapped my father."

Enrique scowls, stepping forward. "You were what?"

Raising her hand, Evelyn stops him in his tracks. "Not now, brother." She saunters closer to Flynn, turning her back on me to focus on him. "And which coven was that? Surely you don't think the Infinity Coven had anything to do with it. Lazlo is a great ally of mine."

Lazlo Infinity. I think the name over and over, finally placing the warlock. He was one of the coven heads to summon Invidia from Lulupoterra. Shit. I know why he's here. I bet the other covens are coming too. Evelyn was going to try to sneak behind our backs to get to Lulupoterra, claiming it as hers.

"It was not," Flynn says sharply, speaking before I have a chance to respond. "It was the Fire Mountain witches. The wolves recognized the magic of their doppelgangers that kept attacking Lunar Crest. Before the Nightstars came in, I had been preparing a tracking spell and finally had a chance to cast it."

"And?" Evelyn rubs her palms together, anxious for his response.

Flynn purses his lips, taking his time to answer. "I failed. Something must've been off with the artifact I used."

"You're trying to locate the Fire Mountain Clan?" Lazlo asks, interrupting whatever response Evelyn was going to give. He narrows his eyes and takes an automatic step back. "What coven are you from, High Priest? I've never seen you before."

Flynn snaps his fingers, and Sterling circles him to sit by his side. "You wouldn't have. It's been over a decade since I've seen Magaelorum. And I'm not a High Priest. I'm a pack mate of the wolves of Lunar Crest."

I finally get Caz to stand down and saunter forward with Sagan by my side. Clearing my throat, I draw Lazlo's attention to me. "I'm our pack leader. I apologize for my mates' reactions, but you disrespected me, and we don't stand for that kind of behavior. I'm not a pet to be admired."

Enrique grumbles under his breath, and I whip my head to look at him. Like the coward he is, he steps behind Evelyn like she'll protect him. I can't resist the urge to fuck with him, so I stride to Flynn and take his hand, meeting Enrique's eyes from over her shoulder.

"I see," Lazlo says from a few feet away.

This fucker. He doesn't even apologize.

Ignoring him, I focus on Evelyn. "Now, before you start celebrating the fact that I betrayed my own species to bring you a she-wolf, I want to make you a bargain. We need help finding the Fire Mountain Clan. I need to find out what happened to Levi. I think he might still be alive."

"How do you know?" Enrique asks, annoyance hardening his voice. "What makes you think the Everdeens will help you after—"

"What do we get out of it?" Evelyn cuts Enrique off, silencing him with magic.

I smirk, loving seeing the shock widening the asshole's eyes. "I want to offer you a piece of Lulupoterra and some wolves who need some training. All you have to do is help us, and it's yours when we take back our home."

Evelyn taps her finger to her lips and shifts her gaze from mine, working her way around the group—from Flynn to Lazlo, my pack, and finally stopping on Enrique. His features sharpen even more. I can nearly feel the heat of his anger toward Evelyn. If one of us does or says one more thing he disagrees with, his head might explode. I hope it does. I never knew how badly I wanted to see someone get ripped apart by my pack. The anticipation tingles across my skin as my she-wolf howls inside me, begging me to let her break free to lead my mates in a fight for revenge.

"I must talk to the rest of my coven," Evelyn finally says, pressing her lips together. "It'll have to wait until after our gathering. Had I known you would be back so soon, I'd have arranged to meet my allies somewhere else, but we have important matters to discuss."

"What a lovely idea," Lazlo says, softening his features and shrinking back down to his short stature. "I'd love to get to know this surprisingly intelligent wolf pack."

This fucker.

Waving at his minions, Lazlo gets the lycan to transform back into his human form. The winged girl lands on her feet and smiles at me like she didn't just try to burn my mates. Dax is the only one of my mates to return to his human form, joining Sterling by my side.

The lycan flicks his gaze to Dax's cock, and I nearly start laughing at his reaction. I bet he regrets transforming now. My guys' equipment can squash any man's ego.

"What do you think, Lyric?" Flynn asks me, speaking to me through our familiar link. "We weren't expecting the Everdeens to have guests."

I don't respond for a moment, considering what will happen when McKayla follows through, alerting the High Council of Magaelorum of the Everdeens deception. We should get a day, but I worry we might need more time.

Remaining expressionless, I nod to Flynn. "I suppose it won't hurt." I straighten my shoulders, purposely keeping my gaze away from Evelyn and Enrique's. I know I shouldn't say my next words, but I can't help myself. I was kidding about wanting to see Enrique's head explode. Smiling, I capture Lazlo's eyes sparkling with his blue magic. "I'd love to talk to other coven heads. You never know when you might need a new ally."

Lazlo's grin widens, showing off all his teeth. I don't have to know many covens to realize how fragile any and all alliances are. All it could take is an argument to start a war. The Everdeens already have one brewing with the Nightstars, and I'm sure Lazlo would use the target my pack's being here put on her to his advantage. What he'd do? I have no idea.

"Perfect," Lazlo says, holding out his elbow for the winged girl to slide her fingers around. The lycan grabs his shoulder. "We will see you inside."

The three of them disappear in a pop of light, leaving us alone with Evelyn and Enrique. She purses her lips in annoyance. Clearly, my small conversation with Lazlo got to her. Enrique claps his hands, disappearing next, and I hug onto Dax's arm.

"You must excuse me, Lyric. Other covens can't know Enrique has been cut off," she says like she can read my thoughts.

I shrug. "Yeah, okay. Just keep him away from us. If you don't—"

Evelyn vanishes without letting me finish my threat.

Dax mutters under his breath and tightens his fingers around me like he can't help ensuring no one tries taking me from him. The rest of our pack transforms, a dozen different emotions crossing their faces and crashing through me.

"Everyone, I need you to stay in control around the covens, okay?" I say, meeting each of their gazes. "It'll only be for a little while."

Flynn bobs his head. "If you don't think you can manage to—"

"We'll manage, warlock," Bastien snaps, fisting his hands. "Don't question our capabilities."

I sigh and brush my hair from my face. "Come on. Let's just go."

14

FRENZY

I TUG AT THE HEM of my gown, wishing I could just go change into some sweats. The last thing I expected from this gathering was formalwear, but the second we returned to my room, Evelyn sent Heather knocking with a purple gown for me and tuxes for everyone else.

I realize this might be the first time any of my guys have ever worn such attire. Sterling messes with the cuffs of his jacket while Dax untucks his dress shirt from his pants. Fidgeting with his vest, Caz pulls at it, trying to stretch it out. Antone flat out takes off his belt, not even caring that Trinity curls her lip up in disbelief. It only makes Bastien follow his twin's lead, and he snaps the leather toward the witch, startling her into her sister. Tipping his head back, Sagan bellows a laugh, shrugging out of his tux jacket. He drops it onto a chair and rolls his shoulders, showing off his bulging muscles.

Flynn touches my outer thigh and draws his finger down the tight fabric, splitting it with magic at the seam. The cool air caresses my bare leg through the thigh-high slit, giving me a better movement. Now if only he could magically turn these dumb heels into tennis shoes...

A soft whistle draws my attention to Dax, and he drinks in the sight of the alteration Flynn made. I shiver under my pack's sudden scrutiny, their intensity getting to me in a good way. Laughter sounds from across the dining room as Lazlo and another witch I recognize—which I hear someone call Allegra—drink from golden chalices like it's the most normal thing in the world.

"Lyric, sweetie, why don't you join us?" Enrique says, waving me closer.

My legs freeze, and I can't help feeling my fear instincts kick on. There is no way in hell I'm about to get within a foot of him. The bastard is already plotting against me. I don't need to make it easier.

"I'll join them," Flynn says, straightening out his tuxedo jacket. "Just wait here."

Instead of arguing, I nod my head and let him take the lead. I don't know what I would say anyway, and Enrique will somehow piss me the hell off and turn me feral.

"And you said we need to stay in control," Caz teases, taking Flynn's place.

"You're the one whose dress is already ready to be ripped off." Sterling takes my other side and traces his finger down the smooth skin peeking out from the slit. "Remind me to high-five my bestie. He always makes things easier, doesn't he?"

I narrow my eyes at him. "He was making me more comfortable."

"Mmm-hmm." Sterling shifts the fabric, trying to take a peek at my ass. "I think he forgot that the only way to make you comfortable is if you're completely naked. I can hel—"

"Pardon me," Lazlo says, causing Sterling to snap his mouth shut. "Flynn mentioned you thought your pack might intimidate Allegra, which is why you sent him."

I smirk at Flynn. "Enrique, too."

Lazlo chuckles and rocks on his heels. "You're absolutely right. There is a reason he didn't step up as High Priest of the Everdeen Coven."

His comment piques my interest. If I were in my wolf form, my ears would perk up. "You knew Eliphas?" I ask, trying to keep my voice even.

"Not well. Only that we shared a passion for powerful creatures like yourself. He loved running with the wolves," he mentions, eyeing my pack.

I touch his arm, redirecting his attention back to me. "And you, Mr. Infinity?"

"Please, call me Lazlo." Nodding across the room, he motions toward his minions, standing together in the corner of the room, having a quiet conversation. "Apart from the fae and lycans, my interest lies in the power of the dragons. I'm assuming you've never encountered one."

Dragons? There is so much more to the world than I can ever grasp. And knowing I've been kept in the dark—hell, even my pack has been kept in the dark because of the separation from Magaelorum—bothers me on a whole other level.

"I haven't." I stare across the room, spotting Flynn now only speaking with Allegra.

Lazlo hums his disappointment as if I'm somehow missing out. "They're quite magnificent."

I bob my head, not really knowing what to say. Blue magic flickers over the vast dining table as dozens of silver dishes materialize along with fragrant courses of food. Damn. The Everdeens really go all out. The arrival of dinner reminds me that I can't remember the last time I ate.

"Please, take a seat. Enjoy. Your hostess will arrive momentarily," Enrique calls, waving at the table. He disappears from his place in the doorway, and I glower at the space he leaves behind.

"How marvelous. Join me?" Lazlo says, offering me his arm.

I don't get a chance to consider whether or not I'll take it because Trinity steps in front of us, placing her hands on her hips, defining the silhouette of her body in her flowing gown. She crinkles her nose as if even acknowledging me pains her, and I heave a sigh, showing that I hate it as much as she does.

"Please excuse us, Lazlo. Evelyn requests a moment of Lyric's time," Trinity says, daring me to object with the magic in her gaze.

"I'll save you and your mates a seat," Lazlo says, turning his attention to my guys.

I glance past Trinity, meeting Flynn's furrowed gaze. He holds out a seat for Allegra and takes one across from her, letting a man and another woman take the spots by her side.

"It'll only take a moment, unless you don't want to know what she found out about the Fire Mountain Clan." A smirk curls the corner of her mouth, the gesture more of a leer with the way her eyes glare.

"You could've just said so," I snap, holding my hands out to Sterling and Caz. "Come on. You're all coming with me."

Flynn stands up from his seat, but Lazlo swats his arm and leans in, whispering something that keeps Flynn in place. I steel my nerves and follow Trinity into the hallway, expecting to see Evelyn.

Spinning around, the witch smacks Sterling and Caz with a shock of power, sending them stumbling back. Her attack kicks me into my fighting stance, and I high kick right at her chest. The second my heel connects with her sternum, the world ignites in light and my head spins. I land on my ass on a rug with Trinity and Enrique glowering at me. Jerking his arm at me, Enrique douses me with some sort of liquid and chants a spell.

My skin tingles as panic courses through me. Catapulting to my feet, I charge Enrique, shoving my hands into his chest. Trinity shocks me with her power, sending me flying toward the wall. Howls and growls echo from outside the door, and it flings open.

"Ti vo lyvina todo og!" Enrique shouts, blasting power into the hallway.

Bright light blinds me, and I shield my eyes. Swiping the potion from my face, I try to clear my vision. What the fuck did he just do? I scramble to my feet, but Enrique and Trinity disappear, leaving me alone and in confusion.

A sharp intake of breath snaps my attention to the hallway, and my gaze lands on Dax, standing in his torn tuxedo, his nostrils flaring and muscles bulging. Sterling shoves past him into the room and rushes to me. He cups my face and looks deep into my eyes.

Something wild unleashes in my soul, my body humming and aching.

I heave a few deep breaths, my mind whirling. "Something's w-wrong." My body buzzes, and I clutch the front of Sterling's shirt. A small whimper escapes my mouth, sounding pathetic as fuck, but the noise is as uncontrollable as my trembling legs. As all-consuming as the deep-seated need, begging me to finish tearing Sterling's shirt off.

And then I do.

Sterling reacts with a deep, sexy grumble from his throat, snatching me by the waist to pull me close. Our mouths crash together in passion as his fingers rip at the slit of my dress. He tears it upward, splitting the side and only taking a moment to move the fabric out of the way. His hard excitement presses into the thin fabric of my g-string until it shifts to the side. He doesn't enter me right away but rubs his shaft to my damp desire, teasing me in a way that I reach down and clutch him.

"I ache," I say, my mind hazy and spinning. "I need my mates."

Warm hands slide around my waist from behind, pulling my gown off completely. Sagan squeezes my breasts, pinching my tight nipples, making me moan. The intensity of their lust is completely consuming, and all I can think about is the pleasure to come. It's the only thing that will stop the ache slowly killing me inside.

"Bring her here," Dax says, the command in his voice making me arch my back so Sagan kisses the base of my neck. "She wants all of us."

Dax joins us and kisses me in Sterling's arms, reaching between us to feel the excitement buzzing through my body, awakening every nerve ending with millions of sparks. Sterling doesn't let me go but falls back on the bed with me in his arms. He gathers my hair and licks my throat, stretching to suck on my earlobe. The gesture sends more explosions through me. I never knew something so simple could feel so powerful, the sensitivity of my skin unlike anything I've ever felt before.

A flash of light flickers, and Flynn inhales a sharp breath, his eyes roving over my naked body on top of Sterling. Taking in the torn and tattered clothes of my mates, all hard and turned on just for me seems to paralyze him in place. I pout my bottom lip and stretch my hands out to him, wanting my soul mate close.

"She needs us," Sterling says to him, wiggling his hand next to mine. "Can't you feel her? Listen to her thoughts. She wants you. Don't deny her."

Something strange crosses Flynn's gaze and he hesitates. His muscles bulge on his arms, flexing as he curls and uncurls his fingers. Lavender electricity dances between his palms, and he swallows, sending his Adam's apple bobbing in his throat.

"Lyric, your body—your soul. I've felt it like this before. What happened? Who did this?" His chest heaves, his fingers absently popping the buttons open on his dress shirt. "It's so intense. More so than before. I feel your ache. It's torture."

"Hurry. She needs us," Sterling repeats.

"I do. Please don't be afraid, warlock," I say, my breath panting. I squirm and drag my hands down my body, rubbing my fingers between my legs, trying to find some sort of release. I'll die otherwise. I know it. "I need all my mates. Come to me.

Save me."

What am I saying? Why do I sound so desperate? Why can't I fucking pull myself together?

"I got you, gorgeous," Sagan says, easing my legs open. "I will not make you wait any longer. He can wait his turn. I claimed you first."

Bending forward, Sagan licks the seam of my body, knocking away the questions rolling through my mind. I moan and arch into Sterling, the sensation of Sagan's mouth easing the all-consuming desire burning me with need. I close my eyes and massage my legs, Sagan's mouth utter bliss yet I still feel on edge.

Antone and Bastien join us on the bed, and I blindly reach out and grab at them, naked and throbbing, completely ready for me. They close in, their cocks within reach of my mouth, and I lick and tease Antone first before doing the same to Bastien.

Flynn groans deep in his throat as he watches me, and I meet his gaze and squirm with the pleasure Sagan creates. I dig my fingers into Dax's firm ass cheek next and glide my tongue over his tip, tasting the tangy desire dripping in anticipation. Flynn's eyes flash with streaks of lavender electricity, and he saunters closer, cautiously, like he's afraid one of our pack mates might bite him.

Caz pushes him from behind, surprising the hell out of Flynn. He strokes his hard-on, stiff with his desire as I taste each of my mates. "She said she wants you. Don't deny her. We're all a pack. It is our duty to ease her aching body. To give her everything she wants and needs."

Damn. My vagina clenches, loving the sound of that.

"Yeah, man. Summon the fucking magical lube and get over here," Sterling calls, kissing my throat. He flexes his boner against my ass, making me gasp. "We're going to need it to fulfill her biggest fantasies."

I moan at his suggestion, my body already clenching and spasming with an orgasm.

All of my guys stiffen and flex, feeling my pleasure with me. Their collection of moans turns me on even more, intensifying the seemingly never-ending ache.

Sagan flips me over, and my boobs press into Sterling's chest. Pulling me up, Sterling buries his face between them and then sucks each of my nipples. The bed shifts as my whole pack piles on around me. Their scents envelop me in mouth-watering fragrances, impossibly turning me on even more.

I whimper again.

Fuck. I wish my mouth would stop that.

"Tell us what you need, Lyric," Dax says, rubbing his hand down my back until he can slip a finger between my legs. "What do you want? Who do you desire first? It doesn't matter. Pick who you need. We all love you."

"We'll give you anything," Antone adds, smacking my ass as I arch my back to look up.

"We're patient," Caz adds, his voice husky.

Sagan moans and leans down, kissing the stinging spot

Antone leaves behind with his lips. "I want what my brother's already gotten," he says, licking his way across my ass cheek.

I hum my agreement, the sensation of his mouth feeling incredible as he uses his mouth and finger to prepare my body. "I want that too."

Cool lube drips over my body, tingling with the familiar magic that arouses me beyond belief, and I wiggle in anticipation.

Flynn kneels next to my head and leans down, kissing me before turning his head to kiss Sterling only inches away from my mouth. The two of them then kiss me together, our tongues gliding and tasting, exploring the excitement of our love as a pack.

"Vi tog al xes," Flynn whispers, sending sparkles of light over the room. "We will share everything as we do our bond."

I bob my head and stroke my fingers over Dax's enormous cock, flexing for my attention. Sagan squirts lube on it, turning it slippery as my fingers slide and warm his up. Everyone moans, feeling what Dax feels as I pleasure him with my hand.

Pressure builds between my legs as Sterling adjusts me, pushing his cock inside and slowly rocking. Sagan holds my ass cheeks, spreading me wider, watching his brother fuck me for a moment. Antone tugs my hair, pulling my head up. He kisses me at the same time Sagan slides into me from behind, and everyone gasps in pleasure. I moan and close my eyes, opening my mouth as I blindly pull Antone to me. He helps me guide his cock through my parted lips, bobbing my head as I lick and suck him. Flynn whispers a spell, sending vibrations across my clit. His magic keeps me in place, so I can feel the extent of everyone. Blindly reaching for Bastien, I slide my other slippery hand over his erection, letting him thrust into the tightness of my fingers.

Another orgasm builds between my legs, the tingles and bliss so intense that my mind turns to mush and all I can think is that I want more.

Sweetness floods my mouth as Antone orgasms at the same time I do, his cum tasting of strawberries and cream, enhanced by whatever magic Flynn uses to ensure I enjoy every second of our frenzy to give and take and just enjoy each other.

Sterling grunts next, his body shuddering with ecstasy. It sets me off again, and I moan so embarrassingly loud that Sagan pulls out and cums across my ass. I don't have a chance to call for my other mates before Dax scoops me into his arms and wraps my body around his. He thrusts inside me hard and fast, so incredibly deep that I feel him penetrating what feels like my soul.

Bastien kisses my shoulder, warming the cold space Sagan leaves behind, and he joins Dax, screwing me how I want and crave and need. I want to smother them in the pleasure we share. Taking care of all of them at once is far more satisfying than I could ever imagine.

Caz stands behind Dax, bracing on his shoulder, guiding his cock into my mouth. I hum and suck, bouncing with Dax and

Bastien, the new position leaving me breathless. Flynn uses magic to set me off again, and I scream my enjoyment, the noise vibrating from my throat and to Caz, making him cum with me.

Each peak my mates reach lessens the painful, all-consuming ache in my body. I moan and pant, turning my gaze up to search for Flynn. He licks his lips, his eyes lusty, and strokes himself teasingly as Sterling kisses him, showing me their love, knowing how hot it makes me.

"You feel like paradise, Ma Belle," Bastien mutters in my ear, pinching my ass cheeks as he thrusts a few more times.

I can't believe another orgasm crashes through me, tensing my body. I clench Dax between my legs, picking up my bouncing and kissing him how he wants. He cums with a whisper of how much he loves me until he eases me off, bending me over the bed.

Flynn joins me last, fucking me from behind while Sagan pulls my hair to kiss the moans from my mouth. Everyone touches my body like they can't help themselves, and I lose myself to the weight of their fingers, to the sensation of love each of them caresses my soul with.

I've never felt so wanted and needed in my life. I feel more powerful than ever, satiating my pack on the level they crave and need.

"I love you, Lyric," Flynn whispers.

He chants a spell under his breath, setting all of us off at once like he had done once before. Warmth splashes across me, the ache in my body finally subsiding enough to think.

And then I tense with my thoughts.

Holy fucking fuck.

"Lyric, what's wrong?" Dax asks, using the blanket to clean me off. "You're scared."

Scrambling up, I try to rush to the door, but Sagan cuts me off. "Move, Sagan. I have a warlock to murder."

"What?" Caz asks.

"Enrique dosed me with some potion. Look what he's done. He broke the spell that was keeping us in control." I heave a few breaths. Turning on the balls of my feet, I meet their gazes. Their sudden worry and guilt bats at me. I lick my lips. "I mean, I loved—I really fucking loved what we just did and I'd do it all over again—but he purposely fucked with the spell controlling my heat to send us into a mating frenzy. He—"

My whole body buzzes with another wave of mind-blowing desire. My mates warned me what mating season would be like, but this is far more intense than what I imagined.

My she-wolf decides she needs my pack's love too, and I can't stop my transformation into a wolf.

Lifting my tail, I whimper and back up, offering my body as a wolf.

Several growls vibrate through my bones, and Sterling mounts me from behind, his hulking wolf body ready to give in to my feral desire.

The door to the bedroom crashes open, flying off the hinges

as Evelyn barges in. "Oh, my fucking fates," she gasps, twisting her mouth.

"I'll fucking kill him!" Flynn shouts, sending magic blasting through the air.

The world spins with intense light.

I pass out.

15

The Witch Chase

"YOU CAN'T LEAVE US HERE," Flynn snaps, his sharp voice cutting through me.

"We already have to move because of this. The High Council will have felt the influx of magic just as I had. It's like her body releases intense energy when she's together with her mates. You should've stopped them," Evelyn responds.

I crack my eyelids open. Swinging her hand, she slaps the

metal door of the strange room.

"You should've kept your coven brother in control. He fucking did this! Now you will take us back. I will not allow you to separate me from my wolves." Flynn gathers power in his hands, preparing to fight.

"No." Evelyn gathers her own magic. "You're too reckless and obsessed with your familiar. You remind me too much of my old High Priest, and what he did—what you're doing—it goes against everything we've spent a millennia trying to accomplish. I will not let your misguided lust for this beast ruin my coven. I don't care if you claim this one. The others are mine. I will control them how I see fit. The Nightstars were right to believe it was time to step in."

Fury explodes inside me, and I launch from the bed, surprising Evelyn. Shoving her back, I slam her body into the metal door. How dare she threaten to steal my pack? I will not let her get away with this.

I pinch her chin and glower into her eyes. "You might think you can destroy us like you had my parents, but you are sorely mistaken. I will rip you apart."

"Teg kab flow!" Evelyn shouts, blasting me with magic.

Flynn shoots his own, sending energy crackling through the room, but Evelyn is already gone.

Rushing to my side, Flynn kneels on the ground and runs his fingers over my naked body. I curl in on myself, the ache and fear trying to debilitate me, and it takes all my strength to push my pain to the back of my mind to focus.

"Where are we?" I ask, pushing my palms into the cold metal ground.

"I don't know. We crossed realms. Somewhere in Magaelorum," he says, scrubbing his hands over his cheeks. "This is all my fault. I knew something was wrong, but I couldn't get my mind to think. It was like your pack's needs consumed my humanity."

I groan and pull him to me, hugging my arms around his. "Don't blame yourself for what the Everdeens did, Flynn. You're not responsible for us. I am. We all are. Even Antone couldn't resist and he is supposed to have the most control over his needs and be able to resist my desires because we haven't shared that kind of bond yet."

Flynn chuckles and sighs. "Whatever Enrique spelled you with was dark magic worse than even the Nightstars used to trigger your heat. He had to have killed someone to complete it."

"Fuck," I murmur, squeezing my eyes shut. My body hums and aches, and I squeeze my legs together. "I'm so out of whack. I feel like if I don't orgasm again, I might die."

"Let me help you." Flynn rubs his hands together, his eyes flickering with magic.

"Control yourself, warlock. We don't have time. If you start, I can't stop." I press the heels of my hands into my eyes.

He strokes his hand over my arms, the softness of his voice trying to ease my rapping heart. "It'll take a second. I don't even have to touch you."

Damn it. "But I want you to touch me. So badly."

He twirls his finger, sending a spark of electricity over my desperate body. I arch my back with his magically induced orgasm, my whole body tensing as I bite my lip, silently rolling with it. Flynn kisses my temple, holding me to him, whispering how much he loves me.

I gasp, my body finally allowing me to breathe. Heat crawls up my neck, and I try not to be embarrassed, but this was a lot less fun than it should be. "Fuck, this is insane. I can barely wrap my mind around any of this. I swear you better work harder in the future."

His chest rumbles in his amusement. "Unless you're just desperate for some quick relief."

I groan. "You are enjoying this way too much, warlock."

"I can't help that I love ensuring you're good. You feel better, don't you?" he asks, chuckling, trying to lighten the mood. "That's all I care about. I need you to be able to focus as I channel your magic to break down the door. I need me to concentrate too, and it's hard when all I want is to satisfy you as your mate."

I inhale a breath through my nose and pout my bottom lip. "Don't think I won't pay you back later. You deserve a reward for dealing with this bullshit."

"You are my reward, she-wolf." Snuggling me close for a moment, Flynn absorbs my love and contentment, using them to get his worry under control. I know he feels responsible, and

I know he feels powerless because of the circumstances, but he's far from it.

So I take charge, pushing to my feet. He can't feel as if he has to do any of this alone, and my damn needs will get themselves in check. I've survived lady blue balls before. Fuck, I've survived things a million times worse.

Snatching a stained blanket from a worn cot, I wrap it around me. Flynn still wears his dress pants, only having taken off his shirt without completely undressing in the mating frenzy, which I'm thankful for. He tries a summoning spell, but his magic bounces back like a firework exploding in the air.

"Can you redirect the ricochet of your magic toward the door?" I ask, striding forward to place my hands against the buzzing metal. "Tap into my power if you have to. I've broken through an entrapment spell before but it took a while."

Flynn dips his chin in a sharp nod. "That's a brilliant idea. I was going to direct my magic at it, but the way the entrapment spell here works is that it triggers at the first detection of magic. The ricochet of power won't be as strong, and if I do it enough, it could break the spell."

My heart lifts with hope. I knew Flynn would figure something out with my help. We're a pack the way the fates have arranged. He's the most determined, strong, intelligent warlock the universe has ever been graced with. And he's mine. All mine.

Flynn takes my hand in his, a smile lighting his handsome face as he feels the confidence I have in his abilities and uses them to lift his own. I lean in and kiss him, imagining taking all of the power in the universe and bottling it up to fill in his hands. Warmth blooms in my chest, rising through my heart to spill through the rest of me. Static buzzes across my skin, dancing from my fingers to Flynn's and our palms light up. He doesn't toss the magic, just letting it battle across the hot field of energy swirling around the walls, shocking the soles of my bare feet.

I shift my weight, ignoring the sting, and imagine our power blending and moving, snaking around us. Lavender light flickers up my arms, lighting my skin in a magical light. Flynn's gorgeous eyes remain narrowed and focused on the door in front of us.

"It's intoxicating," I whisper as my heart picks up pace, rapping against my ribcage, the power filling the cell smothering us in everything Flynn creates. Everything we are together. With me as his familiar, born from the strength of the Lunar Crest pack and the incomparable magic of love, respect, devotion, and desire for a greater future, Flynn is an undeniable force to be reckoned with. He doesn't need the power of a coven. All he needs is our pack. Me.

Lavender electricity strikes lightning bolts from wall to wall, the magic dancing and buzzing, shooting sparks every which way. I expect to be shocked at any second. Possibly knocked out. But all the magic does is fill me up in a way that reminds me of everything at stake. I will not fail my mates. The witches who threaten to tear us apart and leash us will fall at my feet, begging for mercy.

They will get nothing. They will pay for everything they've ever done to not only my pack but my species.

This is no longer a game.

I will hunt them down and destroy them.

This is the starting point of our witch chase, and in the end, only we can win. There is no other option.

"Get ready, my familiar," Flynn calls, his voice whipping around the cell with the electrical currents of his addictive magic.

I straighten my shoulders and brace myself, standing with my feet apart, ready to take on the hurricane of power about to blast through us.

"Erf le tov siensa te cota le ya!" Flynn shouts without releasing the power.

The room quakes and trembles as the powerful shield snaps toward us. Blasting us off our feet, the shield shocks us, stealing my breath away. Flynn flings himself over me and convulses through the magical shockwave ricocheting from us to bounce back at the walls. I grind my teeth as sizzling pain bursts through my very soul, shadowing my vision. I tense and cling onto Flynn, suppressing my urge to scream. The intense magic shoots through the room, returning right back to us, and Flynn drags me up and grips my waist, keeping me on my feet.

"Erf le tov siensa te cota le ya!" he yells again, summoning another round of powerful magic from my soul.

Chucking it forward, he blasts the door, exploding a gaping

hole through the metal. Bolts of red and blue energy crackle and pop, trying to stabilize to keep the shield in place. Once again, Flynn gathers more power and flings it forward, shaking the entire room. The shield breaks, shattering in a firework display of power, raining across the floor and disappearing.

A blaring alarm screeches through the air, and the lights blink off. I groan and cover one of my ears with my free hand, but it does nothing to stop the noise from trying to blast apart my ear drums.

Flynn yanks me forward, not giving me a chance to find my footing, and pulls me through the hole in the door. I don't have a chance to react as a masculine voice shouts over the alarm, the spell lost to the noise. I fly off my feet and skid down the concrete corridor, losing my hold on Flynn.

He yells my name through my mind, his desperation to get to me all-consuming. I slap my palms to the cold ground and push up on my hands, tilting my chin up to peer ahead of me. Enrique ties Flynn in a net of blazing blue magic, forcing him to his knees. Flinging his hand, Flynn points at me, but it's too late.

The fire of a magic collar burns across my throat as Trinity calls her magic, trying to lock it in place. Linking my fingers around the hot chain, tangible by the magic, I force my weight down like I'm about to swing and flip my legs over my head. I crash into Trinity, landing on top of her chest. She shocks me with her magic, but all it does is awaken my she-wolf, setting my inner beast off.

Trinity can't even scream before I transform, my fur exploding through my skin and my senses enhancing, the hunger for revenge turning me wild. I chomp down on Trinity's thigh, sinking my teeth so deep that blood pours from the puncture wounds. She screeches in pain, unable to spit another spell out, and I bite her again. I scramble backward over her body, clawing her with my nails. The second I'm standing over her head, I bow down and lock my jaws to her throat. I don't let go until she stops moving a moment later, the damage I've done to her body causing her to bleed out.

"Id kolraw won," Enrique mutters, stealing my attention away from my kill.

Flynn hollers, his pain so intense that it punches me in the chest. A guttural growl escapes my throat, my instincts to protect the man I love kicking my beast, setting her off. I race forward and narrow my focus on Enrique. He gathers blue light in his hands, preparing to blast it at Flynn. Smashing my back paws into the floor, I launch into the air. Enrique spins and thrusts his magic at me, sending me barreling toward his dead sister.

"You feral animal," he snaps, growing in size, baring long fangs where his teeth should me. Magic sparks like stars in his eyes, and he rushes at me, blasting me again, keeping me on the floor. "I will break you until you lose what is left of my traitor brother."

I screech and yelp as he closes the space and kicks me with a magical force that sends me flying into the wall. Agony bursts through my body, only intensifying as I collide to the floor, landing with my paw twisted. Enrique flicks his fingers and bends my other leg and breaks it completely, sending me dropping yowling.

Flynn hollers, yelling a spell that ignites my soul with his purple light. The magical net that traps him might stop him from fighting back with magic, but it doesn't stop me. Gathering the strength of my pack, the lessons my dad instilled in me that I'm not out unless I'm dead, and I ball it up and push to my paws.

Enrique twists his fingers, knocking my paws out from under me again, and I lay down, letting my mind catch up with me. He blasts me with magic again, sinking it into my skin, trying to burn my humanity away until all I'm left as is a wolf. But he misjudges one thing. He thinks my beast is weak. He thinks that because I'm a she-wolf, he's more powerful than me. But what he doesn't know is that it's not my human half that helps me face the world. It's the power of my wolf, of my mates, of my ancestors that have come before me, working to bring me to this point to change everything.

"Had enough, sweetie?" Enrique asks, acting just like the asshole alpha-mate competitors who never seem to learn that just because I submit now, doesn't mean I won't rise to devour him whole.

"Lyric, get up! The collar!" Flynn yells.

Twisting his torso, Enrique throws a blast of power at

Flynn, sending him tumbling farther away from me. But Flynn wasn't trying to warn me. He was giving me the chance I need.

Flipping up, I land on my front paws and sink my teeth right between Enrique's legs. He hollers and grabs my ears, trying to rip them from my head. I release his junk, smelling the scent of his blood despite not being able to see it, but only to swing my neck and lock my teeth around his wrist. Chomping down, I bite as hard as I can, thrashing my head with all my strength. Enrique shrieks, trying to pull away, but I jerk him into the wall. He slips on his feet, landing on his back.

I don't let go.

I let my she-wolf take complete control, and I tear the fucking asshole's hand off. Blood pours everywhere, the shock of my bite disabling Enrique from even trying to call his magic.

"Wait! Wait, please!" he yells, blocking his neck with his other hand. "This was all Evelyn. She killed your father and took his magic. She's the one collaring your mates. She's the one planning to steal your warlock's magic. Sh—"

I sink my teeth into his arm, cutting off his pleas. He lies helplessly beneath me, screaming and hollering as I tear his other arm off, ensuring he can't ever cast his magic again. Fury courses through me as the asshole stops fighting. I transform into my human self and straddle him, not caring that his blood stains my skin.

"Please," he whispers, his eyes heavy and blinking. "It wasn't my fault."

His words trigger something dark inside me, and I scream in his face. "I don't fucking care!"

Shoving my hand into his throat, I cut off his airway. I press my other hand to his chest and keep him in place, imagining how the world will be so much better off without this fucker in it. Heat swirls around my hand as Enrique's magic climbs up my wrist, zinging through me. I gasp at the strange thrilling sensation crawling up my arms and down my shoulders, gathering around my heart, feeding the necklace I wear carrying Flynn's magic. His soul.

A shock of blue light erupts from me, stealing my vision. My body gives out on me, and I fall over, hitting my shoulder to the concrete. Rolling to my side, I sweep the corridor with my gaze, spotting Flynn pushing to his feet, the net of magic vanishing. I gather all my willpower to get up, my soul craving to be close to his, but I don't get farther than holding my weight on my hands when Flynn lifts me in his arms.

"My fates. My familiar. My soul. You're okay." Flynn showers me with a dozen kisses, not caring that sticky blood coats my body. "What you did...you're the most magical being in the universe. You saved me."

I rest my head to his chest, my body just wanting to be held and cuddled. "One down. Six more to go," I murmur, my heart clenching with the thought of Evelyn hurting our pack. "We need to leave before Evelyn knows."

Flynn nods, gathering magic in his palm, the usually

lavender color blooming indigo. Opening his mouth, he begins to chant a spell, but a low wolf howl catches my attention. I stiffen in Flynn's arms, gripping his shirt in my hands.

"It came from somewhere down the hall," I say, my whole body trembling with a mixture of emotions. "We can't leave him. You know they collared more wolves. They can help us."

Flynn nods without a word, striding down the corridor with me in his arms. We discover another metal door like to the cell we were in, and Flynn opens it without a problem, his new magic tied to the place from siphoning Enrique's.

My heart falters at the sight of the huge tan and white wolf with coffee brown eyes I recognize from looking into them nearly every day of my life. Growling, the hackles on the wolf's back prickle, keeping Flynn frozen in place. But it doesn't stop me.

I wiggle my way from Flynn's arms and limp the dozen feet it takes to cross the room to the wolf. I can't believe he's here. He's really here.

"Dad," I whisper, holding my hand out to him. "Dad, it's me."

Flashing his fangs, the wolf snarls and leaps, colliding into my chest.

I hit the floor and freeze.

"Dad, stop," I say.

He snarls again.

16

MERCILESS

I FLINCH, GRABBING ONTO THE glowing collar around my dad's neck and use all my strength to break it open. Like I've flicked the switch off on his feral beast mode, my dad scrambles back and presses into the metal wall.

My heart breaks at the sight of him. The man who raised me to be strong enough to lead a pack now barely looks capable of standing up without wobbling on his wolf paws. Crawling forward, I open my mind, trying to connect our thoughts, praying he lets me in.

"Dad," I think to him, "I'm here. I'm real. You don't have to be afraid."

Closing my eyes, I shift into my wolf form and turn to glance at Flynn, silently watching from a few feet away. I can sense he wants to be right by my side, holding my hand, but he knows that his presence as a warlock might not be something my dad will accept in his fragile state.

I whimper and shimmy across the floor, nosing his paw. "Dad, please. Say something. I've missed you so damn much. Please."

He responds with a low howl, the sorrow in his voice tightening my chest. "My tough cookie. I failed you. I failed our pack."

Unable to resist, I transform into my human self once more and hug his thin wolf body to me. Where there should be muscles only remains bones. I can feel his ribcage with my fingers, his fur thinning and shedding with his malnourishment and mistreatment.

"Flynn, he needs Bastien and Antone," I say, managing to lift my dad's frail form in my arms, his weight nothing like I remember. I could never have picked him up before, and the fact that I can now...I'm going to kill the fucking witches.

"Will you let me help him? I can give him enough strength to make the journey, but I can only travel with one of you at a time." Flynn cautiously takes a step forward, keeping his hands by his sides. "Is that okay, Levi? I'm a friend and ally of your daughter and the Lunar Crest pack."

Dad stiffens in my arms, and I gently shift him.

"He saved my life, Dad. Let him help you, so we can save my pack. They're in trouble. The Everdeens have them. Everything is a fucking mess." My voice cracks with the words, and I inhale a breath, sucking up my storming emotions.

"Okay," Dad responds, his word a soft whisper through my mind. "I trust your judgment."

Flynn closes the space and guides my hand to rest on one side of my dad's body while he takes the other. His magic tingles against my chest, and I close my eyes at the incredible sensation of our souls mingling and twining as one entity.

Whispering his words, Flynn casts a spell that sets my dad aglow. His muscles don't suddenly fill out nor does his coat turn back to normal, but he manages to shift into a man. Flynn helps him stand on his feet and summons a blanket, wrapping it around my dad's shoulders.

I grip my blanket tighter around me. "You will take me first. I don't want to leave him alone and unprotected at the Everdeen Estate."

My dad grumbles. "I can take care of myself."

I smirk. "And you taught me to take care of you, so don't argue."

A soft smile lights his face, and a whisper of my mom's name flutters through my thoughts. It's strange hearing my dad's voice through the telepathic channel, but I savor the deep rasp of his words, sounding just how I remember.

"Let's be fast, okay?" I tell Flynn, locking my fingers through his. "I can't stand being away from my mates a minute longer."

Hugging my dad one more time, I let Flynn gather me close in his arms, engulfing me with the minty scent of his magic. My stomach flips with the relocation spell, spinning my mind worse than ever. I don't know if it's because I'm hurt or because I'm emotionally drained and magically consumed, but I nearly fall on my ass the second the world stops.

The soft glow of the crescent moon overhead shines only enough to darken shadows around the property. Music hums from the estate, the witches still partying. Annoyance rushes through me. That's how little they think of wolves. Their lives just go on while they try to stop ours.

I've had enough.

Flynn kisses me tenderly, righting me on my feet. He cups my injured leg and whispers a spell, sending tingles through me. The pain, only suppressed by my high adrenaline vanishes, and I puff a breath of relief through my mouth. Fuck, I love my warlock.

"I'd ask you to stay here, but I know you better than that. I brought you as close to your mates as I could sense, using our bond. Go to them." Flynn nudges me toward the back of the property where Enrique had chained them up before.

I rest my head to Flynn's. "Be fast. I'm not giving the witches a chance to fight. We're attacking the second I free our pack."

He tightens his jaw. "Show no mercy. They deserve none."

His command sends a wave of warmth through me, his deep voice so sexy as he disappears. I don't stand in my place long, inhaling a breath, picking up the collection of scents that sets off my she-wolf.

Transforming, I charge through the vast lawn, sticking just outside the path, keeping cover in the trees. If there is some magical shield, I can't sense it. Siphoning Enrique's magic to give to Flynn might've been our saving grace. I don't know exactly how I did it, but I plan to do it over and over until no coven ever dare try to rise against us again.

I reach the back of the property and slow down, my heart clenching at the sight of the empty chains. A soft howl hums through the air, and I jerk my attention toward a huge hedge looking as if it divides the property from another.

"Lyric." Dax's voice whispers my name through my mind. "Don't come any closer. I can smell you. We'll go into another mating frenzy if you do."

Fuck. Me.

"I'm willing to risk it. We must attack now," I say, thinking the words to him. "Control your cocks, okay? You're not mounting me as a wolf."

"But it was so fun trying," Sterling says, chuckling with a groan. "You're just lucky my wolf's kitty tamer is a virgin and I was blindly trying. You never let me get close enough to explore you."

My wolf barks, and I inwardly groan, shoving the thought out of my mind. "You're not helping. Make sure your cock socks stay up or you're getting leashed for life."

"Damn, why do I like when you threaten that?" Sterling mutters.

Bolting forward, I head in the direction of my mates' scents, following the hedge until I reach an entryway to a concrete building—not just any building, but a fucking kennel. I don't believe this shit. I didn't think anyone could be worse than the Nightstars, but it seems as if they're all the same.

"Fuck," Caz whispers. A chain rattles, and I hear my guys start to pace in their wolf forms. "I can't do this. My instincts are—"

Indigo light blasts through the air as Flynn materializes between me and the kennel door with my dad. He doesn't remain in his human form for long, instinctively following my lead and turning into a wolf. He bows to me, his sign of respect and showing he trusts me to lead him fills me with something I can't describe. His pride gives me the confidence to stroll forward through the doorway and into the kennel.

My whole body seizes, just the sight of my mates triggering my intense desire.

Growling, my dad darts between me and them and bares his teeth. "I understand the need, but I will put all of you fuckers in your place beneath me as my daughter's beta if you even think about doing what I think you're about to."

Flynn snaps his fingers, whispering a spell, and I fall over in surprise as the weirdest fucking thing happens in my entire existence. I lie on the ground, staring at my guys in their wolf forms, mirroring my position. Flynn did not just use magic to help us out in front of my fucking dad. If I were a human, I'm certain I'd die from embarrassment.

But fuck it. It worked.

My sudden need dissipates and I get back on my paws only to growl at Flynn. The sexy bastard has the nerve to pet me between my ears as he strolls past and unhooks the collars from my mates, setting them free.

A whimper sounds through the kennel, drawing my attention toward the row of cages my lusty haze never even let me see. I spot Alonzo and a few other wolves locked away like pets, and it intensifies my anger.

"Harlow's inside. I'm worried for her," Alonzo thinks to me.

Flynn rushes to the rest of the cages and one-by-one frees the wolves, adding four more to our pack. I thought I felt powerful before, but it was nothing in comparison to this moment. The strength of the wolves of Lulupoterra courses through me, igniting the magic my she-wolf contains.

Everyone follows my lead, my mates first in line, flanking my sides. Alonzo and the others surround my dad protectively, knowing that he might be a hard-ass but right now, he needs his pack. Our pack. We will work together as one, despite which territories everyone came from and who they wanted to claim as a leader. Because right now, the one thing these witches don't have is unity.

It will be the end of them.

I'll ensure it.

Pounding my paws into the grass, I race toward the estate, my ears perked up as I listen to the party. Flynn blinks into existence ahead of me, standing in front of a grand window. Summoning a basketball-sized orb of his indigo power, he launches it at the window, exploding the glass into a million glittering pieces. I kick off, jumping through the gaping hole and into the middle of the grand living room.

Red power blasts to my right, and I dodge out of the way and duck under the coffee table.

One after the other, my mates and the other wolves rush into the room, snarling and growling. Flynn summons power from me, shooting a wall around us—no, around the witches—caging them in place. Power zaps against the shield as the covens try to break through, but Flynn calls upon me, who gathers the strength of our pack to back him.

I pad my way forward with Dax and Sagan flanking my sides. Evelyn stands wide-eyed and in shock, her all-powerful attitude drained away with her ability to fight back.

Darting her gaze around the room, she stops on my dad, and her features morph in anger. It's now that she also realizes how we escaped her twisted cells. Flynn manages to separate the lavender power from the blue and he zaps Evelyn with it, making her heave.

Stretching my body, I transform into my human self and meet Evelyn's gaze. I don't hide my nudity, not even flinching that I stand here before at least a dozen witches.

"Any witch here who tries to intervene will face the same fate," I say, placing my hands on my hips. "We are not animals to be played with. We are not pets. You will know right this second and remember for the rest of your lives that we are the wolves of Lulupoterra and as the leader of Lunar Crest, I will destroy anyone who threatens my species."

"We saved your species!" Evelyn says, screeching. "Without us—"

My dad launches from his spot, crashing into Evelyn, cutting off her words. She screams, trying to protect herself, but she's no match against a man who lost everything because of her actions.

I turn toward Heather, Samson, and Godfrey. "This is for the death of your High Priest and my mother."

None of them respond or react, standing down without interference.

Strolling forward, I pull my dad back and loom over

Evelyn's bloody and broken body. She tries to call upon her magic, her features twisting into the monster she is, and I slam my palm to her chest and lace my other hand around her throat. My wolf awakens inside me, the strange energy filling me with something I had no idea I was missing. The red power courses over my body, smoothing out the fissures of my soul, damaged by the mess the Everdeens caused. By the pain and heartache, the destruction of my pack, and my life as the fates had intended it. The magic swirls through me, feeling of home and love and everything good that came from my mom's love of a warlock and my dad.

I gasp and remove my hand as the magic settles, filling my soul to blend with Flynn's.

"Blessed are the fates," Allegra whispers, her eyes widening. "The wolves rise again."

I straighten my shoulders, my heart, mind, body, and soul swirling together to remind me of the magic I contain and the power my pack brings.

Turning away from Evelyn's dead body, I face my pack and tense. Green eyes flicker outside the window as a hulking shadow closes in on the estate. Transforming into a wolf, I release a threatening growl.

A lycan launches through the window, snarling and snapping its fangs. It charges toward Samson and crashes through the magic, swiping its dagger-talon across his neck, spilling his blood.

Swinging its neck, it sinks its teeth into Godfrey's throat, ripping it open. Antone collides into the lycan, knocking it away from Heather and bites down on its shoulder.

"The protective shield is broken," Flynn calls out, gathering his magic. "The High Council will come at any moment. We have to leave."

Colored light flashes through the air as the witches scatter and disappear like the cowards they are.

"Move!" Flynn rushes toward me and scoops me into his arms. "Everyone, run to the forest."

"I'm getting Harlow," Alonzo says, his voice calling through my mind.

Panic seizes my heart. I can't believe this is happening.

If we get caught by the High Council, it's over. I know it.

Growls sound from the yard as another lycan charges from the shadows. My eyes widen and I point to it. "Flynn, the lycan. Get him!"

Without hesitating, Flynn blasts the attacking lycan, seizing it with his power. "Go with your pack. I'll meet you in the forest. Run!"

Transforming, I kick into action and race with the others. Bastien nips at my backside, getting me to keep up. I stop at the edge of the tree line, refusing to leave anyone behind. Caz darts behind Alonzo and Harlow, protecting them from behind. Flynn's brilliant magic sparks through the air as he disappears with the lycan.

A strange energy hums over my skin, setting off my instincts.

Shoving my head into Caz, I get him to run with me into the trees.

We don't stop.

We don't look back.

17

RETURN TO LULUPOTERRA

DAX LEADS THE WAY THROUGH the forest, sniffing the ground to track Flynn's scent. My nerves twist and turn, and I stay close to Antone's side, rubbing my body to his. Bugs chirp and buzz through the night. If it weren't for them, the forest would be utterly silent as we pad our way deeper and farther from the estate.

"He's close," Dax says, his thought swirling through my

mind. "I recognize the lycan's scent."

"We should've killed him," Bastien mutters, flanking my other side. "Why did you ask the warlock to save him, Ma Belle? I need a reason or I'll murder him on sight."

I release a low growl, wishing the Nightstars influence didn't constantly make him question me. If I didn't know any better, I'd think he was Antone. "We need the lycan to open the portal to Lulupoterra. We're going home."

No one else questions me, and I finally catch Flynn's minty scent and break away from Antone and Bastien to stalk forward, running ahead of Dax. He doesn't let me get too far ahead, really testing my nature as he noses my backside. I don't think he realizes he's doing it, but damn it. My fear is the only thing keeping my deep-seated nature in check...apart from my dad. I guess that's a cock block I never knew I'd appreciate. It used to drive me crazy how protective he was of me when I was younger.

Thoughts of growing up flee my mind at the sight of Flynn standing over Mr. Remington in his naked human form. He lies frozen on the ground, sparkling with Flynn's magic. I can feel the intensity of his power stronger than ever. He now carries the magic of enough witches to form a coven.

"Something impossible without my beautiful familiar," Flynn whispers, listening to my thoughts wide open to him. "I might be able to break through the gateway as well. If I didn't think the High Council would sense the magic, I would. Have I told you how brilliant you were for thinking of this?"

Circling Flynn in my wolf form, I rub against his legs and nuzzle my nose to his hand hanging by his side. He scratches his fingers between my ears and twitches his fingers, waking up Mr. Remington with a jolt of power. The bastard scowls and tries to fight, his body shuddering with his will to transform. Sterling jumps on his chest and snaps at his face, getting him to stop. Pushing his weight into Mr. Remington's gut, Sterling hops off and takes his place by my side.

"Don't even try it, lycan. Here is how it's going to go. You will create a portal to Lulupoterra or I'll feed you to my pack." Flynn rubs his palms together, dazzling magic raining over Mr. Remington.

He glowers and bares his teeth, the gesture less than threatening with the old man stuck in his ugly human form. "They'll kill me for that. No fucking way am I dying because of that bitch."

Dax growls in his face a second before turning into a man. He fists his hand and prepares to swing it at Mr. Remington's nose for calling me such a name. "Speak of my leader like that again, and I will eat your tongue. Understand?"

Closing my eyes, I transform into my human form, realizing Mr. Remington is far too scared of the Nightstars. He would rather risk his life out here than betray the witches who control him. I cover my breasts while Sterling sits in front of me, blocking Mr. Remington's view of my naked body. I think back to how this whole mess started with his fucking eviction notice on my apartment and how everything just exploded from there.

And then I remember how he was transformed and why he keeps hunting me.

He wants a cure.

Flynn's magic crackles in his hands at my thought, and he thinks, "A cure for a powerful curse will take a huge sacrifice. I don't know if such a thing is possible now, she-wolf. We wasted the Everdeens."

I scrub my face with my hand, wondering if sacrificing others to save myself is worth it. I was already in the position once with Harlow, and I'm not so sure my soul could survive that again unless...

"We will have one," I respond. "A sacrifice so dark and powerful that I'm sure we could make more than one curse."

My response registers with Flynn, and he nods his head, agreeing with my thoughts of destroying the Nightstars being the most potent sacrifice to create something that can change things. There have been so many humans who have died because of the lycan curse and more will come if we don't put a stop to it. Because a cure enables us to strip at least some of the bad magic in the world. It allows us to help those controlled by the evils in the universe. A cure will ensure witches can't use lycans against us again.

Turning to Mr. Remington, I meet his angry gaze. I want to scream and yell at him to stop acting this way toward me, but a part of me knows that he's right. His curse is my fault, and despite his assholeness, he doesn't deserve this sort of life.

I clear my throat. "Mr. Remington, please. I'm sorry for everything that has happened to you because of the circumstances revolving around me. I'm sorry you lost part of your human life and have succumbed to the power of witches. I know you're scared and are just trying to survive this madness, but I'm trying to fix it. I'm done just surviving, and you should be too." I stroke my fingers between Sterling's ears. "Which is why you should help us cross. If you do, you will be fighting back. You will allow us to take back our world and be able to offer you a way out with a cure."

Mr. Remington frowns, his eyes turning toward the trees above us. "They'll kill me."

"They won't," I say, keeping my voice even. "They will keep you as their pet for the rest of your life."

"Just think about it." Flynn drapes his arm over my shoulders. "We will only offer this once. We're getting into Lulupoterra regardless, even if I have to blow up the shield. If I do that, it'll bring more attention from covens with unspeakable powers. They will take you from the Mortal World. They will lock you away for the crimes of the Nightstars. Is that what you want?"

Mr. Remington subtly shakes his head. "So all I have to do is open the gateway, and you will give me the cure?"

I nod. "You can live the rest of your life as the asshole apartment landlord you love to be."

"Okay, I'll do it," Mr. Remington says. "You have a deal,

Ms. Larson."

"It's Lyric of Lunar Crest, Martin," I correct, smirking at Flynn.

He groans. "Whatever. Someone help me up and I'll help you through. Don't expect me to follow, got it?"

"Got it. This isn't your war to fight. It's ours."

The Nightstar Coven is going fucking down.

"Flynn, I want you to take Harlow to her pack," I say, standing within his magical shield on the banks of the foggy lake in Storm Haven. I haven't been here since my aunt's death, and it looks exactly as it had. Dark, dreary, and misting with the rolling fog.

But it's Dax's home, and technically, it was my dad's as well. Before he left with my mom, he was a part of the Storm Haven pack.

"No, Flynn. Bring them to us, please," Harlow says. She stops beside me and takes my hand. "We are leaders together. I will not hide in fear. I want to help."

I bob my head, a smile playing on my lips. I never thought I'd ever hear these words come from Harlow. She wanted a drastically different life when I met her. "Okay, you heard her, Flynn. Bring her pack to us. We will fight together as we should."

Alonzo frowns and touches her shoulder. "But Harlow—"

My dad raises his hand and cuts him off. "The most powerful beings in the universe have something more than themselves to fight for. You will not stand in the way of your leader because of your fear of what could happen. Being a pack mate means using your strength to back her up. Be who she needs you to be and not what you think she wants."

I flick my gaze to my pack, knowing well enough that we've had this discussion several times before, and now they know where I got it from. Without a word, Flynn vanishes. Heat warms my chest as he uses his magic to move between territories.

"We should move. We have a lot of ground to cover." Dad motions to Dax. "Come on, Daxy boy. You lead the way. It's been far too long since I've been home, and I know your dad did a damn good job preparing you for this day."

Dax remains expressionless toward my dad's comment, but his emotions swell to me, the mixture bittersweet. I offer my hand to Dax and slide my fingers through his. He pulls me into him and kisses me, keeping himself in control despite the need to bone my brains out drifting over me.

And fuck. I need this to be over.

"Let's spread out," Dax says, turning toward the others.

"Don't confront anyone. As long as you keep your distance, the shield will remain in place. We're looking for alpha-mates or lycans, anyone we can use to summon the Nightstars out of hiding," I add, bouncing on the balls of my feet. "Sagan and Sterling, I want you to go together. Head east and comb the visitor's community. Antone and Bastien, go west."

"Don't forget to check the tunnel system in Storm Haven

Peak." Dax stretches his torso, preparing to transform.

"Alonzo and Harlow, head south, okay? Be careful because of the leader's den. I don't doubt someone might be there. And Dad, you and Caz stay here and wait for Flynn. Dax and I will comb the northern hills."

"Got it," Dad and Caz say in unison. They look at each other, and I wonder what Caz is thinking. He knew my dad didn't pick him for me, and he had to prove himself. Whether that's going to cause problems? I have no idea.

The others all transform and dart away, following my instructions. Dax weaves between my legs in his massive mahogany wolf form, catching me off guard. I squeeze his body between my thighs, and the bastard takes off, not giving me a chance to do anything but hold onto him, riding him in a way I never imagined.

His laughter sounds in my mind as he practically gallops through the fog, weaving around massive boulders that give some protection from the whistling wind. He's so damn lucky I love him and enjoy hearing his playfulness in a time he would usually be broody as fuck. It's the only thing stopping me from getting him to let me down so I can join him on the run.

After a mile, Dax finally slows and pads his way toward the rock formations where the constant downpour of the rain eroded away the mountainside, exposing glittering minerals. A rumbly voice echoes through the quiet world, and Dax growls deep in his throat, the low tone reverberating through my bones.

"I knew he'd be here," Dax thinks to me, sitting back on his haunches, letting me down. "I'm going to kill him."

It takes me a second to register who he's talking about, but then a familiar man with dark hair, tawny skin and an unkempt beard stomps from the entrance of a cave. Mud covers most of his legs, and he grips a hefty branch in his hand.

"Stand down until we call the others," I think to him, glowering at Luke, the bastard alpha-mate who turned against Trista. Dax's fury sinks into my soul, burning me from the inside out.

"Gather round, pups!" Luke hollers, smacking his palm with the branch. "It's training time. Don't make me hunt you down. Your asses are on the line."

My stomach flips at his comment, and I grip Dax's fur. "Shit."

Another man shuffles his way from behind a boulder, keeping his gaze toward the ground. I can't see who he is or tell if I even know him. A wave of emotion collides into me. Dax obviously does, because the man triggers enough worry to leave me panting.

"They're not training with you," the man—no, he's younger. A teen maybe. Someone stuck between childhood and adulthood. "If you want them, you're going to have to get through me."

Luke tips his head back and laughs. "Is that so, Shep? You ready to fucking be a man and fight? Show me what you got, so I can send you to your new masters? They've been dying to break in a new pet."

My heart clenches at his threat, and I grab onto Dax, stopping him from charging ahead. He growls and warns me with a snap. I smack his snout and squat down, hugging my arms around him.

"Call the others," I say, whispering into his ears.

"He will hear us and run," Dax argues, his thoughts slapping me in the mind with his anger.

"Then we chase him." I dig my fingers into his coat. "We will fight as a pack."

An angry yell echoes through the light drizzle of rain, and I whip my attention toward Luke and the boy. Charging forward, the boy launches at Luke, knocking him onto his back. He gets in one punch before Luke flips him off and tackles him. Luke slams his hands into the boy's chest, pushing to his feet.

The boy tries to get to his feet to fight back, but Luke kicks him in the side, flipping him over. Kicking him again, Luke rolls the boy onto his stomach and scoops up the huge stick, preparing to beat him with it.

Dax snarls and breaks free from me, racing to intervene. I stretch and transform into a wolf, tipping my muzzle toward the sky to release a long, loud howl, calling our pack. Slamming my paws into the ground, I barrel forward watching as Dax collides into Luke's chest. I command my body to work harder, faster, because I spot another wolf slinking through the trees toward Dax.

I cut to the right and circle around a boulder, hoping I'm fast enough to attack the asshole wolf from behind before he sneaks up on my mate. The boy transforms into a wolf and growls, alerting Dax of the bastard. The new alpha-mate snaps his fangs, going after the boy and the two of them collide, biting and snarling, attacking each other on their hind legs. The alpha-mate swings his head and locks his teeth into the young wolf's neck, throwing him into the side of a rock.

"Dax, help!" the boy yells, unable to push up fast enough. "Help, brother!"

Dax loses his focus on Luke as his brother calls for help, leaving himself open. Sinking his teeth into Dax's front leg, Luke yanks him onto his back and pins him down. Rage blasts through me, and I pick up speed, rushing to help the boy. It's what Dax would want as he manages to knock Luke off.

Sagan and Sterling's familiar howls cut through the air, alerting us that they're coming. It gives me the strength to get my ass in gear, and I jump onto a large rock and catapult toward the other alpha-mate. I crash into him, sending his wolf skidding across the muddy ground. I keep pace with him, waiting for an opening to attack. Sinking my teeth into his dark gray coat, I try to rip his throat out, using my anger to set off my she-wolf.

He scrambles back, dragging me with him, and my paws slip out from under me. I release his neck, but he's too fast to dodge, and the bastard slams his paws into my back, shoving me into the mud. He bites my neck, using his weight to pin my wolf body down.

His sick thoughts crash through my mind as his paws lock around me. Shock and outrage course through my body, my muscles spasming and tightening. I transform beneath him and reach behind me, locking my fingers to his fur. A pop of magic crackles through the air like a lightning bolt dancing through the trees, it shocks me, but not in a bad way. It gives me the strength to flip the alpha-mate off and onto his back.

Sagan and Sterling launch from a boulder, landing next to the alpha-mate. They both tear into him at once, and cool hands lock around my waist, hoisting me to my feet. Flynn whispers not to attack him, and I throw my arms around him, shivering in his arms, my mind catching up to me to process what the hell almost happened.

"There are kids here," I say, gasping a breath. "Find them. I need to help the others."

I don't give Flynn a chance to argue and transform, kicking from his arms. Dax snarls, pacing along a wall, cornered by Luke. His drenched, muddy coat stains with dark blood and he limps slightly. Luke isn't much better with blood soaking the fur on his face, his ear chewed and ripped from the vicious fight.

I howl and bark, alerting Luke of my arrival. Just like I expect, he turns his focus to me. It's the split-second Dax needs. Bolting forward, Dax collides into Luke. The two of them roll until Dax pins him, sinking his teeth into his neck. I growl and bite Luke's side, teaming up with my mate to help him get the vengeance he deserves for his uncle's betrayal, being responsible for Dax's dad's death. For his mom's current position as an omega.

Luke falls slack, his body giving out on him. Dax doesn't release him until he's certain Luke can't hurt his pack or anyone else again.

Sinking into the mud, Dax lies on his stomach, catching his breath. Silence falls through the air as Sterling and Sagan subdue the other alpha-mate, keeping him barely alive. But we need him. We can use him to locate the Nightstars.

Transforming into a human, I wrap my arms around Dax's massive body and cradle him against me, showering him with love and strength, and everything amazing in the universe our pack brings.

A soft whimper trickles through the air, I turn my gaze, spotting a dozen boys coming toward us, cautiously leaving their hiding places. Dax's brother, Shep, gets to his feet and lifts the smallest kid in his arms, hugging him with a laugh.

"Look, Lincoln. Look who came home," Shep says, motioning to Dax.

My heart fills with relief, with joy, and with the assurance that everything's going to be okay. Sagan and Sterling join my side, and Caz, Antone, and Bastien stroll through the trees, joining us. Flynn materializes with a flash of light, and he kneels next to Dax.

"Let's find some shelter to wait out the bad weather and

rest," Flynn says, rubbing his hands together.

I push to my feet and straighten my back, gathering strength from my pack. Seeing these kids reminds me of the future I want and one we need. The Nightstar Coven can try to keep us down, but they will fail.

I will bring their world crashing down like a natural disaster, destroying everything in their wake. My pack mates and I no longer just weather the storms. We are fucking hurricanes.

Nothing will stop us.

18

UNSTOPPABLE

I TRACE MY FINGER OVER Dax's spine, unable to sleep. My body refuses to chill out, yet I don't want to wake him up. I don't want to wake up my other mates either. They sleep in their wolf forms near the mouth of the cave and just out of view. Harlow's pack keeps watch, and she and Alonzo cuddle with all the boys under Luke's authority. According to Shep, the kids were brought here to be molded into well-behaved minions while all the females are being imprisoned with the Nightstar Coven.

I hate it.

Thinking about it keeps me up.

Even after all of this is over, I'm not sure how anyone will heal or recover.

"Lyric, keep touching me like that, and you're going to be mine right now." Dax rolls over to his back, pulling me with him.

I land on top of him and straddle his waist, pressing my palms into his hard pecs. Snatching my hands, he links his fingers through mine, raising our arms over his head. My body flattens to his, and he kisses my throat, working his way up my jaw until he kisses my chin. I tilt my head and caress my lips to his, savoring his soft full lips.

"You were incredible today," Dax murmurs against my mouth. "I'm proud to call you my leader and mate. You're everything I've imagined and more, and all I want is to show you how much I love and appreciate you. These last few weeks have been so hard. As much as I love our pack and enjoy our time with them, I also miss our time together."

I hum my agreement, slipping my tongue into his mouth. I try to break my hands from his, but he keeps me restrained in place, so I wiggle lower until I can feel the hardness of his shaft between my legs.

He groans, the sexy noise turning me on even more. "Lyric," he whispers into my mind. "If we start, I'm not going to be able to stop. You're so intoxicating. I crave you."

His words send tingles through my body, my already wild need responding to his. Self-control isn't my strong suit, and after the last few days, I don't care about my heat or the mating season. All I want is for Dax to ease the ache inside me. I yearn to show him exactly how much he means to me and how I feel the same about him as he does me. He's my perfect mate, so caring and protective, and everything I could want. His love fills me and completes me in such a way that I can't get enough of him. I want to give him everything he desires—everything my pack desires too.

Dax finally releases my hands and glides his fingers over the silhouette of my body. "What I desire...I want to give you the perfect future. Love and pleasure beyond belief."

I smile against his mouth. "What? No babies?"

He chuckles. "Is that what you want now?"

Heat blooms over my chest, spilling from my heart. The thought used to scare the fuck out of me. Every time he mentioned it in the past, I wanted to neuter him. But that was before...everything. I don't know if it's because of my crazy hormones or carnal need, but suddenly, the idea of a huge family with my pack doesn't scare me. It makes me want to fight harder. More ruthlessly. I will not let anyone stand in my way.

His smile widens as he listens to my thoughts. "I will stand beside you and ensure it."

I lean back and meet his golden eyes. "So give me half of

what I want today…and maybe all the babies tomorrow," I tease.

His eyes flicker with amusement, which quickly fades into lust as he drinks me in, straddling him naked. I roll my hips, sliding up and down his shaft. He flares his nostrils at my slippery excitement, his mind diving into a pool of lust, dragging me with him, to drown in every hot desire we share.

Releasing a sexy growl, Dax hooks his fingers to my hips and drags me to his face until my knees hit the makeshift bed made of blankets at the sides of his head. His eyes meet mine from between my legs, and I reach down and spread the folds of my body for him, watching him flick his tongue over my clit. I suck my bottom lip between my teeth, trying to suppress my moan. He picks up his speed, kissing and sucking my body, his determination to wake up everyone by getting me to moan incredibly loud seemingly his sole mission.

I cover my mouth with my free hand, rolling and bouncing on my knees, the ache of my body begging for my release. Digging his fingers into my ass cheeks, he grips onto me, keeping me in place. He hums and works his mouth over me like he could happily spend the rest of our lives kissing and tasting me.

And damn. I want to let him.

"Gladly," he whispers into my mind, rolling his tongue at the perfect pressure and speed.

It only takes a minute more for my body to scream in pleasure. Every nerve-ending explodes and buzzes, tightening my spasming muscles. Muffling my loud mouth with my hand, I moan against my palm and scrunch my face. Dax slides me down and yanks my wrist, leaning up to capture my mouth with his. He shivers, experiencing my body on the same level I do, our souls open and exposed and begging for more.

My greedy vagina. She can't get enough.

I release the most pathetic whine as I squeeze Dax's erection between my legs, the sensitivity of my clit pleading for a dozen more moments just like this.

Fuck. I'm greedy too. I'm addicted to cock on the deepest, most natural level of my she-wolf's desire. My mates warned me what mating season would be like, but I don't think anything could've prepared me for this. For the carnal, all-consuming desire. And I don't even care. I don't care what the fuck anyone thinks either.

Dax shifts me on his lap, aligning our bodies. "Far from greedy," he responds, his face alight with amusement.

It reminds me of when we first met, and I couldn't keep my thoughts to myself, especially when it came to my appreciation of his enormous cock.

"You're the most giving woman in the world. You give me exactly what I need, every time I need it. I never feel as if you divide yourself among the seven of us. If anything, you bring us something I never knew I desperately needed—a pack I can count on," Dax adds, cupping my face. "Now kiss me. I'm going to make love to you until you can't think."

Damn.

I nearly say, yes sir, but Dax does exactly what he planned and crashes his mouth to mine at the same time he thrusts into me. Our tongues glide together, exploring each other's mouths, a battle of desire and love, utter passion that sends goosebumps over my skin. Holding my hips, Dax bounces me on him hard and fast, hitting me exactly in the right spot to steal my breath. I touch his hard pecs and caress my fingers up his shoulders, feeling his flexing muscles while losing myself to the mind-blowing intensity of our lovemaking. There is nothing sweet or sensual about this moment. It's wild, raw, and erotic.

I comb my fingers through his hair, twisting the dark strands in my fingers. Tilting my head, I silently beg for him to kiss my throat, my shoulder, my collarbone. Anywhere and everywhere his mouth can reach. I gasp and cling onto him, resting my head to his shoulder. Sucking his skin, I mark him with a hickey, and then I do it again and again, wanting the whole fucking universe to know that he's mine.

He moans and pushes me back, changing positions curling my legs over my head until my toes touch the ground. Bracing one palm on the blanket and his other arm around my knee, he thrusts so deeply that I'm nearly certain he's going to fuck my brains out in the best way possible. My muscles ache with the stretch, and I give up on being quiet, my mouth wanting to declare our ecstasy. I scream my pleasure, my whole body buzzing. My toes curl and I scratch my nails into my outer thighs, feeling myself cum hard enough to get Dax wet.

And damn him.

He loves it, whispering, "Hell yeah," under his breath as his own muscles flex. Pulling out, he cums across my ass and the backs of my legs harder than I've ever seen him do it. It's my turn to grin, my she-wolf pretty damn proud of being the reason.

"My beautiful mate," he murmurs, sliding next to me to pull me into his arms.

We face each other, the heaviness of the world no longer smothering us so hard that we can barely breathe. A lightness lifts my soul, and I lace my fingers around Dax's neck, kissing him and shifting close, ensuring no space gets between us.

The soft padding of paws draws my attention, and I watch Sterling stalk closer like he's hunting for a bone too. His gray eyes flash in the sparkling of lightning, and he dramatically flops by our feet and sprawls out on his side with a pathetic whimper.

"I'm dead, blondie. This killed me," he thinks to me in his wolf form, rolling on his back with his belly exposed. "I have the worst blue balls in all of existence smelling you right now. Give me one of those blankets so I can detonate my weapon of ass destruction over there."

I grimace with my laugh. "If that's what you want to be known as...you will no longer get anywhere near my booty button."

His ears perk up and he crawls forward, only to transform into his cute bastard self. "Sorry, I mistook myself for Dax for a second. This fucking bond. I'm ready to mount or be mounted.

I don't care. Everything you arouse in me is so fucking hot."

Dax tips his head back and laughs. "It's interesting, to say the least. Let's just say I can empathize with you, fucking horn dog."

I pat Dax's chest. "He's the cutest horn dog, though. Don't you think? Look at those puppy dog eyes. I thought yours were bad."

Sterling play-whimpers. "Does that mean you guys will let me join—"

Scrunching his face, Sterling grunts and stiffens. He narrows his eyes and slaps his palms to the floor, pushing up. "Bestie, I swear to the fucking fates. You need to work on your damn build up before the climax. You better watch out. I don't have magic, but I'm damn well determined to get you back—"

Lavender light illuminates the back of the cave as Flynn materializes beside Sterling. He covers Sterling's mouth with his hand and pulls him to his feet. Sterling doesn't thrash or fight, and with one look into Flynn's eyes, I know something is wrong.

"Something triggered the traps I set," Flynn whispers, keeping his voice low. "I don't want to scare the children, but we need to check things out and prepare to move."

"I'll go with you," Sterling murmurs, grabbing onto Flynn's arm.

Flynn shakes his head and looks at me. "If it's the Nightstars, it's better if you stay close to me, Lyric. My magic depends on you."

I tighten my mouth with a nod. He's right. They'll be more concerned about the two of us anyway. We could even lead them away, keeping the kids safe while we hunt them down and strategize a plan.

"I'll take the children," Harlow says, her soft voice drifting over the sound of the rain. "My pack and I will keep them safe. We can make it back to Lunar Crest."

"I will go with them." Dad meanders along the wall of the cave, stopping several dozen feet away to keep his distance. "I hate to admit it, but I'll slow you down, Lyric. I'll serve our people better getting our young to safety."

I don't argue. My dad knows what he's best at, and he's not the type to act strong when there is even the slight possibility he could endanger us. Some men would think him to be weak for admitting as much, but to me, it makes him the smartest, most caring man in the world.

"We should move. Another trap was triggered," Flynn says, rubbing his palms together.

Dax lifts me with him and sets me on my feet. I'm a hot mess, but I'm also still riding the high of being with my mate. It makes me dangerous, deadly, more possessive. Whoever tries to sneak up on us will regret ever facing the Lunar Crest pack.

"I'll lead our pack and meet you two at the next trap. Distract them for as long as you can until we get there, okay?" Dax hugs his arms around me, kissing me below the ear.

"Don't get your hopes up about another fight. I plan to

destroy whoever it is before you can even catch up." I smirk, loving his reaction, his hot emotions lusting for me because of my threat.

Sterling kisses me next. "You better. I'll reward you any way you like for being my badass blond bombshell."

I swat his naked ass. "Careful what you say, horn dog. You've given me a lot of fun ideas."

Stepping into Flynn's arms, I don't wait for Sterling's response. Flynn envelops me in a hug and the world turns blinding with his transportation spell. My bare feet sink into the mud before my mind orients itself and my vision adjusts. Thunder booms with the ever-present rain that gives Storm Haven its name as the pack used the mountains and caves to shelter from the weather. It also gave Dax an incomparable ability to track, because with the rain, you must rely on many other things besides scenting to find your way.

The ground quivers with the heavy, familiar clomping of lycans. Branches rustle, and a tree crashes nearby. I drag Flynn from our spot in the open and take shelter under the cover of some low-hanging branches.

"Let them pass us, and we will sneak up from behind," I say, communicating through our telepathic link. "If they're here, they've either come for us or to speak with Luke. Either way, I don't think we'll be able to follow them back to where the Nightstars hide."

Flynn dips his chin. "If they're anything like Martin, they're new, probably created with the help of Paige. I think we should give them—"

Lightning strikes, illuminating the world around us. I spot a lycan standing a dozen feet away as he catches sight of us, the rain destroyed branches bare and barely providing shelter. Tensing, I transform into a wolf, the threat prodding at my instincts. I never thought I'd ever get to the point of feeling the most powerful in this form, but I do.

Flynn gathers magic between his hands and builds a shield around us instead of attacking. The lycan gallops forward on four legs, running in our direction. The ground shakes and water cascades from above, streaming down my hair and face. I stand tall and ready, refusing to back down.

Magic zaps across our invisible shield, lighting the world in swirling colors of red, blue, and lavender before merging into one, creating the most beautiful magic I've ever seen. The lycan roars, his green reflective eyes widening at the sight of the shield. He scrambles to stop, sliding in the mud, impaling his dagger talons into the ground to slow down.

His body slams into our protective shield, and the lycan falls to the mud on his back. He doesn't get up, stunned from the shock, and Flynn drops the shield. I launch onto the lycan and get in his face snarling.

"Emat eht nacyl. Peek mih atu devo li ta!" Flynn shouts, whipping a magical chain across the lycan's throat. It slithers like a snake, alive with Flynn's power, and winds around the rest of the massive beast's body, constricting him.

I growl, refusing to get off. "Offer him the cure in exchange for a guide to the Nightstars," I say, thinking the words to Flynn instead of transforming.

Flynn looms next to me and glowers at the lycan, remaining in his beast form. "I'm giving you one chance, so think about what you plan to do carefully, beast."

The lycan tries to thrash, but it only tightens the chains even more.

"Give us the location of the Nightstar Coven, and we'll let you live," Flynn says, curling and uncurling his fingers with flickering light. "Agree to turn on them, and I will give you a cure. You will no longer have to bow to a coven."

Again, the lycan roars. He flashes his fangs with his frothy jowls and narrows his eyes at me. "A cure? You think I'll take a fucking cure?"

Shit.

The ground quakes around us, and the lycan releases the creepiest, wet, guttural laugh. I jump off the beast and spin in place, flicking my attention to the dark, storming world around us. Another lycan stands tall on two legs, howling as if he wants to scare us. All it does is give me more time to figure out a plan.

Barreling forward, I abandon Flynn and the other lycan, charging at the new beast. The monstrous half-man, half-wolf drops on all fours. He charges me, accepting my threat, but I don't stop. I push harder on my paws, racing as fast as I can.

The lycan roars in anticipation, his massive form three times my size. I use the difference between us to my advantage and cut off the path and under a low branch. The lycan skids, jerking his body to chase me, and rams into the branch, flipping over it. I launch at him and sink my teeth into his throat, ripping a chunk of fur and flesh away as I rush to get off before he can overpower me.

I scramble away and dart in the opposite direction of Flynn, trying to split the lycans up. While this beast plays a game of chase, I consider it a run of predator and prey—except I'm the predator in disguise. And I'm not alone.

Dax's howl cuts through the downpour, and I pin my ears back and pound my paws into the ground, gaining speed. I respond to his call with a quick yip, afraid to waste even an ounce of my energy.

Antone and Bastien howl next, sounding closer and off to my right. I swerve and bolt between two trees, determined to meet them halfway.

I feel the tremble of the ground before I spot another lycan, but it's too late. I can't stop fast enough, skidding across the mud, trying to scramble out of the way.

The beast rises on two legs, towering over me.

All I can do is brace for the oncoming pain of his claws.

Tilting its head back toward the sky, the lycan releases a blood-curdling roar.

19

SACRIFICE

"LYRIC, RUN!" PETE YELLS, HIS guttural voice clicking recognition in my mind. I hadn't even had a chance to think about the lycan and what Evelyn had him doing. Leaving him in Lulupoterra is like she wanted the Nightstars to know we were getting close to the war she waged. "Run! I'll catch up."

Without hesitating, I scramble away, jetting between Pete's muscular, hairy legs. He charges the other lycan with another threatening roar, and the two of them collide into a tree, knocking it over. The crack snaps through the air, louder than the thunder and lightning dancing above us. I narrow my focus on the world in front of me, trying to remember how to find my way back to Flynn. The rain does nothing to help, muting my senses.

"Cherie, this way!" Antone launches from the trees, his massive black frame, cutting off my path. I skid across the muddy ground. I nearly lose my footing, but I manage to catch myself and stop before bumping into my mate. His dark eyes flash with the lightning, and my heart fills with relief. If I were in my human form, I'd throw my arms around him.

"Help Pete. He went after another lycan," I think to him, my wolf barking in command. I nudge my head into his hind quarters, shoving him toward the loud fight. Pete and the lycan crash into another tree, cracking it in half. "Hurry! He's not a trained fighter, and we need him alive. I'm going to find Flynn."

A muddy wolf races from the trees, circling me with a bark and a nip to my backside. He separates me from Antone and growls at my mate, getting him to abandon me to help Pete. "He's this way, Ma Belle. Come on. I need you to keep up." I nearly didn't recognize Bastien's beautiful white wolf with the mud coating him. He nips me again, shoving me with his head before taking off without me. "Get your thoughts together and run. Hurry up. You make me question your capabilities as my leader."

Instead of responding, I suck up my annoyance and follow his lead, racing behind him. He dashes through the forest just ahead of me, and I flank his side, our positions not going unnoticed. He used to always stay slightly behind me, playfully nipping me and keeping me moving, strengthening me as his leader instead of questioning my worthiness. I try not to let it get to me, suppressing the thought the best I can.

"Ma Belle, that's an unnecessary thing to mourn," Bastien comments, pushing into me with his body. "I will strengthen you in other ways but you must earn them."

I don't comment, closing my mind off to him, annoyance rushing through me. It kicks me into gear, and I run faster, harder, getting ahead of Bastien. A part of me fears that the Nightstar Coven's influence only enhanced his inner feelings. I hate how insecure it makes me, my heart hurting and longing for the tender side of him I need and crave in a world of dominance.

He tries to match my pace, but my fury shoves me forward. If this side of him needs proof, I'll give him fucking proof. I'll teach him never to question my position again. I don't want to have to force him into submission, but I will. I just need to get to Flynn. We can find the Nightstars, so I don't have to act in a way with Bastien I have no desire to. The witches are fucking dead. They will regret what they've done to my sweet Bastien. I will get him back. I will get my territory back. Our lives and my pack will be free from this bullshit.

I vow to it as a leader of Lunar Crest.

My parents did everything they could to change things, and I won't let them down. My species will get the lives we deserve, untainted and controlled by those who will do anything for power. They'll learn the wolves of Lulupoterra don't need to do anything to gain power. We embody power and strength, and we will no longer let anyone take that from us.

The pop of colorful magic catches my attention through the trees, and I race forward, nearly crashing into Sagan. He jumps over me as I skid across the ground. Whipping around to grab the scruff of my neck, he hauls me upright, holding me tight until I steady myself on my paws.

Sagan yips at me, trying to climb on my back. "Careful, gorgeous. Next time I find you under me—"

Dax growls and shoves Sagan off me, not allowing him to mount me in a show of dominance. Locking his jaw to Sagan's neck, Dax flips him onto his back and pins him down with his heavy paws. "Save it for later. You might've blocked her from your thoughts, but you forgot about the rest of us, and I will not stand by and let you think for even a second that she needs to submit and breed with you. We have shit to do."

Fuck. I'm glad I didn't hear that thought. I bet it was dirtier than Dax lets on.

Sagan thrashes under Dax and growls. "Don't act like she's yours alone. You had your time."

I transform into a human and get to my feet. "Enough! We

have to move in case more lycans show up."

"That's not happening," Pete calls, raising his voice over the storm.

He strides through the trees in his human form, naked and muddy. Antone slips through two trees behind him, watching his back. Stopping in front of me, Pete kneels and bows, kissing my feet. I automatically step back and out of his reach. I want none of this weird-ass business.

"These lycans were the last two," he adds, tipping his head up to glance at me. "The Nightstars are planning to open a gateway to bring through more humans as soon as..." His words trail off. "Come on. We have to hurry. I've done what I could to keep the coven busy, but I'm no match. My goddess was supposed to come already to take me home and—"

"Evelyn was never coming for you," Flynn says, speaking up. He strolls to me and slides his hand around my waist like he needs to be close. "If it's okay, I'd like to cast a spell for the information you contain."

"Anything," Pete says, bowing to Flynn next. At least he doesn't call him master.

Flynn releases me and helps the lycan up. "Over here. It'll only take a moment."

It's now that I realize the lycan Flynn captured no longer remains bound in magic. Drag marks cut across the ground, and I don't have to ask anyone to know my pack got to the beast-man. If he claimed allegiance to the Nightstars, then he's against us. I can't feel bad for someone who seeks to hurt my species. He had no business getting dragged into our world in the first place.

Pete frowns at Flynn, but he doesn't resist, doing as he asks. I thank the fates that Flynn insisted on helping curse Pete. If he hadn't, I don't know where we'd be.

"We'd be just as close to taking our home back as we are now, Lyric," Caz says, slinking up beside me. I shift my weight into him, relieved that he's here and unharmed. He licks my hip and nuzzles his nose into my hand, quietly assuring himself I'm okay.

It doesn't take long before my pack surrounds me. I kneel in the mud and savor the power of their wolves. Sterling licks my cheek and neck, and I ruffle his wet fur. The scent of the dirt and rain, the hum of magic, and their wild protectiveness engulfs me in a wave of hope, keeping my heartbeat steady. I take a minute to give each one of them my attention, kissing their cold noses and muddying my hands by petting them.

"Lyric, fuck," Flynn snaps, dragging my attention from my mates. "We need to go. Now."

Fear crashes through me at the tone of his voice, and I tense. Whatever information he extracted from Pete feels almost life-shattering. Flynn's emotions overwhelm me, and I hop to my feet.

"The Nightstars are planning a sacrifice," he adds, rushing to me. "We might be too late."

My eyes widen and I turn to my pack.

"I'll show them the way," Pete says, standing near Antone.

Flynn doesn't give anyone a chance to respond. Scooping me into his arms, he takes charge and relocates us again. My heart crashes against my ribcage, and my stomach twists. The potent smell of something rancid wafts through the air.

"We call upon the fates to accept this offering," a man shouts, his short white hair making him look bald in the dark.

The warlock from the Nightstar Coven stands in front of the former leader of the Dawnlit Bay territory and Bastien and Antone's mom. Bridgette kneels before him, keeping her back straight and eyes trained on something in the distance.

"The power of the wolves of Lulupoterra has grown far too great over the last few days, and we must put a stop to it. We offer the last females of their kind as a gift to summon the Lunar Crest pack before us," the warlock continues.

I clutch Flynn's hand. "Fuck, stop them."

"Ekat eth flow. Evig su rewop, great fates!" The warlock holds an athame in one hand and gathers blue power in his other.

Two white-haired witches step up behind Bridgette and douse her with some sort of potion. She flinches, trying to move, but one of the witches grabs Bridgette's hair and yanks her head back.

"Blessed by the fates," the three Nightstar Coven members chant.

"Ekat eth flow. Evig su rewop, great fates!" the warlock

chants again, stepping closer to Bridgette, glowering in her face.

The other women whimper and cry, pleading and begging for the Nightstars to stop. Flynn shouts a spell, gathering magic in his palms. He throws it at the two witches, but it collides into a shield. Sparks crack and pop, lighting their circle aglow and they stand in the middle of the former leaders they forced into being omegas.

I transform into a wolf, charging after Flynn as he gathers more magic, blasting it at the shield.

"Ekat eth flow. Evig su rewop, great fates!" the warlock shouts, grabbing Bridgette's shoulder.

Panic clenches my chest, and I howl, my wolf call echoing through the night. Flynn shocks the protective shield, trying to smash it into pieces, but the other coven members call on their power, deflecting his attack.

And then the warlock swipes his blade across Bridgette's throat, spilling her blood down her chest and across the ground. Shock and disbelief battles inside me, watching Bridgette's body fall forward. Fire burns across my chest as Flynn calls upon our link for more power. I charge the barrier, feeling the crackle of magic across my skin. Smashing into the shield, I crack it open, and Flynn blasts it again, shattering it into pieces.

"Ekat eth flow. Evig su rewop, great fates!" The warlock rushes and grabs onto one of the younger leaders, Zerena from Galaxy Peak, and slits her throat next, sending her sprawling on the ground.

The women scream in horror, their grief stealing my breath. I use it to push me forward, and I collide into the closest witch, chomping my teeth into her shoulder. Emerson shouts for the women to run, and she flings her arm out, knocking the other witch's legs out from under her. She falls into the warlock, giving Flynn the chance to attack with magic. I snarl and sink my teeth into the Nightstar witch beneath me, ripping at the flesh on the back of her neck.

Bright blue light flashes through the air, and I blindly bite and tear, attacking the woman until she stops fighting. Launching away from her, I land on top of the other witch, flipping her onto her back. She tries to block my bite, and I sink my teeth into her arm, shaking it so hard that I dislocate her shoulder.

Blood coats my paws, and I growl and snarl, anger and rage rushing through me. I can't believe what they've done to my species. I can't believe they've gotten away with it for this long.

"Daed ti foli cantanu og!" Flynn shouts, sending his power raining over us. "Don't kill her, Lyric! We need her for the cure. Bring her here. Quick!"

His command snaps something feral inside me, and it takes all of my control to do as he says instead of seeking justice for the packs. The witch screeches and tries to call on her power, but Flynn shoots a bolt of energy at her chest, winding her. Using my teeth, I drag her closer to him, rushing to rearrange the altar, setting up his spell.

"I can contain the power of the sacrifice for the spell later.

Set her in the center of the circle and transform. I need you to ground my magic." Flynn races around, throwing the spellcasting tools the warlock left behind until he finds what he's looking for. Lifting a metal bejeweled dagger in his hands, he waits until I shift into my human form to hand it to me.

My mind whirls, a thousand emotions battling through me, demanding my attention. Everything happens so fast, I can't even process what's happening in front of me as Flynn shouts unfamiliar words, summoning power so intense that my hair catches in the static. My heart aches, and my legs threaten to give out on me.

"Lyric, hold on for a bit longer. I'm almost done," Flynn says, standing before me, his hands covered in blood and blue light as he takes the witch's heart from her chest.

A soft whine steals my breath, hearing Dax in his wolf form somewhere behind me.

"Help her, she needs our pack's strength," Flynn says, his voice ringing through the air. "This will test her power as my familiar."

Two hands slide around me, hugging me from behind. "We're here, blondie. We got you."

I sink against Sterling, letting him hold my weight as I close my eyes, my mind begging for me to block the world out. Power bursts from my chest as Flynn summons magic, and it takes everything in me to grasp the metal box in my hands.

"Mi vo le tientivo su Nightstar witch," Flynn chants, his

presence closing in on me, lighting the inside of my eyelids red.

Still, I don't look.

I can't.

The box shifts as he sets the witch's heart in it, and I tighten my jaw, trying to ignore the feeling of it beating, the thrums tapping against my palms through the bottom of the container. Sterling hugs me tighter, whispering how fucking insane this all is. Dax and Caz stand by our sides, flanking us, and I focus on the weight of their fingers grasping my arms. Sagan, Antone, and Bastien stand behind us, and the six of them fill me with love and strength and everything I need to stay upright as Flynn seals the box with magic.

Cool fingers touch my forehead, drawing a symbol across my skin that I can't see. Flynn whispers a spell under his breath, and magic spills through me. Easing the box from my grip, Flynn takes it away from me. The thrumming sound disappears, and I fall limp in Sterling's arms. Exhaustion consumes me.

I try and fail to open my eyes, listening to the quiet murmurs of my pack as they finally let what happened here sink in.

A low growl sounds through the air. Antone's distinct guttural noise stabs me through the chest, splitting me open with a wave of despair.

"*Maman*," Bastien whispers, his soft voice caressing my ears. "What have they done to you?"

Arms pull me from the ground, and I groan in pain and heartache, mourning the death of the two women along with the rest of my pack. Soft howls sing in a melody of sorrow as the other women slink from their hiding places to join us on the hillside overlooking Dawnlit Bay.

I flutter my eyes open as tears burn and streak down my cheeks. From Sterling's arms, I reach for Bastien and Antone, my need to smother the sadness away all-consuming. Sterling carries me closer and Bastien doesn't say anything, suddenly steeling himself from me. Antone remains in his wolf form and licks his mother's head.

Tipping his head back, he releases the most unbearably grief-filled howl, breaking my heart along with his. He bolts away and darts through the forest, disappearing into the shadows of the ending night.

"Antone," I whisper, struggling to get to my feet, my exhaustion betraying me, making it impossible to go after him.

"I'll get him," Caz murmurs, kissing my forehead.

I reach out and touch Bastien's arm, silently begging him to let me hold his hand. The shift inside him tries pushing me away. The Nightstar Coven's influence trying to manipulate him into thinking that feeling anything in this horrible moment makes him weak.

"Bastien, I need you," I say instead, prodding at his alpha nature. "Will you take care of me?"

He slowly nods his head, leaning down to kiss his mom's cool skin. "Yes, Ma Belle. I will help you get cleaned up."

"Will you cuddle me too? I'm so exhausted. My soul hurts,"

I whisper.

He takes me from Sterling and lifts me into his arms. "I'm here. I will be your strength."

Sighing, I rest my head to his chest, quietly sending him all the love I have to give. Strolling down the hillside, he carries me to the expansive bay near the community he grew up in. He holds me in silence, and together, we stare at the lightening sky.

Rays of early morning sunshine streak brilliant colors of gold and orange through the sky and across the surface of the bay. I inhale a deep breath of the crisp air, trying to remind myself that not all is lost.

The sun rises on us, giving us another day.

20

THE CURE

"LYRIC, WAKE UP. I NEED your help." A minty puff of breath tickles my ear. "It won't take long, but it's better if we get this done with now."

I blink the sleep from my eyes, my body aching with exhaustion and grief. It takes everything in me not to curl myself around Bastien again and hold him like he needs, despite his whirling mind telling him otherwise.

I ease up, and Flynn helps me off the bed, flickering magic to mute any sounds we could make. It took forever for our pack to fall asleep, despite the shield Flynn keeps in place protecting us and the she-wolves from any threats.

Peering around, I search for Antone. He and Caz are still gone, and it hurts that Antone chose to deal with his grief without me.

"They're not far," Flynn murmurs, knowing who I'm searching for. "I checked on them just a bit ago."

I try not to frown. "I wish Antone would let me be here for him. He doesn't have to hide his grief from me."

Sighing, Flynn pulls me into a hug. He tilts his head and meets his lips to mine, kissing me sweetly, sensually, just giving me the affection I need to ease my broken heart. I hurt so badly for my mates that it's as if their loss is my own. And the fucked up part of all this is that the last Nightstar warlock is still out there. He gathered magic from the sacrifice of two powerful women, and in doing so, he also ripped a hole in the hearts of everyone. Bridgette and Zerena might not have only been leaders of Dawnlit Bay and Galaxy Peak, but they were part of Lulupoterra. They had mates and children—family. Losing them really shows me the importance of a strong alliance between territories. If only it didn't have to take a tragedy to bring everyone together.

"He'll be okay, my familiar. Give him a moment to process, and I'm sure he'll be ready." Flynn touches my cheek. "Even the toughest men can't resist the warmth of your arms and the comfort your closeness brings."

Flynn's right. At least he allows Caz to be there for him, even if it's only to silently support him from nearby.

I offer a sad smile and bury my face into the crook of his neck, squeezing him tighter. Our hearts beat against each other's in perfect sync, and I let Flynn lift me up. Wrapping my legs around his waist, he carries me from the room and into another down the hall, set up with a makeshift altar on a heavy polished wood table. I spot the dreadful metal box, half-expecting to hear the witch's heart rapping against the bottom.

I shiver and wrap my arms around Flynn's neck. "Are you sure this is safe?"

Flynn sets me on my feet and summons Eliphas's grimoire into his hands. Flipping through the pages, he stops midway through and traces his finger over the page. "I'm certain. I've studied the spell all day. We have everything we need."

"So what do I have to do?" I step toward the altar and look at the collection of crystals, herbs, and two different athames.

Flynn comes up beside me and picks up the silver athame. "Just give me a drop of blood and a lock of your fur. I'll do everything else."

Damn. I already hate the sound of this, but I know it's for the best. I owe it to Mr. Remington. And if something happens, and witches try to bring more lycans into the universe, we'll be ready.

I bounce on the balls of my feet and shake out my hands.

Flynn abandons my side only to walk around to the other side of the altar. He shifts the box over to make room for a stone mixing bowl and starts placing the ingredients inside it, using his electric magic to set the herbs ablaze until they turn to ash. A small cloud of smoke wafts from the bowl, and Flynn swipes the other athame, made of some sort of black stone, through it. It sparks, reacting to the magic, igniting with a lavender glow.

Like the blade hypnotizes me, I reach out, the urge to touch it consuming my thoughts. The power draws me closer until I press my finger to the point. A shock zaps me to the core, and I gasp, the sensation buzzing through every cell on my body. I stand frozen as Flynn eases the blade from my finger. A drop of blood clings to the point like the athame turns magnetic, locking to the iron in my blood—but that's not right. It's the magic of the blade capturing a piece of my essence, refusing to let it go.

I bring my finger to my mouth and suck the tip, tasting the tang of blood as I staunch the pinprick wound. Flynn carefully flips open the metal lid on the box, and I turn my gaze to the heart, still pulsing and beating as if it still remains inside the witch's body Flynn cut it from.

"Blessed the fates, I give this sacrifice to bring hope to the future of the wolves of Lulupoterra and the Mortal World." Flynn lifts the heart with his free hand, the soft tissue still magically pumping blood, spilling it into the bowl.

Setting it on the ash, Flynn scoops up the crystals and arranges them in a circle on the thick rim of the bowl. His eyes light with his lavender magic, and he summons an orb in his fingers, filling it with blue, purple, and red. The magic blends and sparks, flickering with electric light.

"Please transform, my familiar," Flynn says, lifting his gaze to meet mine.

I close my eyes and transform into my she-wolf, standing on my hind legs to rest my paws on the edge of the table. Flynn wiggles his fingers, calling me closer, and I lean in until he bows and presses a kiss to my nose. Pinching his fingers to the fur on my neck, he yanks a small clump away, pulling it straight from my skin. I whimper and shake my head, knocking away the blip of pain. Once more, Flynn kisses my nose and whispers an apology.

"Eht vu lovio ki tani flow," Flynn chants, glancing at the spell book as he chants the spell. "I offer the fates the power of three covens and the strength of the Lunar Crest pack to give us the magic we need. Eht vu lovio ki tani flow."

Dropping my fur onto the heart, Flynn sets it ablaze with his mixture of magic. He chants the spell again under his breath, sending energy humming through the air. I remain guarded in my wolf form, watching the heart light up with the magic. Holding the glowing athame with my blood, he points it downward and stabs it through the heart. Power explodes from the organ, sending bolts of electricity to each crystal until it forms a dome of magic, the strikes of power creating a star.

"Eht vu lovio ki tani flow. Evig em eth eruc." Flynn grabs

the second athame and brings it to his palm.

Energy circles around us, dancing over my fur to the pendant around my neck. I howl, the sensation awakening my wild nature, and I lean forward, staring in awe at the blazing crystals glowing like the stars come to earth to bless us with the power of the fates and the universe.

Squeezing his hand, Flynn drips his blood into the middle of the dazzling star, triggering explosive magic to shake the room. I instinctively hop back, scrambling away until I crash into the wall. The light intensifies and Flynn shouts the spell again, flicking each crystal into the bowl. A shockwave of energy ripples across my skin, stealing my breath, and I curl in on myself and peek at Flynn from my paws.

Silence falls over the room as the light disappears, and Flynn releases a deep breath, pressing his palms to the table. He drops to his knees and slumps his shoulders. My body kicks into action and I jet from my place and under the table to his side.

I lick his face, climbing up to rest my paws on his shoulders. A dozen emotions crash through me as I wait for him to move or speak, to give me some sort of sign that he's okay.

Tipping his head back, he howls like my wolf nature possesses him and releases a loud laugh. Engulfing me in his arms, he pulls me onto him and scratches his fingers into my fur. I bark and lick his face, wagging my tail. He flips me off and scrubs his hands into my chest and down to my stomach, making me thrash and wiggle like crazy until I shift into my human self.

He doesn't even give me a second before our lips crash together, and he kisses me with hot passion, sending tingles zinging between my legs, our excitement over completing the spell turning us both on.

"Fates, you're so magical. Brilliant. The perfect leader our world needs." Flynn combs his fingers through my hair, pushing the messy strands away. "We did it. I can't believe we fucking did it."

I kiss him again. "We have to tell the others. They need this news. Something good to wake up to."

"And you delivering it like this will be appreciated," he teases, rolling off me. Pushing up, he helps me to my feet. "Go on, my beautiful familiar. I'll bottle this up and put it somewhere safe. Just save me some time later?"

I pat his chest. "Always."

My heart swells with love and relief, pushing away the anger and grief that's been clinging to me. I saunter away from him and peek over my shoulder, beaming a smile. He flicks his fingers, swatting my ass with magic. I laugh and rush to the door.

I step into the hallway and close the door behind me, striding the few doors to where I left my pack mates. Soft murmurs trickle through the wood, and I hesitate, hovering my hand an inch away from the door handle.

"We can smell you, blondie. Brace yourself if you plan to come in. We all need a major distraction, and that python syphon is exactly what we want. My nope rope throbs for you."

Sterling groans from inside the room. "Get your ass in here so I can slither in the place that feels most like home."

I crack open the door and lock my gaze to him as he sits naked on the edge of the bed, cock in hand, while everyone except for Sagan remains fast asleep. "You sure know how to seduce me," I say, quirking my mouth in a smile. "But it's going to have to wait."

Sagan pushes from his spot on the floor and flexes, showing off his bulging muscles and massive hard-on, teasing me as bad as Sterling. "You sure about that, gorgeous? I think I can change your mind."

He stalks closer, stroking himself with a wicked smile on his face. I hold up my hand, motioning for him to stay back. He doesn't, rushing closer. I laugh and squeal, dodging out of the way. Sterling opens his arms to me, but I hop on the bed and out of his way. I jump up and down, bouncing my boobs, and Dax snaps his eyes open and swings his arm to grab my leg. I jump again, landing next to Bastien. He rubs his hands over his face and glances up at me bouncing by his head. A strange look crosses his face, and I drop to my knees and hug him.

"I'm sorry to wake you all like this, but I couldn't wait to tell you." I roll off Bastien and get to my feet, curling and uncurling my fingers. "Come on. We need to find Caz and Antone. They need to hear this too."

Dax snatches me by my waist, stopping me from rushing away from him. "Is everything okay? Your excitement...what happened?"

I press my finger to his lips. "Please, I want our pack together."

Transforming into a wolf, Sterling tips his head back and releases a loud howl, the noise echoing through the room. "Fuck, they can get their asses in here. It feels like we're about to celebrate."

I can't stop the smile crossing my mouth as I nod. "Not exactly celebrate, but I have good news."

A growl sounds from the hallway, and the excitement swelling through me snuffs out, spotting Antone slinking into the room, his tail low and his ears pinned back to his head. Caz quietly follows behind him, and I break away from Dax and rush them, tackling Antone with my whole body.

Transforming into a man, he wraps his arms around me, burying his nose to the crook of my neck and inhales a breath of my scent. "Don't pity me, Cherie. Tell me the good news. We could use it."

"We did it! We made a lycan cure!" I hop up and down in my spot, excitement spilling through me.

"What? The fucker did it?" Antone asks, raising his brows in surprise.

"You say that like it wasn't our mate who made it possible," Bastien mutters, sitting up to rest his elbows on his legs. Something about the comment feels backhanded. I know he and Sagan have both been a bit moody toward Flynn since we brought them home, but this is getting ridiculous.

"Bastien, we did it together. As a pack," I say, trying to hold tightly onto my excitement.

"A pack? Gorgeous, things have changed. There is one Nightstar Coven asshole cowering somewhere, and we'll find him. This is over. You don't need to play around with the warlock. Send him home." Sagan narrows his blue eyes with his words. "There's already enough of us having to shar—"

Sterling growls, swinging his fist, clocking Sagan in the jaw. The two of them explode into their wolf forms, fighting on the bed, snarling and rolling, sending fur scattering. Bastien follows suit and catapults at Sterling, knocking him away from Sagan. I stare in shock at the fight. Why is this happening? Things were just getting better. They—

Blue light ignites in the corner of the room, and I shield my eyes a second before Dax plows into me, shoving me back with his wolf head. Antone and Caz growl at the same time, and I hoist myself up, using Dax's back.

"My pets, I hope you didn't think I've forgotten you," the Nightstar warlock says, building a shield of magic around him.

Sagan and Bastien freeze in their wolf forms and drop down, bowing forward. Sterling snarls and charges the warlock, crashing into the shield. It sparks and sends him flying across the room and into the wall. Pain explodes through my back as he fails to block his feelings and emotions from me.

"Now, be good little beasts and bring me the she-wolf," the

warlock says, elongating his fangs and glowering. "She will be punished for what she's done."

"Yes, Master Ingram," Bastien and Sagan say in unison, their minds still open for me.

The warlock claps his hands, igniting chains of blue magic around their necks. He whips them, sending my mates snarling. Antone rushes Bastien, trying to get in his way, but the warlock lowers his shield and chants a spell, twisting Antone's front legs hard enough to crack his bones.

"Lyric, run!" Dax says, his voice in my mind kicking me into action.

But I don't run.

I'm done running.

Summoning my she-wolf, I howl a call through the air, alerting Flynn, and dodge around Sagan and toward Ingram. A leer widens his sharp smile, and he gathers power in his hands. Jerking his arms out, he throws his blue energy at me, but Flynn materializes in the room, deflecting it.

His appearance distracts me enough that Sagan manages to sink his teeth into my tail, ripping me back. I shriek in pain, scrambling to break free. Dax rushes me in his massive wolf form, but Bastien whips his head, sending his magic chain into Dax's side. He howls in pain, the magic singeing his coat and knocking him back. Power pops and crackles, and instead of attacking Flynn, Ingram shouts a spell, sending blinding light through the room. He pops into view next to Bastien and grabs him by the collar, pulling his chain. Sagan circles in front of the two of them, growling and snarling, protecting the asshole.

"Come to me, she-wolf, or your mates will die," Ingram says, using magic to grab Sagan's chain. "Their sacrifice will be sweeter than the she-wolves who just refused to fall in line."

Dax pushes to his paws and wobbles, turning his golden eyes to mine. "Don't do it, Lyric. They wouldn't want you to."

"Is that so?" Ingram asks, twirling his fingers and summoning a blade. "Shall we see? Transform."

Sagan and Bastien transform on his command, their eyes glowing with the magic he controls them with. My heart slams around my ribcage, threatening to throw itself in their direction. They grip the magic chains, trying to loosen the hold on their necks.

"Are you willing to die for the she-wolf, so she can continue to live in the beds of those unworthy?" Ingram asks, standing behind Bastien first.

Bastien flares his nostrils, fighting against the magic.

His silence speaks volumes.

But it also sets the warlock off.

Raising the dagger to Bastien's neck, he pricks his flesh, sending a trickle of blood toward the collar. "Last chance."

I heave a few breaths, my emotions waging a war inside me. I know my pack mates don't want me to sacrifice myself on their behalves. Even under the control of the Nightstar warlock's magic, Bastien and Sagan refuse to back down. They're still my mates. We still share a bond. The warlock is out of his damn mind if he thinks that could ever be broken.

"Lyric," Flynn whispers, growing magic in his hands. "Do you trust me?"

I blink my eyes, clearing my vision. "What do I do?"

"Bow to him. Do it, quickly." Flynn tightens his jaw with the words drifting through my mind.

Raising my hands, I step forward, ignoring the anger of the rest of my mates. I clear my throat. "I'd do this for any of you. Respect my decision as your leader. Trust in me."

I slowly drop to my knees and arch forward. "I bow to you. I will do what you want. Take me and spare him."

Ingram shoves his hand into Bastien, pushing him toward Flynn. "You took too long, she-wolf. I will spare him but not the other."

I don't have time to react as the warlock swipes his blade across Sagan's throat, spilling his blood all over me.

Screaming, I jump to my feet and rush him, but Ingram grabs me by the throat.

The world turns white.

Power Struggle

DAMN IT. I SWEAR TO the fates Flynn better have a fucking plan. The only thing keeping me from panicking is that the warlock had terrible aim, and I can feel Sagan's guilt over not being able to do anything to stop this asshole from taking me.

I grip tightly to my guys' emotions, battling through me even with whatever the hell distance lies between us. I know I'm still in Lulupoterra, but I'm not sure where at exactly. All I know is that when I tear this fucker apart, I'll make it my mission to learn and memorize every damn inch of our lands.

Heat burns between my breasts, the sensation of Flynn summoning magic speeding up my heart. I can't move as I lie naked on a smooth stone, chained with ropes and magic, and even a damn cursed muzzle, stopping me from fighting. Because this shit hurts.

The energy in the cave shifts, and I stiffen, hearing the thuds of footsteps crossing the stone floor. Ingram takes his time coming to me, gathering magic between his palms as if he's scared I might've broken free from my restraints. The fucking asshole. He's lucky I haven't, because he surely would piss his damn pants if that were the case.

"If you need a sacrificial virgin, you caught the wrong shewolf," I snap, hoping the heat of my voice startles him. I growl and crane my neck. I can't see much, but I know there is only one way in and out, which means I'll have to fight with everything in me. This fucker will not let me go easily.

The warlock scoffs at my comment, the gruff noise bouncing off the walls. "A bred one is far more useful for what I need right now. And one who contains powerful magic? It is an even better treat. No wonder so many crave to collar and leash you, but I don't care for that. I prefer my pets more malleable." Ingram stomps closer, using his magic to grow taller and broader, trying to intimidate me. Leaning over me, he leers, his fangs on full display. "This kind of magic is far more rewarding. Your pain will be sweet."

I don't let his words get to me and steel myself. "Yours will taste as magical as the rest of your covens. My wolf has a thing for power, you know."

His face contorts in anger and he roars, growing even taller, like he thinks his sheer size could possibly make me cower.

"Maybe you should've protected your lycans better. At least they know how to trigger a blip of fear." I smirk, yearning to get under his skin. "I'm used to everyone towering over me with a mouth full of fangs, so if this is a threat, you've failed. Now if you let me go, I will—" My voice cuts off with a wave of his hand. The muzzle tightens, stealing my breath, ensuring I can't speak for a minute.

"Shut up, beast. I don't have time for this. I know what you're doing. I want to get this over with before your pack finds us and does something stupid. Your magic is mine. That little soul on your neck will rip out with your beating heart." Ingram traces his finger over my collarbone like he can see Flynn's necklace. "You might've killed my sisters, but there are other covens who would love to add to the power I will claim from you. The wolves will always be mine." Ingram holds his hands out and mutters a spell, summoning a bag out of thin air.

Shit. I'm sure I can name a few covens who would take him up on the offer.

"You're fucking wrong," I say, managing to fight the tightness of the muzzle, continuing in my attempt to distract him even if he realizes it. "I'll prove it. This is your last chance to leave me the fuck alone. Leave now and I won't devour you."

Widening his mouth, he roars again, squeezing his fingers in the air above me. Shadows edge my vision as he chokes me. I force away my panic to fight and struggle and instead relent to his need to control me and play faint until the power eases up instead of knocking me out.

I shift and move, trying to loosen the ropes on my ankles first. If I can get those free, then I can concentrate on breaking through the magic. Pointing my toes, I slowly stretch my leg, pulling my knee toward my stomach. It rubs the rope against the anchor, doing exactly what I need. It's made of some sort of material, a torn shirt or something, because Ingram is dumb enough to rely on his power, thinking that because he's a warlock and I'm a wolf that he's better than me. I would think after knowing I've killed the rest of his coven mates that he'd think otherwise, but I suppose that's better for me.

"I do hope it's the big brute whose offspring you carry," Ingram says, setting up his altar. He doesn't look at me with his comment and adds a few ingredients to a cauldron.

Ice spills through me, freezing me from inside out. I repeat his comment over and over again in my mind, trying to make sense of it.

What. The. Actual. Fuck.

He did not just say what I think he said. I am *not* carrying anyone's offspring. I would know, right? I'm still in heat. I can feel the burning desire rushing through me every time my guys are near. They can smell it too. Even today.

There is no damn way I could be pregnant. The thought alone freaks me out. This is some sick, twisted way to torture me. He seems like the type to do that, especially because I've refused to give him the fear and panic he craves to see from me. My power makes him uneasy, and we both know it.

"Whoever put this mark on you was quite clever." Ingram shifts my hair and drums his fingers to my shoulder. His eyes flash with his magic, and he penetrates me with his gaze, waiting to devour my reaction.

I don't give him one. The fucker is bat-shit crazy like the rest of his coven. I will not feed into his bullshit even more. Instead, I work at my restraints, not caring that he can see me. If he notices, he doesn't do anything, the confidence in his power making him cocky. It might be my saving grace. Those who underestimate me find out in the worst way what kind of beast I can be.

"I wouldn't have even noticed it if it hadn't been for this." Ingram waves his hand over me. Something cool presses against my skin and blue light illuminates in my periphery. A stinging sensation crawls over my arm, and I clench my jaw, using it to push me harder to break free. "My coven and I love rewriting the fates set forth by others. It's far more entertaining watching the mess it makes in the order of things, and you, beast, have been kissed with the mark of the fates to trick your mates. There is nothing like the wild abandonment that comes with the mating season to manipulate a pack. It's been a long time since someone dared to play these games."

My breathing quickens as I think about his words. It's a lot to process and decipher what he even means. Because if I'm right. It's fucking impossible. It doesn't make sense. The only one who has rewritten my fate was Invidia when she spelled the she-wolves to bring mating season early.

Ingram leans over me, peering down through the muzzle and into my eyes. He flicks his fingers, removing the gag that keeps me silent. "You look like you have something to say." He smirks with his words, enjoying the confusion I can't stop from puckering my brows. "Go on. I'll allow it. Seeing your reaction is priceless. I bet no one even knows."

He continues setting different stones around me, waiting for me to find the nerve to speak. I don't know if I should, if it's even worth the effort it takes. But it consumes me. All I can think about are his words and what they mean. What it means for me and my pack. He's wrong. He has to be. I won't stand for it any longer. He needs to know I won't allow him to treat this all like a game.

I growl in my throat, trying to summon my she-wolf. Heat swells through my heart, and I thrash in anger, fighting the restraints. "You're lying about everything, you fucker! I won't fall for this. Your sister triggered this heat, and I'm not pregnant. I would know. My mates would too."

He presses his palms to the stone by my head, setting it aglow. "You can think anything you want. The magic says otherwise, beast. Maybe it was that warlock you've bowed to. He is far smarter and more strategic than I expected from a man who should've burned by dragon fire like his High Priestess." How does he know? Fuck.

The feeling of hopelessness threatens to weaken me, but it only pisses me off. My inner beast growls and howls, desperate to break free. Anger ignites inside me, and I jerk my legs, my sudden strength snapping the ropes, but the magic shocks me, sending my heels slamming against the stone.

I fight harder, yearning to bite this fucker's head off. "He would never do something like that! His coven is innocent, you bastard. We have proof."

"Oh, yes. Indeed, you're right. I heard of the resurrection of the former Liohts' High Priestess," he confirms, locking his fingers to my shoulder, trying to hold me still. "It was...interesting. Which is why power is more important than ever."

I struggle, pulling at my limbs, trying to release my beast.

Ingram's nonchalance digs under my skin. He sets up his spell without even stopping and taps his finger to his chin. "Oh, I know. I bet it was your family to make you the perfect vessel for me, then." This fuckhead. How can he just keep going on and on? "The bastard Everdeens thought all it took was a little blood bond to tame a wild wolf. Did you have fun tearing them apart?" he asks, wagging his eyebrows at me. "I wish I had been there to see the mess you caused."

I thrash again, yanking my wrists, trying to summon the strength of my pack. I can't stand this discussion a moment longer. I thought I could steel myself from his attempts to get to me, but the more he talks the worse it gets.

Flicking magic at my face, he silences me once more, shooting agony across my neck. "Never mind. I don't really care about anything you do. You're a wild animal, and I already sense the answers from a beast who can neither be tamed nor reasoned with. Now hold still. I need a good look to make sure I target the power of different bloodlines properly. You would hate it if I missed. I'm not that cruel."

Holy-fucking-I-don't-even-know-how-to-think.

I buck and twist, fighting with all my power. Ingram sighs dramatically and bows over, pressing his hand to my naked belly. My stomach clenches, my body heaving at the horror his words ignite inside me. My whirlwind emotions devour me whole, making me dizzy and sick. Jerking my chin to my chest, I throw up all over myself from panic. This is far worse than I thought. A part of me begs for him to be lying, but the dominant, desperate part of me knows he's not. The witches fucked with not only my world but my future, and this shocking revelation sends me over the edge. Had I known...fuck! I don't know what I'd have done.

Ingram growls and slaps my leg with his palm. "Damn it. You must be clean for the incantation. I should punish you, you fucking animal. You should be thankful I've given you the chance to know."

Summoning magic in his palms, he prepares to throw it at my chest. I tense, my muscles clenching, and I manage to transform only my hands into paws, pulling myself free of the restraints on my wrists. My wolf fights to break free, pushing against the power of Ingram.

If only the magic didn't pin me down. Breaking the restraints doesn't even matter.

"Stop fighting!" he shouts.

Thrusting his power, Ingram shocks me in the chest, winding me, and the edges of my vision shadow. I open and close my mouth, but the air refuses to come. It steals the fight from me, placating my body. He chants a spell, and a waterfall of ice water cascades from the ceiling above, pouring over me, washing my sickness away. It's so cold that it feels as if it burns my skin. The shock to my system jolts my energy awake, and I buck my body, the sheer pain of this torture giving me the fight I need.

The magic bindings snap, and I arch my back and catapult to my feet. I slip on the wet stone and slide off, landing hard on my ass. I cry out and do my best to get my shit together. I can't waste even a second. That's all the time the bastard warlock would need to stun me.

Ingram shouts, calling upon his magic, but I roll out of the way of his power. I knew it. Our battle of wills turns us both desperate, but I have more to fight for. I have more important things to keep me going. The thoughts that scared me before now only kick my ass into gear. I will not let him control me. I will never let him steal the beautiful future I now know is already in my reach.

Transforming into a wolf, I growl and snarl, skidding across the cave floor as I whip around to launch at the warlock. My nerve-endings prickle with the buzzing magic pulsating through the air. It teases me, swirling around me. I can nearly taste it as it awakens the deep-seated hunger of my wolf. I want to devour him whole and take his magic as my own.

I will take it.

This fucker is dead.

I crash into his gut, knocking him back, and bash the muzzle as hard as I can into his face. He howls and shoves me off of him with a zing of magical force to the chest. I fly a few feet back as he puts space between us. Growling, I charge him again. My hunger for power won't stop until I get what I want. Ingram will learn the true ruthlessness of my she-wolf as the leader of Lunar Crest.

Bringing his hands up protectively, he blocks his face from getting smashed in the nose with the muzzle again. A flash of light pops through the cave, and he disappears from the spot beneath me like the coward I knew he would be.

I don't waste a second and bolt toward the wide mouth of the cave, launching out of the opening. I land with a thump in the soft dirt and skid a few feet. The expansive tree line of the dense forest lies just a dozen feet ahead, and I bolt for it. The light fades fast with the sunset, giving me an advantage. My wolf has far better vision and my senses bring the world to life around me. I know the warlock wouldn't have gone far. He's probably lying in wait to see if he can sneak up on me. But I plan to find him first.

Pushing hard on my paws, I race deeper into the trees, my mind concentrating on the fact that the damn bastard will be back. It's the one thing that pushes me to keep moving. I will call for my pack's protection. I won't let him capture me again.

I slow down and tip my head back, inhaling a breath of air. Fuck. I can smell his musky scent, swirling through the forest with something sweeter. I won't make it to my pack in time, if they're even close. It's been who knows how long. If I wasn't worried that Ingram would pop up if I make noise, I would release a howl.

Except I don't have to. Howls trickle through the air, sending my heart racing. I trudge deeper into the woods, sniffing the ground, trying to pinpoint where the warlock's scent comes from. It seems everywhere and nowhere, confusing my wolf, leaving me on edge.

I don't think the fucker is far. If my mates are in the vicinity, he won't waste time in a game of hide-and-seek.

I can't keep going without alerting my pack. I'm going to have to risk it.

Racing forward, I release a howl through the forest,

responding to their calls.

A flash of blue light illuminates the forest ahead of me, and I jump behind a tree, taking cover. I know it's not Flynn. I'd sense him. His soul calls to mine, and the magic within the portal warns me to keep far, far away.

"She-wolf, you're only avoiding the inevitable," Ingram calls, speaking as if his words will somehow lure me out. "I will get you."

I circle in my spot next to the tree, peering around. I need to run, but any sort of movement will catch the warlock's attention. All he'd have to do is touch me to steal me away again. Who knows which territory we'll end up in next? This one is already unfamiliar, but I'm picking up the scents I need to navigate. Any sudden relocations will disorient me and leave me weak.

I need to be strong to fight. Clear-headed.

"Lyric, say something again. Flynn got me close, but there are shields, and he can't pinpoint where you are located. Are you hurt?" Dax's thought enters my mind, flooding me with relief. "Tied up? Caged? Give me as many details as you can. I'm coming."

I pant, thinking about the shitty situation. "I was restrained in a cave, but I managed to break free, and now I'm hiding in the forest. I can't fight well as a wolf. I'm muzzled. The fucker—he—shit. I don't know where I am. He's close by, though." I can't even speak the thought of what Ingram said about me, and

I'm not even so sure I believe it now that I'm free and able to think more clearly. He obviously seems like the type of tormentor to say anything he can to break me on more than a physical level. He will slice my soul to shreds given the chance.

"Listen for my call again, Lyric. We will get to you." With Dax's words comes a wave of tranquility, easing the panic in my heart.

A howl sounds through the air from a distance, and I focus on narrowing down where it came from. I wish with everything in me that he was closer. I want so badly to make a run for it. I almost consider it, but then he howls again.

"Lyric?" Dax asks. "Want me to call again?"

I spin in a circle. "No, I heard you, but you're still far away." I look down at the shadows of the trees as the sun sets, trying to remember everything my mates taught me about navigation during the She-Wolf Games. "I think I'm east of you. A couple miles."

Another flash of blue magic sparkles through the trees, and I tense, transforming into a human. My humanity cages my wolf out of desperation. I have to figure out how to get this muzzle off me, and until I do, I'm going to need my skills as a human fighter to protect myself if I can't use my teeth.

"Pretty beast, I know you're nearby. Don't make me sic my pets on you. If they catch you, they will bite. I promise." Ingram's voice calls through the forest, and he blasts power at a nearby tree.

Two familiar growls reverberate through my bones, and I rip leaves from a low branch and shove them between the collar and my neck to protect my fingers the best I can from the burning of the metal. I dig my thumbs under the collar and try to work the buckle, the pure agony of the cursed metal smoldering the flesh of my hands even through the leaves. I gasp and grind my teeth, refusing to give up. It's my only chance to fight. I can defend myself against men, but when they're wolves? Fuck.

A howl cuts through the air, and I startle at Bastien's closeness, my instincts kicking my ass into motion. I never thought I'd ever run from him in fear, but I know Ingram isn't lying. I can feel the intensity of his beast, collared and chained by magic, forcing him to bend to another's will. If I face him, I'll have to fight. I won't have a choice. One of us will end up hurt or worse. The thought alone is enough to shove thoughts of defending myself away.

Instead, I flee.

22

Magaelorum

I GIVE UP ON TRYING to loosen the muzzle and run west, hoping and praying to the universe that I was right about Dax's location. If I hustle, I can meet him halfway. I'll have a better chance with my pack backing me. They can tame the feral wildness of Bastien if they have to.

"Dax, where's Flynn?" I ask, sending my thought to him. A cramp seizes my side, trying to slow me down. This is worse than any race for my life. It's as if my own heart betrays me and is out to cut itself free.

"He's coming, Cherie. Just one more of us to go. He needs you to have the power of our pack." Antone's voice fills me with his demanding presence. I try to capture the intensity of his nature and bottle it up inside me through the link of our souls. His toughness steels me a bit more, suppressing the rolling panic trying to destroy my insides.

I push my feet to move harder, keeping my quick pace the best I can as I navigate through the darkening forest. The greenery grows denser, and I find myself having to climb over branches and vines to get between the trees. It's nearly suffocating as a human, but still, I must keep my she-wolf at bay.

"He shouldn't have brought Bastien and Sagan." I need to keep talking to my mates. It's the one thing motivating me to keep hustling through the harsh terrain. My desire to find safety within our pack prevents me from stopping and trying to hide, an impossible task when it comes to Bastien—any of my mates for that matter. Right now, it's just a race of who can get to me first, and Bastien has a greater lead.

"He didn't," Caz says, speaking into my mind next. He keeps his voice even, not giving anything away.

"Well, they're fucking here and hunting me." I don't mean to snap, but it's obvious from Caz's lack of response that he knows this already.

"Just keep moving, blondie," Sterling commands, his voice

deep and lacking the lightness I'm used to. "I know you, and if you even think about turning around and trying to talk sense into them, I will spank you until next week. They're too far spelled. The warlock pulled in the reigns and there isn't anything we can do about it this second. So just keep going."

"I am," I snap, whipping my anger at Sterling through our mind link. "You hustle your damn ass too."

Peering around the forest as I run, I stick to racing between trees and weaving around anything that could get in Bastien and Sagan's way. I duck under low branches and pull vines free, hoping they won't see them and get tangled enough to slow them even a little. It almost feels like the first time I ran in the She-Wolf Games, but this is much, much worse. There isn't any teasing and banter. This isn't a damn game with me as the prize. They're not after me to seduce into a wild night of lovemaking. Bastien and Sagan have been spelled and turned against me. With their arrival will come pain—unbearable agony as they're forced to fight against me.

Several howls echo through the air as my mates call out to me once more. They're trying to help me find them since I can't call out. I focus on the direction the howls come from and turn and adjust the route I run, changing from directly west to northwest. It shouldn't be long. They're racing toward me far faster, my fear dragging them in my direction.

I don't see Bastien until it's too late.

Crashing into my side, Bastien knocks me to the ground,

sending me rolling across the forest floor. He snaps his teeth and snarls, his eyes flashing with the blue light of Ingram's spell. I swing my fist, punching him in the snout, trying to block his teeth from me. The only time I've ever seen him fight so aggressively was to kill a lycan. Now, I'm afraid he'll try to kill me.

"Bastien, stop!" I yell, locking my fingers into the white fur of his chest. "Please, you don't want to hurt me. I'm your mate."

"Ma Belle." His pleading voice caresses my mind. "I can't stop. Fight me. Hurt me. Kill me if you have to. If I do something to harm you, I'll never forgive myself. Please, you have to fight!"

Fury and sorrow battle through my heart until my rage wins. It ignites a wave of all-consuming determination inside me at his desperate pleas. I summon the strength of my pack and grab Bastien's front legs, using him to brace on as I bash my muzzled head forward into his. He yelps and tries to get away, but I do it again. The cursed metal burns him, sizzling his fur and the skin of his nose with its heat, and he whips away with a screech of pain, giving me the chance I need to get to my feet.

I dash away, making it only a few feet before heavy paws ram into my back, knocking me forward. I screech at the pain exploding through me as nails scratch down my back as I'm forced down. I land on my hands and knees, my sudden instincts wanting me to protect my stomach, and I swing my heel up and kick Sagan in his furry belly. I do it again, sending him jumping away, but all it does is piss him off. Snarling, he rushes me and sinks his teeth into my ankle, dragging me back. I claw at the ground, trying to find something to hold on to, but the strength of my mate overpowers me. I'm defenseless. I can't even manage to make it a foot away.

"Lyric, fight! Don't stop. We're almost there," Dax says, his thought getting me to flail my body. He calls a howl through the air, stealing Sagan's attention.

I take his second of distraction and use it to my advantage. Flipping over, I toss Sagan with the gesture, getting him to release me. I grab a handful of dirt and chuck it into his eyes, hoping it gives me the chance to get back up. Bastien sinks his teeth into my other leg, sending me sprawling again.

I swing and kick out, thrashing and throwing dirt, doing everything I can to keep them away. I will do everything I possibly can to ensure they don't have to live with the guilt of being forced against me by power out of their control. I know it'll eat away at them for the rest of their lives. I, on the other hand, will take the guilt upon myself. I know they'd rather me kick their asses any day, and right now? Fuck. I have to. For everyone's sake.

"Stop, please! Stop! You don't belong to him!" I manage to push up on my hands, gathering my strength. If I stay down, they'll attack me at full force, seeing my weakness as their opportunity to give the warlock what he demands of them.

Sagan skulks forward, his blue eyes locking onto my gaze. He growls deep in his throat and licks his lips like he can't wait to sink his teeth into every inch of me. My heart races, my stomach twisting. Fuck. He's going to devour me and not in the way we both enjoy.

"Sagan, stop!" I snatch the front of his fur and get in his face.

Snarling, he tries to bite me, but I summon all my strength and keep him inches away. I smack his nose and shake him, hoping it'll knock sense into his wild, deadly beast. His teeth nip my hand, setting me off with a wave of pure and utter desperation.

I smack my muzzle into his face, knocking the growls right out of him, the force enough to split the metal frame. I rip it away and grind my teeth, threatening to smash it into him again. "Stop it, Sagan! I said, *stop*! He can't order you around. Fight it. Fight for me. You're mine!"

Sagan freezes, the flickering magic in his eyes faltering and dimming in his blue gaze. He relaxes his jaw, hiding his teeth, and the saddest, most pathetic whimper escapes him. "Lyric," he whispers through our mind link.

Gnashing his frothy jowls, Bastien latches his teeth onto Sagan's tail and drags him back, shoving him out of the way as he tries to attack me next. Sagan transforms into a human. He snatches the muzzle and lunges at Bastien, wrapping his arms around his big wolf body in a bear hug, trying to shove his snout in the muzzle to stop him.

"Bastien, no! Don't!" Sagan shouts, squeezing him tighter. "Don't make me do this."

I scramble forward and grab Bastien by his ears, holding him in place. "Resist the bastard's magic. You don't belong to him. You know this. You're mine. All fucking mine."

A blast of power sends dirt shooting into the air, and I grab Sagan and Bastien, pulling them to me. Ingram materializes a few feet away, his face contorting in anger as he realizes what I've done.

"My pets, come bow to me," he snaps, raising his hands toward the sky. Electricity zings between his palms dancing and crackling. "Do it now."

Sagan's muscles flex and he grinds his teeth as Ingram tests the strength of his magic. Bastien skids on the ground, scrambling to get control of his paws. Magic drags him toward the warlock, and no matter how much he fights, he can't escape.

"To vita benitata le og eht be!" Ingram shouts, sending a bolt of magic at Bastien, shocking him in the heart.

He falls to the ground going limp, and I gasp as the magic steals my breath and sizzles across my skin.

"No!" I scream, catapulting to my feet. My insides twist, and my heart feels as if it splits in two.

Pain swells through me, but instead of leaving me weak, it only pushes me forward. It smacks my ass like Sagan would, and I hustle, charging at Ingram. He calls another spell and shoots his magic at me, I squeeze my eyes closed, bracing for its impact.

"Don't stop, she-wolf. Keep going." Flynn's voice erupts in my mind as he deflects Ingram's magic with his own.

Ingram's eyes widen a second before he scowls in anger, summoning more magic. Shooting it over my head, he aims for Flynn from somewhere behind me. I watch as the warlock opens his hands, ready to clap and disappear, so I push off hard on my feet.

Flynn realizes what I plan to do, and magic light engulfs me in a protective orb of all his power and love, and I transform into a wolf midair, thrashing my head to send the muzzle flinging off and into a tree, broken by the magic spilling from my bond to Flynn. Ingram clenches his jaw, losing focus. I ram into his chest and stop him from running.

This chase is over.

I've won.

Sinking my teeth into his arm, I shake my head and tear at his flesh. He screams and zaps me, trying to blast me with magic, but it bounces off the shield. I snap and snarl, gathering all my grief, hurt, and anger, unleashing it on the warlock like a force of nature, here to consume and destroy anything in my path.

Static and wind from the whipping magic blows around us, and Ingram pours his power into his hands, throwing it at my protective shield in a wave of bright light. The ground quakes under the influx of magic, and I fight against his defensive spell, snapping my teeth inches from his throat.

"Lyric, the shield protecting Lulupoterra is breaking!" Flynn calls, his voice ringing over the zinging magic.

Panic smashes into me from him, trying to overwhelm me.

I shove it away and tense my body, gathering everything in me.

"Lyric, stop!" Flynn yells. "It's too much!"

But I don't stop.

I won't.

I can't.

Fire explodes in my chest as I draw on Flynn's magic, using every last ounce of it to shatter Ingram's. His eyes widen as his power sputters out, blending and joining the energy surrounding me. I snap my teeth hard into his neck, tearing at his throat.

Flynn's magic snaps back, flinging me into the air, the whole world jostling. I crash into the dirt and scramble to my paws. My pack surrounds me in silence, and we stare in shock as bolts of magic cut across the sky, seemingly breaking pieces of it apart.

"Holy fuck," Sterling says, his voice trickling to all of us.

"Is that..." Dax can't finish his sentence.

The world in front of us crumbles, revealing an expansive forest of emerald trees going on for miles and miles. Golden clouds glow in an indigo sky, and I watch as a huge creature flaps its wings along the horizon.

"Magaelorum," Flynn whispers, his shock and awe pouring through me.

And then he panics.

"Lyric, grab the warlock. Quick!" he shouts, pointing at Ingram, twitching and writhing on the ground. "If I can't fix the shield, our lives are over. You'll never get Lunar Crest back."

Ah, hell. I can't let that happen.

Dax rushes past me and locks his teeth into the warlock's shin, dragging him toward Flynn for me. Using a stick, Flynn draws a circle around Ingram and claps his hands, summoning Eliphas's grimoire like he knows exactly what he's looking for.

"Everyone circle us. I need you as an anchor to ground the shield while I rebuild it." Flynn motions to everyone, and my mates take their places. He points to me. "Lyric, you will offer the sacrifice. It is for your people, and must come from you."

I transform into a human and stride to stand by his side. It's hard for me to take my eyes off the wondrous world before us. I thought Lulupoterra was incredible, but it's hard to compare to the sight of dragons flying across the skies in the distance.

"It's the Dragon Lands," Flynn says, flipping through the pages of the spell book. "Just beyond it is the Witchlands and my old home. The High Council will have felt the rip. We need to hurry. They will come."

Fuck. "What do I do?"

Flynn reaches into Ingram's jacket and pulls an athame free. Holding the bejeweled hilt to me, Flynn waits for me to take it. Magic buzzes in my fingers, and I adjust it in my hand, aiming it at Ingram as he scowls at me.

"Take my hand," Flynn instructs, lacing his fingers through mine. "This requires five different covens, but I'm going to try my best, she-wolf."

I swallow my nerves and nod my head.

"To mos vida le si te be wolf, Lulupoterra," Flynn chants, gathering magic in his free hand. "I call upon the fates with the offering of power from the skies, the flames, the water, the earth, and the spirit of wolves. Blessed be the packs of Lulupoterra and help build the shield they need."

Energy buzzes through my body, erupting goosebumps over my skin. My mates howl, tipping their heads back and calling to the strength of the packs before us.

"Et nac nus vet covi nad." Flynn shoots a beam of his lavender magic in the sky, sending sparkles raining through the air. "Et nac nus vet covi nad," he chants again, tossing a ruby orb of the power of my biological father.

I gaze at the blending of red and lavender, my heart soaring as it rains down in a breathtaking lightshow.

"Et nac nus vet covi nad," Flynn continues to chant, sending up the blue light taken from the Everdeens. It brightens the sky, the magic so palpable that if I were to fly up and reach out, I could gather it in my palm.

"With the power of our pack, I offer the fates this sacrifice, bringing justice to the wolves." Flynn motions to me, and I inhale a deep breath.

"This is for Bridgette and Zerena. For my parents, for the wolves broken, for hurting my mates, and threatening the child you claim I carry. This is for the bettering of our future and the strength of my pack." I stab the athame into Ingram's heart and he opens his mouth in a silent scream as his blue power joins the rest in the sky, rebuilding the broken shield.

"Et nac nus vet covi nad," Flynn whispers, his eyes locking to mine, a dozen emotions crossing his face. But he doesn't stop. He keeps going. "Dear fates, we ask of you to strengthen our world with the power of the she-wolf, and let her spirit grow to protect us all. Et nac nus vet covi nad."

Warmth blossoms in my chest, and I gasp as light erupts from my heart, soaring into the air, feeling as if I come apart yet still manage to stay grounded, the strength of my mates tethering my soul to theirs.

The broken shield solidifies, returning the sky to normal, cutting off the view of Magaelorum and the Dragon Lands. Arching my back, I howl as my body morphs into my wolf form, and my pack mates join me in a victorious melody.

I drop to my belly and flop over. My soul fills with love and strength, yet my body is so tired that I can only whimper and peek through my heavy eyelids.

"Lyric," Flynn says, kneeling beside me, joining my pack as they nuzzle me and lick me in their wolf forms. "Lyric, stay with me, my soul. My beautiful familiar."

I groan and stretch, caging my wolf even though it's the form my body craves to take. I lick my lips and open my arms, hugging my pack mates the best I can.

"I'm not going anywhere," I whisper to Flynn. "I'll never abandon you. Any of you."

With my words, I close my eyes.

All I can think about is how it's finally over. I've taken control back from the witches. The packs are free.

And best of all, with my seven mates and the beautiful adventure of our futures stretching out before us, our lives together can finally begin.

23

The Future of Lunar Crest

I LIE ON THE FLOOR, surrounded by the she-wolves of Lulupoterra. The leaders—with me now among them—each touch a hand to my body. Silence fills the air as they open their minds and all of us connect on a level I never knew possible.

"I sense triplets," Trista says, smirking from her seat. Stroking a hand over my arm, she closes her eyes and inhales another breath, sniffing the air. "I always knew Dax would—"

"Dax? Have you forgotten my sons? I'm nearly certain she carries the Night Forest line in her womb." Simone chuckles and pats my hip. "I also think it's quadruplets."

"If I was to guess, I'd say you're both right about your packs," Harlow teases, wagging her brows at me. "I wasn't sure you had it in you, but I'm glad I was wrong. This is so exciting!"

I frown and bolt upright, clutching my stomach as if I can sense what they do. I bat everyone away and cover my heating face. This is crazy. "I am so not carrying a litter."

Laughing, Harlow doesn't let me get far and throws her arms around me. "It wouldn't be unheard of, hon."

"Especially considering how powerful your mates are," Emerson adds, hugging my other side. "We're she-wolves. We accept multiple mates for this reason."

I crinkle my nose and curl my knees to my chest. "You guys are nuts. I'm going to need an ultrasound or something. Do you not have pregnancy tests around here? Like I don't know what the hell you all smell on me, but it's definitely not a thing. I feel like I'm still in heat."

"Perhaps because there are still more to come," Viviana says, speaking up from near my feet. She brushes her red hair from her face and twists it into a bun. "Wouldn't that be something? It usually takes two spring cycles but maybe she's experiencing one abnormally long one because of the magic."

I groan and shake my head. Their talk of multiple babies and long heat cycles, litters, and whatever the hell plans to liberate from my vagina makes me want to run for the sake of my poor body. I really am turning into a baby dispenser.

Tugging from Harlow and Emerson, I rush to my feet and step out of their circle. "Thanks for the confirmation and all...but I really need my fucking pack right now. Some air. A good run."

"That's expected, dear. Try not to worry. We're all here for each other." This comes from Nessa, the younger leader from Sky Canyon. "Even more so now."

I bob my head and whisper my thanks, the need to escape grabbing ahold of my essence. Jogging from the leader's den in Dawnlit Bay, I ignore the she-wolves calling my name and bolt in the direction of the lapping shoreline.

Crisp air cools my clammy skin, and I dip my toes in the water, feeling my crazy emotions wash away in the crystal clear bay. Stripping off my shirt and shorts, I stroll deeper, loving the sensation of weightlessness swimming brings. It's been so long since I've done so for fun, the last time being when I still worked at Ripped Fitness in the indoor pool. But this is far better. The pure water cleanses me as the sun shines overhead, pushing the cold away.

I float on my back, just hovering on the surface, watching the golden clouds crawl overhead. A blip of sadness trickles through my whirlwind emotions of confusion, shock, and a teensy bit of unexpected joy. I lift my head up, catching sight of Antone curled under a tree in his wolf form. He's remained more beast than man the last day, and my heart aches as his grief laces around my soul.

Pursing my lips, I blow a soft whistle, calling out to his wolf. Antone lifts his head and searches the area, his gaze landing on me in the bay. I saunter back to shore with rivulets of water streaming down my skin. I squeeze the moisture from my hair and rub my hands up and down my cool arms, watching as Antone transforms into a man. His dark eyes travel the length of my body, devouring the sight of me and the hardness of my nipples peeking through the thin fabric of the first bra I've worn in what seems like forever.

"Want to swim with me?" I ask, bouncing on my feet.

Antone tightens his mouth in thought. "Not here. Can I take you somewhere else?"

My eyebrows peak on my forehead and I offer my hand out to him, but he doesn't let me help him up. Instead, he pulls me onto him, my wet, cold body pressing into his hot one, and I automatically curl myself around him as he lifts me with him, getting to his feet.

"The bay's fucking freezing year-round. I want to take you to my favorite place in Dawnlit Bay. My secret paradise." His voice rumbles against my chest.

I rest my cheek to his shoulder and hug him, savoring the sensation of our hearts beating in perfect sync. Picking up his pace, he strides into the forest of towering trees in shades of emerald and olive green. We head deeper into the woods until I catch the sound of trickling water. I swivel to peer behind me, spotting a stream.

Antone trudges through the damp forest floor alongside the stream, never putting me down like he can't stand the thought of my body being even a foot away. I tease him by kissing his throat, excitement coursing through me. I love the idea of this adventure with just the two of us. I've yearned for more time alone with him, getting to enjoy the side of him he doesn't often let others see.

And in this moment, his hard-ass façade cracks open, letting me feel him on a level we've never truly shared.

"It's beautiful out here, Antone," I say against his throat, taking my time to explore the scent and taste of his skin.

His beard tickles my temple, and I imagine the sensation all over me as he explores me with his mouth. Fuck. My body turns out of whack at the thought. Antone groans in his throat and drops me an inch, flexing his hardening arousal against my damp panties.

"I hope we can rebuild Lunar Crest to be the same," I continue, trying to push aside the thickening lust between us.

We haven't been alone much since I claimed his soul as mine, and the thought doesn't go unnoticed. I can feel his anticipation and need coursing through him. He even thinks about all the ways he can take me, claiming my body as his—his good little brat that keeps him on his feet.

"We already are," he finally responds, his voice low like he struggles to say anything at all. He flips me onto his back as he climbs up a steep hill, probably more used to the terrain as a wolf. It doesn't stop him or slow him down though. If anything, it intensifies his desire and pushes him to move faster.

I tilt my head, pressing my breasts into his back and stretch to meet his gaze. "Really? Is that what everyone's doing?"

His jaw twitches. "It was the only thing I could do to get our pack to stop pacing outside the leader's den. It's supposed to be a surprise, but I know you prefer to be included."

"They were pacing? Fuck," I whisper. "I'm not ready to deal with this."

"Which I knew as well, so I gave them all something to do. We're alike, you know, Cherie. We need space to process." He rubs his warm palms on my forearms. "Some distractions to keep our minds occupied."

"So that's what this is about." Grinning, I clutch his face, turning his head to kiss him, awakening the lust he struggles to keep at bay.

He hums from his throat, the guttural sound so sexy coming from his lips. He pulls me from his back in one quick motion that I can't help deepening our kiss, sliding my tongue into his mouth.

"It used to annoy me how you knew things about me I never thought much about myself," I think to him, refusing to pull away. His sensual kiss awakens my wild nature, and all I want to do is kiss him so passionately until I have to yank myself away to breathe. And then I want more.

"I know," he responds, rubbing his palm down the length of my spine until he squeezes my ass. "But you also love it. You still love it, Cherie. I know how much you enjoy being my naughty girl, wanting me to take control and tell you what to do. What you need. It helps with your stress when I take control and put you where you want to be with me. I know it's hard being an alpha."

I whack his shoulder. "Don't start, Antone."

"But it's so fun." Bending forward, he yanks a thin, long vine from the ground. "You'll love it when I tie you up. Get dirt in your hair. Possibly get your she-wolf to come out to play."

Scrunching my nose, I narrow my eyes. "Well, that's not happening any time soon. I mean, the wolf."

He chuckles and slows down, the sound of rushing water growing louder and louder. "I guess we'll see."

I turn my attention from his handsome face and gawk at the expansive waterfall, cascading crystalline water into a bubbling, steaming pool. I expect him to set me down, but he carries me all the way to the natural spring and strolls into it, dipping me under. I moan at how amazing the bubbling heated pool feels, the scent of something fresh, like morning dew on grass, wafts from the water.

I wiggle in his embrace until he lets me go, and I touch my toes to the bottom, grazing my feet over smooth rocks. The sound of the waterfall muffles the world around us, this secret spot of Antone's feeling like a private piece of heaven made just for us.

"I'm glad you like it," he murmurs, coming up behind me. "I'll bring you here whenever you want." His aroused body tests my resolve. His cock presses against my lower back as he treats any sort of space between us like an enemy, fighting to keep it away.

Sliding his hand up my arm and to the wet hair on my shoulder, he grips the strands and tugs, tilting my head to the side. His lips caress the crook of my neck, working up until he nips my ear between his teeth. I grab his hand and pull it around, guiding him lower until it dips under the water and stops short of touching between my legs.

I release a breath, his sudden resistance igniting a throbbing ache in my sensitive skin, one only Antone can heal.

"Is that what you want, Cherie?" he asks, drawing his finger lower.

"Mmmhmm," I mumble, trying to guide his hand between my legs but he resists.

"I need complete control over you to do so." He retracts his hand and grips my arm, squeezing my bicep to show his strength. Tugging my arm behind me, he pins it between us and presses his weight to my back, slightly bowing me forward. "Is that something you're willing to give?"

I sway my hips and wiggle my fingers, trying to tease him as he restrains me. "Only if you restrain me. I can't promise to behave and allow you otherwise...*sir.*"

He sucks in a breath between his teeth and releases the sexiest growl in response to my teasing. He might know how to press my buttons, but I damn well sure know how to smack all of his, giving him exactly what he wants and needs. And who knew how much I need it too. His protectiveness. His dangerous wild beast, willing to test my strength and will, my power, unlike any of my other mates.

"You're my sexy little brat, aren't you, Cherie?" he says, grabbing my other arm and tugging it behind my back. "Now hold still or I promise that ache will stay."

I jerk my arm out of his hold. "Make me."

A rumbling growl escapes his throat, and he grabs me again, locking both of my small wrists in one of his hands. He slides his knee between my legs, surprising me, the pressure of him lifting me like this making me moan desperately for more of his touch. He eases me onto a rock shelf near the waterfall, and cool mist prickles over my heated skin. He climbs next to me, still restraining my wrists, and rips the flimsy fabric of my undergarments right off. Pulling my arms higher behind my back, I have no choice but to bend forward to his will. He spanks me, the slap of his palm against my ass cheek sounding over the rushing water.

The misty air cools the sting and my heart races as he stretches beside me and tosses a vine over a sturdy branch, sending leaves raining down and sticking to my wet skin. Excitement zings through my body, the different sensations caressing my skin awakening my body in anticipation. Antone uses everything the forest offers around us, his creativity in securing my arms together at my elbows and again at my wrist, looping and knotting vines until I'm secure and stuck exactly how he wants with my body exposed and open and ready for what he has to offer.

My muscles ache in a good way, and I try to test his restraints, anchored to the tree branch overhead only once. Usually, being bound and vulnerable out in the woods and unable to easily break free would scare me. But Antone's all-consuming presence, his sensual touch and protectiveness, makes me feel incredibly safe. Relaxed. I desperately want more of him.

"Ask me, Cherie," he murmurs, responding to my thought, standing behind me in the deeper section of the water, admiring the curves of my body.

I fake glare at the steaming water, wanting to resist and test him to see how long he can keep up his dominance before giving in.

He shifts closer at my lack of response and grabs my legs, spreading them open wider, placing a few heavy stones by my ankles. It prevents me from repositioning my body, and he climbs to my level and teases me with his hard cock before denying me the ecstasy of sliding into me. I shiver as his finger follows the line between my ass cheeks and explores my skin, tracing every inch of my sensitive body, making me clench. When he reaches my clit, he spreads my body open with his hand and taps me with his middle finger, intensifying my aching desire.

I give in, craving to lose this war of dominance because what I want is for him to have his way with me.

He hums. "Ask me, Cherie."

I pant a few times and squirm, trying to bring my ankles closer to squeeze my thighs together, the intense anticipation driving me wild. "I ache so badly for you," I say, my voice whining in desperation. "Will you please help make it stop? I want you. I need you."

With my words, he puts pressure between my legs with his hand, rubbing my sensitive clit with his fingers, making me moan so incredibly loud, the universe might hear it over the waterfall.

"That feels so good," I say, my wet hair hanging around my face. "Give me more. This is torture. I know you're teasing me."

Bowing into me, he kisses my spine, sucking my skin hard enough that I know he leaves his mark. I moan, my legs trembling as the pressure of his touch intensifies until tingles explode between my legs with my orgasm. He doesn't stop or slow, extending the pleasure until my legs feel as if they'll give out on me at any second.

"Tell me you're mine, Cherie," Antone says, lining his body to mine, just teasing me with his tip.

I bite my lip in consideration and decide to say, "But you're mine."

He play-growls and pulls away, thumping his erection to

my ass. "My perfect brat. Never making things easy for me."

I grin and sway my hips. "Absolutely not."

"I fucking love it." He swats me with his hand next. "Like I love you and that disobedient mouth of yours."

My heart soars at his admission, and I nearly give in and tell him what he wants to hear. Almost. "I told you so. You're mine, Antone. All damn mine."

He spanks me again and scoops up a handful of water, dripping it across my back. I shiver as he swipes it off, the different sensations he creates driving me crazy. My body trembles and I whimper in need, knowing he'll keep this up until I obey. Reaching around me, he pinches my tight, cold nipples, aligning his body to mine again, moaning at the warmth of my excitement between my legs.

He sinks in more, just teasing me again. "All you have to do is admit you're mine. Tell me the words, and I'll show you exactly what it's like for me to stake my claim on you."

"I'm yours." My rebel mouth. How dare she relent.

Antone thrusts into me with my words, the immense pressure and pleasure banging the thoughts from my mind. I roll my neck and close my eyes, unable to move as he takes me how he wants while giving me exactly what I need. His hips slap against my ass, the position allowing him to thrust hard and deep, rough, and go completely wild like the beast inside the both of us. My moans turn into screaming bursts of pleasure, and he purposely snaps the vines and brings my arms down to hold my hands. His body slides in and out, rubbing me in all the right places until an orgasm builds again, and I tense and squeeze my eyes shut through the electrifying wave of bliss.

He flips me over to face him and pulls me close, smashing his mouth to mine in a battle of lust, using our lips, tongues, and teeth as our weapons. I snap my hands free of the vines and scratch my nails into his smooth ass, yanking him harder into me until we end up on the side of the natural spring, the misting waterfall drenching our skin, the soft light of day sending rainbow colors through the air.

Antone moans and scrunches his face, cumming with a few more intense thrusts. He rolls and tugs me with him, letting me lie on top instead of on the muddy, coarse ground. I kiss him again, my body flush to his, the warmth keeping the chill away. I rest my head over his heart and savor his arms around me, cuddling me close, showing he has a softer side saved only for me.

"You're mine, Lyric. Body, heart, soul. I've imagined this moment a million times, and it still was more than anything I could've dreamed of." He strokes his fingers down my back, drawing circles. "You're my powerful, feisty, addictive as hell mate, and I vow to follow wherever you choose to lead and spank you if it's somewhere I don't like."

I laugh and tip my head back to smile at him. "My cute little omega. I love it when you talk all tough to me."

A smile lights his face, and he carries me back to the natural spring to rinse the dirt and leaves away.

I sit on his lap, enjoying this piece of paradise he claims is now ours until I sense the familiarity of our pack drawing near. Antone lifts me from the water and kisses me, ensuring my silence as he carries me away. I grin, loving how he really meant what he said about this place being ours, and I can't wait to see what my other mates have in store for me. With the witches gone and the shield we built as a pack, no one can ever invade our home again.

Five howls—no, six—echo through the woods and I grin at Antone's scrunching expression at Flynn embracing his wild side as a part of our pack. Tipping my head back, I howl in my human form, projecting my voice through the forest.

Sterling, Dax, and Sagan jet from between the trees in a race to get to us. Bastien launches from some rocks on the hillside and cuts them off. A flash of blue light ignites a few feet in front of us, and Flynn and Caz pop into view together. Spinning around, Antone plays keep away with me, throwing me onto his shoulder...no, wait. The fucker is totally exposing my ass.

Sagan swats me with a laugh and Sterling kisses the spot soon after. I wiggle and break free, only to fall into Dax's arms. Bastien steals a kiss before he can close the space, and Antone whacks Bastien between the shoulders. Heat blooms across my chest watching them bump fists, unashamedly bonding over our claim. Caz shakes his head with a smile and kisses my temple as Dax meets my mouth. Flynn snaps his fingers, stealing me from Dax's arms, and he spins me around, making me squeal.

Our pack engulfs us, hugging and loving up on me and each other, filling my heart with so much joy that tears escape my lashes. Silence falls between us, my wave of emotions stealing the words from everyone's mouths as I think about how perfect this moment is, knowing we've faced the universe out to get us and won. The strength of our pack will never be broken. We finally get what we want from life—to be together, to ensure a beautiful future, and to do more than fight just to survive.

"All right, blondie. You're killing us. This is torture. What did the other leaders say?" Sterling asks, nuzzling his nose to mine. "Did my baby blaster fill your kiddy carriage?"

I close my eyes and laugh, my tears still streaming down my face. "You guys are in so much trouble. I might be having a fucking litter, but they couldn't *sense* how many. *Sense.* Don't get too excited."

Dax inhales a breath, his eyes widening in the purest happiness I wish I could bottle up and save. "So you are pregnant." It's not a question.

"Hell yeah!" Sagan shouts, tipping his head back with a howl.

The others follow his lead, and I wipe my eyes with the backs of my hands, their crazy-intense wave of the most beautiful, loving, exciting emotions not allowing me to dare worry about what this means. Because it could never be anything bad, carrying the babies of the men who love me more than anything in the universe. And now, our love will bloom and grow outside us, bringing more strength, brilliance, and power the world will ever see.

"I knew your sweet succulent was made of magic," Sterling teases, squeezing my thigh.

"She's made of magic," Flynn corrects, kissing me.

Sterling tilts his lips downward and shrugs. "Think your swimmers cheated and transported to the land of wonders?"

I screech an uncontrollable laugh, unable to handle hearing this talk any longer. Sagan hooks his arms under me and punches Sterling in the gut.

Spinning, he bolts away with me in his arms, running hard on his feet as the others transform into wolves. Flynn materializes in our way, but Sagan dodges him and tosses me forward, shouting to transform and run.

I hit my paws to the ground and bolt forward, howling through the word, leading my pack through the forest. A whistle sounds through the air, and I perk my ears up. The familiar call to gather the wolves pushing me to keep up my pace even as Bastien sneaks up behind me.

Nosing my ass, he says, "Faster, Ma Belle. Don't let those assholes think for even a minute they can beat you in a chase."

I bark my excitement, savoring the sweetness of his voice, the gesture taking me back to the first days of the She-Wolf Games.

Running hard on my paws, I spot a familiar dark wolf standing next to Dad's tall frame. He looks stronger than before, and

I howl and call out to him.

"Show those assholes who their alpha is, girl," Dad thinks to me, barking his command. "You can beat them by miles."

"At least give us a little wag if you're going to tease us with your ass," Caz calls in my mind.

The others catcall and howl, egging me on.

"This way, Lyric," Trista calls with a howl, shoving into my dad to take off without him.

I race through the trees, catching up to Dax's mom and run beside her. She brushes my body with hers, barking with joy unlike I've ever seen. The other she-wolves join us on our run, bringing all of the packs together as we bolt toward the river.

I dive in, transforming into a human in the water. Shimmering blue light sparkles with the gateway, and Flynn laces his fingers through mine, helping me lead the way.

I pop my head through the surface, gasping a breath of cool air. Swiping the water from my face, I stare in awe at the emerald lawns stretching for miles, the trees lush and full climbing toward the azure sky. The white, whimsical buildings look exactly as I remember them, and I trudge through the forest edge and down the hillside.

"What do you think, she-wolf?" Flynn asks, grinning at me.

"I love it. You fixed everything," I say.

He rubs his hands together, sending sparkles through the air. "With our pack's help."

"It was fucking hard work telling my bestie what to do."

Sterling hugs me from behind.

"Welcome back to Lunar Crest, gorgeous," Sagan says.

I turn around and hug them all the best I can. "I love you all so much. I love it. It's perfect."

No place has ever felt like this before.

We're finally home.

24

THE TENEBRIS COVEN

I SIT ON THE RED couch long enough to seat my whole pack in the cozy living room of the three-bedroom family suite in the main building of the Lunar Crest community. The fireplace burns with orange and white flames, warming the crisp air trickling in through the open window. The wood-beamed roof and tan tiles give the living space a homey feel, and I already love everything about it.

I had never been in this unit before, but after going from room to room—over two hundred, which Dax teased we were going to need—this one was my favorite.

Before, all my guys had their own rooms. They are still free to their personal spaces, but I sure as hell won't be stepping into the damn pink room again. Here, everyone can still have separate beds for when we need space but it's also close enough that we'll never feel separated.

I've claimed this suite as all of ours, and my mates happily chose their beds without complaint, though they might've wrestled for the spot next to me for the night. I have a feeling I'll wake up in a dogpile no matter what, and the thought makes me incredibly happy.

"I'm so proud of you, Lyric," Dad says, plopping down on the red curved couch beside me.

He leans in and drapes his arm around my shoulder, pulling me into his side like he's done all my life. I sink against him and feel my body relax, recognizing the comfort my dad brings, his scent and warmth reminding me of all the years we had together.

"I'm proud of you, too," I say, turning my head to grin at him. "You haven't threatened a single one of my mates in a few hours."

My comment lights his face with amusement, and he pats my knee. "That you know of."

I crinkle my nose and laugh, shaking my head. "Dad!"

Okay, so maybe my pack didn't complain because my dad

showed up and asked for some time alone, and there was no way I was turning him away. I've missed him so damn much that I will cherish every moment I get with him.

"I'm just teasing. Those knuckleheads remind me of myself at their age, so I'll go easy on them. I know you have it handled." He squeezes me closer. "You know, you've grown into everything your mother and I had hoped for, Lyric. I just wish I could've been here to help you through it all."

He releases a sigh and presses his lips into a line, hiding them. His scruffy beard helps obscure his expression, but I know my dad. It will bother him for the rest of his life that things hadn't gone as he had hoped. He wanted to guide me through all this when he thought I was ready.

"You picked a perfect starter pack for the task," I tease with a smile, hoping to lighten his mood. "You overprotective bastard."

"You'll understand soon enough." He chuckles and wags his eyebrows, motioning to my belly like he can't wait for it to grow.

The excitement in his eyes warms my middle as he imagines what will come, being a grandfather. I'm so happy he's here for this. The idea of him not being here? I can't think about it anymore. He's safe now. I'll ensure it as I will with my pack.

"And so you know," he adds. "I do approve of your chosen additions. It was never that I thought they were unworthy to begin with, but the rules were the rules."

I raise my eyebrows and play-punch him. "Sheesh, Dad.

You say that like either of us ever follows them."

That gets a loud laugh out of him, and he covers his lips, his shoulders shaking with his amusement. "I bet those boys had to experience a few good fights to prove themselves."

I pretend to squeeze something in my hand. "And me threatening the hell out of their balls."

"Especially the warlock, huh? He had his hands full with you probably growling and snapping the second he got within feet of you."

"Damn straight, I did. You would've been cheering me on." That day seems like so long ago despite only being weeks. I'll never forget how Flynn arrived in a flash of light and followed me around like a sexy, creepy stalker you know you shouldn't trust but there was no rationale with my attraction to him.

Dad punches his hand into his palm. "My tough cookie. I told you all my training would come in handy. Still will if they don't pick their shit up or shed every-fucking-where. Even if they do ensure everything is perfect, it's always good to remind them whose daughter you were before they claimed you as their mate."

"I'm sure they'll never forget it." Laughing, I hand him the plate of cookies Flynn protected with magic to stop my mates from consuming if I left them unattended. "I have a few new tricks of my own now too."

"I'm not sure I want to know." He winks at me, making me blush. "As long as they remember that just because I'm not an alpha-mate anymore, doesn't mean they can do whatever the hell they want here. This was your mom's territory. I'll do what needs to be done, so you get to enjoy it like we never could." He snatches a cookie and hands it to me first, the gesture not going unnoticed. He's done simple things like this all my life, and I never really thought why. There were plenty of dads at the gym who'd shove ten cookies in their mouths in a hurry as to not share. "Your mom would've loved the hell out of them. Knowing so makes me love them even more. She used to go on and on, telling me about her visions of your future."

My heart aches a bit with his words, and I don't even know how to begin to express my feelings about everything. This is more than anything he's ever shared at once with me about her. It was always just little words here and there, like how we looked so similar, especially when my hair was up and out of my face, or how I loved staring at the stars like she did.

He'd even beat himself up if I got upset by something he did, because apparently he thought it would've upset my mom just the same. Like when he let some kid pick all the flowers from the flowerbeds outside the gym to keep her busy, and I cried over the petals scattered over the sidewalk, saddened by the fact that something so beautiful could just get plucked and thrown away.

He shifts with the weight of my silence as I lose myself to my thoughts. "She knew you'd change things around here, and I'm so happy she was right," he adds and smiles, his eyes dreamily staring into space with his memory.

But with him bringing up my mom and her desires for my future as a she-wolf, I can't wait any longer to bring up what's been on my mind since learning the truth from Enrique. I have so many questions about her and Dad—about Eliphas and the Everdeens. I'm afraid if I don't ask now, I might never get a chance to ask again. He might close down and try to keep things locked in the past.

"Dad, about mom...and Eliphas. About everything," I start, setting the plate of cookies on the coffee table. I turn and look at him, but he averts his eyes. "Please, Dad. I have to know the truth. Why didn't you tell me Mom loved another? That he was my biological dad? I know you kept my nature from me to ensure the leaders and the packs couldn't easily find us and influence me to turn like them, but—Eliphas and Mom? I think I deserved to know. It might've helped me understand things, knowing what I do now about how encompassing love can be." I try to remain expressionless, matching my dad's reaction as his eyes flick over his weathered hands, calloused and rough from years of fighting. "I'm not mad, but I just want to know. It doesn't change anything between me and you. You're my dad..."

I don't know what else to say or if I should try to think of more. My swirling emotions crash through me, and I reach my arms completely around him in a hug.

He clears his throat and eases me away to scrub his hands over his face. The emotions threatening to break his hard-ass façade vanish. Gathering his thoughts, he exhales a long breath through his lips. "I wish I had a better reason than I do, Lyric. Back then, things were complicated. I was on another pack and Eliphas wasn't supposed to be here at all, but your mom's soul drew him to us the very first time we snuck away together to the Mortal World and every time after. I didn't know for certain, and honestly, your mother and I, Eliphas, we didn't care. It didn't matter. You were our daughter regardless. All I know is that I loved them both very much and they loved me. You were ours together no matter how you were conceived. I just wish—I wish they could've been here through all this. I feel like I let them down, but we agreed I'd protect you until they had things handled..." His voice cracks and he closes his eyes. "I'm sorry."

I throw my arms around him and hug him, hearing the soft emotion in his voice seemingly like the first time ever. Sighing, he pulls away and kisses my forehead. His face remains even and hard, just like always, and I turn away and swipe my tears away. He doesn't show his grief, but I can feel it just as tangibly as I do my own. It's strange. I don't remember much about my mom, but in this moment, her absence hurts me more than it ever had before.

Sucking in a shuddering breath, I meet his gaze. "Me too, but I'm so thankful you're here. I'm sorry I didn't find you sooner. Everyone thought the Fire Mountain Clan had taken you. If I had known—"

He nudges my shoulder with his fist. "Stop it with this shit. You can't hold onto things out of your control. It's not good for your soul. It's my fault I didn't think about those assholes. I thought they would move the hell on after—after what they did."

"No one in Fire Mountain even knew..." With the thought rises an image of the witch who swore she'd help us. I've been so consumed with everything else that I haven't stopped to think more past fleeing the Everdeen Estate. I know she got through to the High Council because Ingram revealed as much, but now what? "Fuck. I need to do something. McKayla—"

"What about her? What can I do? I know you have your pack now, but you can still come to me." Lacing his fingers around my wrist, he stops me from running to Flynn. "I know a thing or two about Fire Mountain."

"I need to see if we can still use the gateways to the Mortal World," I say, bouncing anxiously. "It's important."

"Ah hell, tough cookie. We don't need to wake your pack for that. I'll take ya. I might be old and off my game a bit, but the Mortal World and Fire Mountain are the two things I know best. Plus, Eliphas didn't leave us with nothing. He was one powerful bastard and gave us a way to communicate. I'll show you." Dad tugs me with him to the door. "We'll be fast. You can show your mates exactly what to expect from the daughter of Melody."

I smirk and raise my eyebrows. I can already hear my mates freaking out and threatening to spank me for being naughty. An idea I suddenly really fucking love. "And what's that?"

He bumps me with his shoulder and stands, helping me to my feet. "You're wild, fierce, and strong-willed."

"Maybe a pain in their balls, too," I add.

Dad barks a laugh. "Like mother, like daughter. I couldn't have asked for more."

I wiggle my fingers, curling and uncurling them. "Keep up, you guys. We don't want to be late." I can't believe I pulled this off without anyone even figuring it out. I'm going to enjoy the fuck out of it, because the second they realize the extent of it, they're going to up their game, probably sleep with one eye open, or learn to sleep with a part of them always gripping me.

"Late for what? Remington got his cure," Bastien asks, his voice trickling through my mind. His white wolf weaves through the trees, and he gets in front of me to meet my gaze. "Right?"

"And a memory wipe. He can return to living his life as an asshole with poor Pete," Sterling answers for Flynn. "I wish we could've kept him."

Hearing his response makes me so glad I wasn't there to see Mr. Remington off. I'd have probably left him naked outside my old apartment complex in Evergreen Beach with a sign saying the first month's rent is on him.

Dax weaves between my legs, lifting me off my feet in a teasing game of ride his massive wolf. He trots like a damn horse, bouncing me on his back, loving every second of this bullshit. I laugh and clutch his fur, squeezing him between my thighs. My voice echoes through the dark forest, and I lean, trying to get him to shift closer to Sterling until I can smack his backside.

Sterling whips around and licks my hand, and I laugh louder. Antone growls at me from the right in warning. His cautious nerves try to steal my excitement, but I kick my heels into Dax's hind quarters and lean forward, making myself laugh again as he picks up his pace to run ahead of our pack. He howls with me, the noise of our voices bouncing through the trees.

"Cherie, you're going to bring someone to us," Antone says, finally telling me what's on his mind. "If that happens, I can't control what happens to Dax."

I twist and glare at him. "You guys are far too tense. I never thought I'd have to tell you to follow Dax's lead and chill the hell out. We're safe. Right, Flynn?" I glance over at Flynn, strolling a few feet away with his protective shield firmly in place around us. "Another hour out here won't hurt. Don't you guys miss it? I know you enjoyed the Mortal World as much I did."

Flynn bobs his head and rubs his palms together, sending magic glittering through the air. "I'd feel better if you'd tell me where we're going. This is farther than I thought you meant by going on a quick walk. I never thought we'd stay this long in the Mortal World again."

I cock an eyebrow at him. I know things haven't been easy for us, but I believe in the power of our pack and how well we protect each other. Plus, it'll be so worth it. "Really? You lived here almost as long as I had. The gateways to the Mortal World even open only for us, bringing us directly here. If that's not a sign from the fates that we're meant to travel, then you have some serious convincing to do to make me believe otherwise. Trust me. All of you."

"Don't you even pull that card, Ma Belle," Bastien says, yipping at me. "You know we trust you with our lives."

"And balls," Sterling teases.

"Are we not going to discuss the fact that our pack leader snuck out while we were sleeping to test her theory?" Sagan asks, trotting up to match Dax's pace. He noses my hand and licks me.

"You should punish me. I want someone, anyone, to spank me. I deserve it." I stick my tongue out at him, loving his reaction, his surprise morphing into lust. It feels so amazing to tease him. "I mean, you haven't seen your favorite shade of red in a while now, have you, Sagan?"

"That naughty blond bombshell," Sterling mutters, his silver coat gleaming with the pale moonlight through the trees. "You're asking for more than a spanking, and I will gladly assist with that."

I giggle and scrub my fingers into Dax's ears, listening to his mind's reaction as well. I squeeze his big body between my legs again, because he doesn't think about spanking me with his hand but something that I'm damn certain is more powerful.

I shiver and lean forward, wishing he was letting me ride him in his human form. The thought weirdly excites me as I imagine pressing my boobs into his back and teasing the hell out of him from behind, where he couldn't easily get his hands on me. "Tell them to lighten up, Dax," I say, blowing a soft breath in his ear, making it twitch. "They act as if I went alone and unprotected. My necklace shields me just as good as Flynn does."

Several growls hum through the air.

"You went with her, asshole?" Bastien asks, his voice humming through my mind. He tries to suppress his annoyance, but even as a wolf, it's obvious. "That explains a lot. No-fucking-wonder you're not on edge."

Dax chuckles in my mind, swaying his body side to side, turning the ride a bit wobbly. "See what you did?" he thinks to only me. "They're going to think I need to be punished now too."

"You know you're okay bending over beside me." I flush at the thought.

He barks, his laughter filling me to the soul. "Always."

"All right, who's going to help me pin him?" Caz darts in front of us and bares his teeth in a play-threat.

Antone bumps into Dax enough that I hop off and sidestep keeping out of their oncoming wrestling match. Dax whips around and snaps his teeth, trying to nip Antone for making me move.

"Block his right, Caz," Antone says, howling with his words.

I lock my fingers into Caz's fur and haul him back before things get out of control. I wouldn't put it past them to

transform to roll around naked on the ground. And if that happens? Fuck. Me.

It's only been a week, but their protectiveness runs wild, and
with it comes their raging desire. They already act as if I'm going
to start shooting babies out from between my legs, and being out
here doesn't help with their anxiousness to keep me safe.

"Enough, you guys. Don't make me be the one to pin you.
I know it sounds fun, but I promise otherwise. It wasn't Dax
who went with me to test the gateway. It was my dad," I say,
speaking up since Dax obviously loves teasing them. "If you have
a problem, take it up with him."

That gets them to stop.

Growling, Dax nudges Caz away with his big head and
adds, "Yeah, I only caught them after. Lyric was lucky she left a
note on the pillow, but don't worry. I know it wasn't enough,
and she should've let us come, but Levi made sure I knew he was
capable of protecting his daughter. I wasn't going to argue with
that, but you can be my fucking guest."

Sterling groans. "No thanks, but I still want to spank her."

Dax returns to me and noses my thigh, trying to get back
between my legs to lift me onto his back, but I don't let him.
The cute bastard nips my ass cheek. "That's been covered...and
then some. The second Levi retreated to his suite, I punished
Lyric exactly how she likes."

Tingles burst between my legs at the memory. He's right
about that. I lick my lips, trying to get my lust to chill the hell

out. It still consumes me in the best, yet seriously distracting, way. "That's enough. I mean it. You can all take up your complaints with me later, because right now, you all need to chill. We're almost there, and I want to make a good first impression."

Whoops. I guess I should've waited to mention that. I might have to transform and dash ahead as fast as I can to get us all where we need to go. My words slow everyone down as they realize that I imply we're meeting someone, and I bet they hadn't planned on doing something like this again. We might as well hang up a sign in our living room with what is surely our new slogan: *If we don't know you, go away. We bite hard.*

Flynn stops completely, blocking my way. Searching my face, his eyes dart back and forth, his brow puckered together with his confusion. I think he out of everyone might be extra cautious. We know exactly what others are capable of, and he likes to be ready for anything and anyone at all times.

"Trust me, warlock," I say, using the words he has said to me over and over again every time I was worried about a plan he hadn't fully given me information on. "You owe me that. Trust me to know what I'm doing. I wouldn't drag you all into danger. I made absolutely certain this was safe."

Flynn narrows his eyes. "Lyric."

It's Sterling who pounces, resting his big paws on Flynn's shoulders to meet his gaze. "Don't *Lyric* her, bestie. You know she's right."

Sighing, Flynn pats Sterling's head and he returns his

affection by slobbering across his face, making Flynn push him off.

I grin, taking Sterling's place, and shove my hands into Flynn's chest, getting him to move again. He only walks backwards for a few feet before lacing our fingers together. Silence falls through the forest, my mates going on high alert.

When Flynn tries to slow down again, sensing the familiar buzz of strange magic, I lock my fingers through his and drag him forward. I pick up my pace, forcing him to run beside me. The others keep up, circling us in their protective formation. Dax nips at Flynn's legs, getting him to move faster, and he finally lets me lead us all to an opening in the trees.

I release his hand and open my arms. Spinning on the balls of my feet, I let my hair blow around me as I tip my head toward the glittering, star-speckled sky. I inhale a breath of crisp air and just savor this moment.

It's so exciting.

I can't wait.

Kissing Flynn's cheek and petting Bastien between the ears, I slide between them and out of the circle. I hold my hand up, motioning everyone to stay where they are and saunter forward, peering over the ground until I find the leather bag I'm looking for. McKayla came through just as she promised she would when Dad put me in contact with her through the magic of a looking glass not far from the portal that took us into the forest near our old home.

I scoop up the bag and hand it to Flynn, bouncing on my feet in excitement. "I know you all have been busy, so I took it upon myself to arrange this."

Flynn cups the bag between his palms. "What is this, Lyric?"

I wave my hand and motion for him to open it. "A gift from McKayla. She said you'd know what to do." I bite my lip with another beaming smile and shift to wave the rest of our pack around us. "I wasn't sure if she had followed through, but she did. A magical den isn't the only thing Eliphas left behind. He ensured my dad could contact the Fire Mountain Clan from the Mortal World...just open it. Hurry."

My voice fades as Flynn stares at the bag for a moment longer before emptying the contents onto the ground. They scatter, caught in magic, and streaks of blue portal light explode through the world in front of us.

I gasp, not sure what I was imagining to happen, and I grip Flynn. "Shit."

My pack surrounds me protectively, and Flynn cautiously steps forward as three figures emerge through the portal. I hold my breath, clutching onto Sterling while absently scratching my fingers between his ears.

"Who are they?" Sagan asks quietly, rubbing his head into my hand. "You're nervous. Do we need to prepare to fight?"

I shake my head and pet him. "Just wait a second. You'll see."

The portal light disappears, and I stare in silence as two

women and a man glance at each other in confusion. I break away from my mates and take Flynn's hand, standing beside him. He trembles in my hold, his eyes never breaking from the group. His Adam's apple pops in his throat, and a wave of intense emotion crashes through me—relief, surprise, awe, and gratitude.

"Tasha, did they say anything else to you?" the woman with reddish-brown hair asks, looking at the woman who unmistakably reminds me of Flynn with her chestnut hair and lavender eyes.

"No. Only that our convictions were overturned—the first time in history—but that the Liohts were missing and they'd alert us when they found them," Tasha responds, turning her gaze in our direction. She doesn't notice us standing before them, Flynn's magic in place.

"So they just threw us into the Mortal World?" The man with them links his fingers behind his head. "I don't care if we don't have magic. We don't belong here."

Tasha shakes her head. "No, we were supposed to—"

"You're exactly where you're supposed to be," Flynn says, waving his hands, spreading the shield to encompass them.

Tasha squeaks and covers her mouth with her hand. A faint flicker of purple magic dances across her irises, but nothing happens when she twitches her fingers in surprise. The woman launches herself at Flynn and engulfs him in a hug I can feel even not being a part of it.

"Little brother! Oh my fates! You're okay!" Tasha starts sobbing on Flynn's shoulder, and I blink my eyes, becoming overwhelmed by her emotions.

Flynn wipes his own eyes and eases away, meeting Tasha's gaze. "I'm sorry it took me so long. I had to wait until the fates gave me the most magnificent gift in the universe. I want to introduce you to my pack, and my beautiful, breathtaking familiar. It was her fate that led me back to you."

I lick my lips, praying with everything in me that this doesn't turn into my worst nightmare with witches who think we're Flynn's pets.

"Lyric, this is my coven. Meet my sisters Tasha and Sadie and my brother Artemis." Flynn takes my hand and pulls me closer, draping his arm over my shoulders. "And this is the rest of our pack. Dax, Sagan, Caz, Bastien, Antone...and that naked bastard is Sterling."

Sterling strolls up next to me in his human form. He nods his head. "I'm Flynn's official bestie. Lyric is our mate, carrying our future children, and if you're cool with it, we'd like to take you all the hell home."

I elbow him in the side. "Sterling, seriously?"

Flynn laughs. "I don't think I could've said it any better." Turning to his coven mates, he adds, "What do you say? Do you want to go to Lulupoterra and meet the rest of the wolves? They're the most incredible beings I've ever been blessed to have been welcomed among them."

Tasha reacts first, blinking the tears from her eyes. She steps closer and offers her hand to me. "I can't believe it. Wolves. A she-wolf. You're my brother's familiar?"

I nod. "Also his mate."

She slowly nods her head, a smile splitting across her face. "I knew he was destined for the greatest magic in all the universe. I'm so happy he found you."

I pull her into a hug, and she sinks against me, feeling as safe and pure as Flynn. "Me too."

"All right, let's move out. We might still make it in time for the games," Dax says, braving to transform into his human form.

"The games?" Sadie asks, speaking up.

Flynn shrugs his shoulders. "Pack life. You'll soon find out."

25

THE PACK MATE COMPETITION

"I CAN'T BELIEVE YOU SURPRISED me like this," Flynn says, rubbing my shoulders. He pulls my hair from the robe and shifts it to kiss my neck. "It means the world to me, though our pack might never sleep again."

"You all will have to get used to sleeping in shifts, anyway." Smiling with my words, I bounce on the balls of my bare feet. I tilt my head to the side, silently begging for his lips to travel down my throat. "Might as well start now. They should know your coven is important to us. I had to make sure McKayla kept her word."

"I don't know how I'll ever thank you, she-wolf." Flynn spins me around to face him, peering into my eyes.

Sliding my hands over his shoulders, I drape my arms around his neck. "I can think of a few ways."

His eyes flicker with magic, his desire igniting under my insinuation. Teasing my pack like this will never grow old. "I will do anything you want. Give you whatever you can think up. What you've done for me, Lyric. I don't think I'll ever be able to repay you, but I'll damn well try. You have given me a life I never imagined possible."

I stand on my tiptoes and meet his lips, kissing him softly. His hand snakes around my waist, pulling me into him. It takes everything not to get carried away and ask him to transport us somewhere else to enjoy each other for a while.

I ease away and smile, enjoying how much he craves me. "We gave each other this. Don't give me all the credit."

"Hey, we helped too. Now get your ass over here, bestie. You're running with me," Sterling shouts from behind us. "Get ready to experience the power of my wolf. I hope you're prepared for the ride of your life."

Flynn chuckles, shaking his head. "You're going to make our mate jealous."

"Whatever. Blondie loves every second of this bromance.

Can't you hear her filthy little thoughts? She's totally thinking about getting in on a warlock sandwich. Adding her cock pocket to this meat market."

I crack up and bury my face into Flynn's chest. "I love you, Sterling. Always making my warlock feel welcome."

"What can I say? I'm a horn dog. Gotta get creative with your army of dicks, sword fighting for a slice of your pussy paradise. I'm not picky." Sterling laughs loudly enough that his voice echoes through the night despite his thoughts humming only to me. "No shame in discovering new magic portals to Pleasureland."

A loud whistle sounds through the air, dragging my attention from Sterling's wild imagination that leaves me squeezing my thighs together and Flynn's hard-on really testing my restraint.

"Damn," Caz murmurs in unison with Sagan.

Dax groans with lust. "We gotta fucking hurry and get this over with. Our mate needs her favorite kind of prize."

Flynn chuckles again and kisses me once more and jogs away to join the others, waiting a hundred feet away within the line of trees. Shrugging out of my robe, I drag it down until it piles at my feet. Several wolf-whistles and catcalls sound through the air from behind me, and I stretch my hands above my head and sway my hips from side-to-side, feeling the intensity of my pack's gaze burning over my naked body.

"Keep teasing them, and you'll never finish the course,"

Emerson says, strolling up to me, gracing me with a dazzling smile.

Harlow drops her robe to the ground and stretches her leg behind her. "I think that's the idea. I know it's mine. You have no idea of the sort of fun my boys plan for our pack. It's unforgettable every time. Their love for each other is better than any tough guy competitor ever could be."

A soft chuckle sounds from beside us. "I can't wait to find out. I never thought this sort of thing would ever be possible for me." Trista pulls her silver-streaked mahogany hair from her ponytail and lets it cascade down her back. "Who knew I'd love getting a complete say in who joins my pack. No peace at stake. No fighting or manipulation. You've given us so much, Lyric. Your mom would be so proud that you finished what she started."

I smirk at Dax's mom. "I know she would be."

Simone steps up beside her friend. "It is something, isn't it?"

"Nerve-wracking too, right?" Trista says, peering behind her at every remaining wolf in all of Lulupoterra, some that never dreamed of getting this opportunity again.

"You will be great," I say, squeezing her hand. "A nosy little wolf might've mentioned a former Stargaze Hill pack mate is desperate to catch the interest of the stunning leader of Storm Haven."

Trista beams brighter and bows forward, turning into a

wolf. The other she-wolves, including those girls mature enough to transform, follow her lead until we're a pack of fourteen, ready to compete in the first-ever Pack Mate Competition.

It's no longer a game of chase the she-wolf for a day claim. It's now a way to train with our mates and future mates, learning how to build strong bonds and relationships as they were meant to be. No restrictions. No prize she-wolves. Those who play will do so only to help the leaders of the territories they wish to join. Winners are lady's choice. Whether she chooses anyone at all is up to her. We're no longer competing for territories or positions of power. We're here to work toward building a better, brighter future for all of Lulupoterra.

"Get ready, gorgeous. I'm going to ensure you make it across that finish line first," Sagan thinks to me, already in his wolf form.

"You can count on me and Flynn for last," Sterling teases, yipping with his words. "I already have everything set up in the woods to entertain us all night long."

"It's a good thing you can entertain yourselves." Dax howls with his jest, causing all the other wolves to join in on his excitement. "I have my own plan for our mate. I'm going to test the leader's theory about my babies. They already need more brothers and sisters."

I groan and cover my face. "Can I at least have this litter first?"

Dax play-growls in response, and I jog in place, shaking my

muscles. With the ring of the second whistle, I transform into my she-wolf and bolt forward, allowing my instincts to take over. Howls, barks, yowls, and yips echo through the woods as the wolves run behind us, letting us know they have our backs.

Emerson darts ahead of me, and I push harder on my feet, chasing her red wolf. It takes only a second to catch up to her. She runs alongside me, brushing her body to mine, and we don't slow down, weaving and racing through the trees along the course.

"All right, gorgeous. At the boulder up ahead, make a sharp right. I'm taking you through a shortcut," Sagan says, his voice swirling through my mind. "It'll shave off seven minutes."

"You're going to have to figure out how to make it at least fifteen if you want to celebrate properly before everyone else at the finish line." I break away from Emerson and follow Sagan's instructions, darting through the dark forest.

"Deal. The river's up ahead. Keep going until you reach it and then transform. I'll meet you there." Sagan howls, egging on our pack, and my heart fills with joy at their responses.

I bark in excitement, loving hearing the other wolves calling out to encourage and help push the other she-wolves forward. Their strength lifts up the leaders, ensuring our species can now thrive.

"Thirty seconds," Sagan calls through my mind. "Get ready."

I push hard on my paws, the world jetting by with my

speed. The ground softens the closer I get to the river, and I slow down. The rushing water hums through the air, and I stare at it sparkling and glowing with turquoise light. Closing my eyes, I transform into my human self, staying on my hands and knees for a moment to look at my reflection. My blue eyes sparkle, and I can't help smiling at myself.

Sagan howls. "Uh-oh, gorgeous. Incoming."

I don't get the chance to react as magic lights the air with Flynn and Sterling's arrival. Flynn flies forward over my head, Sterling's quick stop thrusting him off and into the river. Paws lock around my sides, and Sterling's huge wolf-body mounts me from behind, sneak attack humping me right into the river. I land in the icy water beside Flynn, and he pulls me to the surface.

I gasp and laugh in surprise, watching as Sagan launches at Sterling and the two of them splash under together. Dax, Bastien, Antone, and Caz all laugh from various spots, jumping into the river, joining us. Flynn gathers magic in his palm and whispers a spell in my ear, engulfing us in light. I wobble on my feet in the middle of the heated pool within my parents' old den. I touch my hand to my chest in surprise. I had no idea Flynn fixed it, rebuilding the private sanctuary that was passed down to me as the new leader of Lunar Crest.

Water splashes behind me, and I twist on my feet and watch the rest of our pack break through the surface. Sagan lifts himself from the icy river and joins us, sneaking his arm around my waist to lift me in his arms, carrying me to the den.

"This is incredible," I say, wiggling in Sagan's arms until he sets me on my feet.

Dax shakes the water from his hair. "We know it's not exactly the same, but—"

"We really needed a fucking bigger bed," Sterling says, cutting him off.

I laugh and lay down on the massive double king, feeling tiny in comparison. I spread out and make a snow angel in the blankets, snuggling within the warmth of the most comfortable bed I've ever felt in my life.

"You're right about that," I tease and rest my hands on my stomach, unsure if the fluttering is my excitement. Things happen fast as a she-wolf. Thank fucking-fuck I have my pack to get me through. I don't know how I would deal otherwise. "I mean, I'm not even sure I'll be able to fit in this one in the next couple weeks."

Sagan beats everyone and flops beside me, rolling on top of me, cocooning us in the blankets. His hardening body rests right between my legs, and I hum and kiss him, losing myself to the sudden lust and desire filling the air.

"It is kind of a tight squeeze for the two of us. You guys go wait outside. I'll take care of our mate," Sagan says, kissing me with a smile.

"I think what Sagan means is that we'll make room if you want to join." I ease my body open wider, rocking my hips to tease him with my warmth. "I have plenty of love for all of you and want to show you as much. I can't wait any longer. I want to celebrate our pack now."

The bed shifts beside us, and I catch the intoxicating fragrance of Dax nestling in beside us. Tugging the edge of the blanket, he joins me and Sagan and kisses me. Desire rushes through me, and I reach for Dax, lacing my fingers around his cock, making him moan. The blankets shift again and Bastien joins my other side, and I grab him in my other hand, exploring his hard desire.

Caz kneels by my head, bowing down to kiss me, and I savor the taste of his mouth as Dax slips his hand between me and Sagan and plays with my clit, and Sagan sinks inside me. I moan at the pressure of his cock, stretching my neck so Caz can kiss my throat.

"Damn, she loves this," Antone murmurs, drawing my attention to him. "Your pleasure is so intense. It feels good." He strokes himself, watching the others work me up.

Flynn and Sterling catch my attention with Flynn's flicker of magic, and I moan, watching them kiss before Antone surprises the hell out of me and joins in, the three of them getting so turned on by my lust, that nothing matters in this moment except being together as a pack and enjoying everything we can offer each other.

Flynn whispers a spell, intensifying our connection, and I lose myself to the pleasure and need we explore. No one is left out as my mates devour my attention, enjoying everything I offer.

I work my mouth over Caz, licking and sucking him, getting him to moan. Sagan thrusts hard and fast as Dax helps him bring me to my peak, and I arch my back with my orgasm, setting Sagan off too. Bastien fills the space he leaves and rolls me onto Dax. I press my breasts into Dax's hard chest, arching up to let Caz slide his cock in and out of my mouth. Dax aligns his body to mine, and I moan in bliss, feeling him enter me and cool lube pours down my ass from behind, Bastien joining us in our haze of lust and desire, setting off our pack's ecstasy even more.

My mates take turns making me cum, working together to ensure I experience nothing but immense pleasure that we all can share. I find my back pressed to Antone's chest and he moans as he enters my ass, squeezing my breasts in his hands. Sterling kneels between our legs and lowers himself onto me and Flynn positions himself behind him, kissing his shoulder before leaning over to kiss me. Our moans and lust fill the air, and Flynn sets everyone off even more with his magic as we get carried away in our frenzy to experience pleasure on new levels better than ever before. I've never felt so good in my life, and I scream in bliss with the sudden jolt of magic that gets all my guys off with me.

Holy fucking shit. I can't believe this is my life.

My perfect life with my incredible pack.

The sudden need to announce my chosen ones consumes me, and instead of sinking into the sexy dogpile my mates create around me, I scramble to my feet and grin. My thoughts crash through them, exploding happiness, joy, and love through the room.

"See you at the finish line," I say, blowing them a kiss.

"You're really going to hit it and quit it, blondie?" Sterling asks, rubbing his hand over his cock, his arousal never-ending.

I stick my tongue out at him. "No, I'm going to hit it, enjoy it, savor it, love it, and fucking announce to the universe that you're my pack, and I can't wait to spend my life with you by declaring my official claim."

Without waiting for them to respond, I rush from our den and dive into the river, letting the freezing water push me faster than ever. Howls and cheers sound from behind me as they race to catch up with me.

A whistle blows, declaring the beginning of the she-wolves crossing the finish line, and I run from the river, transform into a wolf, and bolt toward the finish line at the edge of our community in Lunar Crest.

I spot Emerson hugging a few wolves just over the finish line as the older she-wolves join her with all of the men interested in starting a new life and pack together. I push harder on my feet, catching sight of my dad with Flynn's coven mates, passing out robes. The little boys and younger she-wolfs howl in excitement, sending a wave of pure joy flooding through me. This is the start of the future they deserve, learning how to work together, teach each other, and form the strong packs our species needs.

Slowing down, I wait for my pack mates to barrel up beside me, and together, we cross the finish line as the Lunar Crest pack. Cheers, whistles, and howls fill the air and my very soul, giving me hope and faith and trust in the fates to always guide toward the life we deserve. The life we want. The future of our dreams.

"Congratulations, Lyric of Lunar Crest," Dad shouts, his voice bellowing through the crowd. "Please announce the mates you have chosen to stand beside you, lift you up with their strength, and help you lead your territory toward great prosperity and power."

"You forgot unforgettable pleasure!" Sterling yells with a howl.

I laugh and whack him in the gut, sending him bowing. Dad laughs and holds his hand out to help me onto the winner's podium. He drapes his arms around my shoulders and kisses my temple.

"That's my tough cookie. Keep him in his place," he jokes.

Straightening my shoulders, I meet the dozens of gazes as our packs gather around, waiting in anticipation.

I clear my throat and meet my mates' eyes. "It is an honor to stand before you today, celebrating our first ever Pack Mate Competition. The seven men I've chosen to officially claim to help me grow Lunar Crest are some of the most incredible, loving, magical beings I am lucky to call my mates."

I take a moment to look at each of my guys. Trista puts her

arms around Dax and hugs him before moving to Caz, Antone, Sterling, Sagan, Bastien, and lastly Flynn.

"Please join me to celebrate the union and official claim between Lyric of Lunar Crest and congratulate Dax of Storm Haven, Caz of Meadow View, Bastien and Antone of Dawnlit Bay, Sterling and Sagan of Night Forest, and Flynn of the Tenebris Coven for coming together to not only save our lands but also our futures," Dad says, opening his arms to greet each of my pack mates with a hug. "Welcome to our family. You have all proven yourself worthy of my daughter, and I'm honored to call you all my sons."

Tears rim my eyes, but I blink them away and join my mates, hugging and kissing each of them. We stand together as one and watch as the other she-wolves announce both permanent and potential mates, no longer having to be a prize and given the chance to bond and grow together, ensuring the best life has to offer.

I sigh in contentment, resting my back to Dax's chest. "I never knew this is all I ever wanted."

Sagan laces his fingers through mine. "And more."

Grinning, I kiss his cheek and bump my shoulder to his, touching my hand to my belly. "You're right. It's much, much more."

26

UNSTOPPABLE

"YOUSSEF, DON'T LEAVE YOURSELF OPEN," I call, circling around one of Bastien and Antone's little brothers. I stand behind him and re-adjust his arms from his sides and nudge his right calf, getting him to step his leg forward. "He might be bigger than you, but you're twice as fast. Don't let the bastard try to intimidate you."

Dax releases a tough-ass growl and shows off a few of his

moves. "You're going down, little buddy."

"You got this, brother," Bastien calls from the sidelines. "Show Lyric the new move we've been working on."

I smile and place my hands on my hips. "You guys have been practicing without me?"

"That's their mistake," Dax teases, bouncing on the balls of his feet. He jabs the air and growls, baring his teeth at Youssef. "You should've come to me, little buddy. I'm the best."

The little guy doesn't even flinch, narrowing his eyes. A breeze catches on his light brown tresses, sending his hair in his face. All he does is blow it and bare his teeth right back at Dax. "Watch it, big man. Bas says you're all bark. Keep it up and you're going to embarrass yourself in front of your mate. I won't go easy on you." Performing a high kick, Youssef accepts Dax's challenge.

It takes everything in me not to smirk. The little boy is so damn cute.

Dax can't resist and howls a laugh, his face lighting with his handsome smile. I especially love seeing him working with the young, helping me teach them the skills they might need in the future, though I hope they never have to use them.

I adjust Youssef's position just a bit more. "You better not. Someone has to put his smug-ass in his place every once in a while, and I want you to do it today. Now show me what you got."

"Yeah, little buddy. Bring it on," Dax says, reaching out to ruffle Youssef's hair.

He growls at Dax and whacks him, stepping back to give himself the space he needs to strategize what he plans to do.

Dax winks at me, and I blow him a kiss.

Youssef takes an offensive position, charging forward to get him in the gut. Like the cocky bastard Dax can be, he stretches his arm out and catches Youssef with a palm to the forehead. Like he was expecting Dax's move, Youssef locks his hands around Dax's wrists and swings forward, kicking him in the gut. Heaving, Dax bows forward while Youssef propels himself between his legs and kicks Dax in the back of the knee, dropping him.

I clap my hands with a cheer, calling his name. Several howls sound through the air, and all the young boys from Lulupoterra gather around us, shouting their glee. Dax huffs as he hits the grass and flattens his body. Youssef climbs on top of him, pinning him down.

Rushing to them, I grab Youssef's arm and pull him to his feet, giving him a hug. "We have a new champion!" I call, patting his back.

The other boys cheer some more and howl, tipping their heads back. I join along with Bastien and pump my fist in the air. Dax remains flopped on the ground, dramatically groaning.

"Take a celebratory lap, guys," I call out, shooing the boys away. It'll be something when they can actually transform in a few years.

The group takes off, racing each other up the hillside and into the forest. Wrapping his arms around me from behind, Bastien lifts me off my feet and kisses my throat, carrying me to Dax. Rolling over, Dax grins up at me, reaching his hands out. He hooks his fingers around my knees, dragging me and Bastien to the grass with him.

"You should've seen your face," I say, straddling him. "Just wait until he's fifty pounds heavier."

Dax chuckles and whacks Bastien on the back. "Nice work with him. I almost lost my breath."

"I guess I'm going to have to ensure it." Fisting his hand, Bastien leans over and jabs Dax in the gut between my legs.

I hop off them and roll, getting out of the way before they wrestle with me in between them. If we were inside, I would, because being in the middle of any of my mates always leads to an amazing time, but we don't need a bunch of boys catching us. Sterling would never let us live that one down.

"Damn right, blondie," he calls, his voice echoing over Dax and Bastien's fighting noises. "Especially because I'd be so fucking jealous not helping to educate the future pack mates, though I had a lot of fun playing chase the warlock. Our girl's getting damn fast. Look at her go."

I twist on my feet and crouch down, opening my arms wide as Sterling sets Aria on her chubby legs and she toddles toward me, stretching out her little arms. I smile and clap, my heart filling with so much love that I could survive forever on it. Scooping

Aria off her feet, I lie back with her on my chest and kiss her rosy cheeks, rubbing my fingers through her golden hair.

"Dogpile Mommy!" Sagan shouts, racing with both our handsome boys in his arms.

I laugh and squeal, cuddling Jaxson and Jett close. They giggle, the sound of their voices chiming together the most melodious things I've ever heard.

"Hey, Junior. Come to Daddy," Dax says, crawling closer. He stretches over me to scoop up our beautiful dark-haired boy in his arms, nuzzling his nose to his. "Did you have fun with your uncles? I hope you gave them a hard time."

Flynn materializes into view, and I sit up, wiggling my fingers. He cradles our daughter in a lavender blanket, stitched with the symbols of the Tenebris Coven bloodlines. I take Sabina in my arms and bring her sleeping face to mine, kissing her.

"You look like you have your hands full, brother," Bastien says, hopping to his feet. "Come here, boys. Give your uncle a rest."

I grin, watching Antone and Caz strolling together with the rest of our brood. Tobias and Blade swing from Antone's biceps, giggling with their excitement. Antone lowers them to the ground and Bastien lifts them up and spins them around. Adjusting our daughter in his arms, Antone rubs his hand over Bridgette's tiny body and she sleeps on his shoulder, her black hair matching her grandmother and namesake. Caz plops down next to me with Milo, and I kiss them both, loving being smothered by my mates and our children.

The first day I was dragged fighting into Lunar Crest, confused and shocked to discover myself as a she-wolf, I would've never in a million years expected my life to end up as it is in only two seasons since we changed everything as a pack—nine new members of our family, strong enough to lead the next generation of pack mates, and a life of utter and endless love and devotion.

The thoughts stir the strength of my she-wolf, rousing the power of every leader who has come before me and every leader who will come after, awakening the wild beast inside me. My spirit howls, filling me with the determination to never, ever, let anything bad come to my species again.

Sterling groans and kisses me. "I love when you get all alpha in your thoughts. Protective mama wolf. It makes me want to hump the hell out of you, slide my sperm baster in your baby baker, and—"

Sagan covers Sterling's mouth. "Careful, brother. Pretty sure all we have to do is say the words and—"

"Boom, pregnant," Dax says, poking my side.

I crack up and squirm away, finding myself in Flynn's arms next. I hum and kiss him, his sparkling power buzzing around us and our pack in the waterfall of the magic we share. I hug and love up on my mates and our pack, feeling the warmth of everyone around me, satisfying me on every level with everything amazing in the universe.

I stare at the azure sky above me, appreciating the small moments now more than ever. I daydream of our future as it stretches before us, full of everything beautiful and breathtaking, and completely magical. I savor each day as we grow stronger than ever. The pack mates of Lunar Crest are an unstoppable force and will never back down from a challenge. We fought hard for this life, and no one will ever take it from us. That's a promise.

I vow to the fates, to my pack, to the universe. This world is ours.

~The End~

Author Note

Dear reader,

Thank you so much for taking a chance on The Pack Mates of Lunar Crest! I hope you enjoyed the world of Lulupoterra and all the magic that hides within it. As an author who loves writing big universes, you can expect other books in the Mates of Magaelorum World. If you haven't checked out Maximum Magical Penitentiary, you definitely should. Our favorite pack will make an appearance in that series.

Happy reading!

XOXO,

Ginna

OTHER REVERSE HAREM NOVELS BY GINNA MORAN

THE WOLFPACKS OF SHADOW MOON ISLAND:
Wild Wolves
Savage Wolves

THE VAMPIRE HEIRS WORLD

La Vega Vampire Showstoppers
Vampire Nights
Bloody Nights
Renegade Nights

The Divine Vampire Heirs
Blood Match
Blood Rebel
Blood Debt
Blood Feud
Blood Loss
Blood Vows
Blood Holiday

The Royale Vampire Heirs Series:
Rebel Vampires
Rebel Dhampir
Rebel Match
Rebel Heir
Rebel Fight

Academy of Vampire Heirs Series:
Dhampirs 101
Blood Sources 102
Coven Bonds 103
Personal Donors 104
Blood Wars 105

THE MATES OF MAGAELORUM WORLD

SERIES IN THE MATES OF MAGAELORUM WORLD

The Pack Mates of Lunar Crest:

The She-Wolf Games

The Wolf-Mate Trials

The Omega Hunt

The Witch Chase

Fated Mate of the Dragon Clans

Caged by Her Dragons

Freed by Her Dragons

Saved by Her Dragons

SEVEN SINNERS WORLD

The Seven Sinners of Hell's Kingdom:

Her Personal Demons

Her Deadly Angels

Her Darkest Devils

Her Sinful Saints

Her **Twisted** Sinners

SAINT VISTA PACK REGIMES

The Knotty Girl Club

STANDALONES

Fame

Rise from the Flames

About Ginna Moran

GINNA MORAN IS the USA Today Bestselling author of over seventy novels including the popular The Pack Mates of Lunar Crest and The Seven Sinners of Hell's Kingdom reverse harem novels.

She always carried a fascination for all things paranormal and wrote her first unpublished manuscript at age eighteen. Her love of the supernatural grew stronger through her adult life, and she now spends her days with different creatures of the night. Whether it's vampires, werewolves, dragons, fae, angels, demons, or mermaids, Ginna loves creating and living in worlds from her dreams.

Aside from Ginna's professional life, she enjoys binge-watching TV, crafting and design, playing pretend with her daughter, and cuddling with her dog. Some of her favorite things include chocolate, mermaids, anything that glitters, learning new things, cheesy jokes, and organizing her bookshelf. Ginna is currently hard at work on her next novel and the one after, and the one after that.

www.ingramcontent.com/pod-product-compliance
Lightning Source LLC
Chambersburg PA
CBHW031619180726
48284CB00005B/1611